THE LIES
WE TOLD

ROBERTA
KAGAN

MARGOT'S SECRET

4

ISBN (eBook): 978-1-957207-64-3
ISBN (Paperback): 978-1-957207-65-0
ISBN (Hardcover): 978-1-957207-66-7
ISBN (Large Print): 978-1-957207-67-4

Title Production by The Book Whisperer

DISCLAIMER

This is a work of fiction. Names, characters, businesses, places, events, and incidents are either the products of the author's imagination or used in a fictitious manner. Any resemblance to actual persons, living or dead, or actual events is purely coincidental.

PROLOGUE

He loved the smell of gasoline. As a child, he adored the fumes so much that he often started small fires in trash cans. That sharp odor that stung his nostrils also made his body tingle. It tingled because it was a silent reminder to him that he was in control. He had power. The power of fire, the power to kill. And often, he did. His need for power began when he was an awkward, heavyset boy of thirteen. One of his classmates taunted and ridiculed him mercilessly. However, he was too weak to fight his tormentor. So, instead, one afternoon he waited at the playground for the boy's younger brother. The brother was only five years old and very trusting. It took a few pieces of candy to lure the child into the woods. There, he got his revenge. He burned the child with matches and beat him until he was dead. He felt better about himself with every burn and every punch or kick. It was as if he was actually killing the little boy's older brother. When it was over, he was spent but vindicated. Carefully, he covered any evidence of his crime. No one in town even suspected him. They thought it was probably a drifter who had murdered the child. Inwardly, he smiled as he joined the rest of his neighbors at the little boy's funeral, where he watched as the child's family, especially his hated older brother, grieved.

But today, he felt ten feet tall, like a giant of a man, as his mind traveled back to the woman he had left tied up in the room upstairs. A smile tickled his lips. She was a true beauty with her ivory skin and golden curls. *It would have been a great pleasure to watch her die.* He thought. He would have branded the picture of it in his mind and forever cherished the look on her face when she knew that her life was about to end as the wild flames leaped up with the wind into the dark, starless sky. But alas, he had not been able to stay and watch her terror. A laugh bubbled up in his throat. For several moments, he'd stood in her room, mesmerized by the sight of her. He had even considered sacrificing his own life for the pure pleasure of watching her suffer. She would have looked exquisite as her skin melted away from the fire. But he'd had to leave. The room was getting too hot. He turned and took a last look at her. She was crying. Her lovely, perfect face was covered with tears. Black mascara ran like a dark river down her cheeks. He knew she would beg him. It was worth getting caught to hear her begging. So, he removed the gag from her mouth, but only for a second. And he was right. She did plead for her life, and he enjoyed it immensely, but then she screamed and ruined everything. A moment of fear shot through him. He couldn't risk anyone hearing her. If they did, they might try to stop the fire before it could finish its work. So, he quickly shoved her panties back into her mouth. She choked and gagged, pleading now with her eyes, but he didn't remove the gag. This time, he would finish her off. This woman deserved to die. He knew her for what she was, a liar and a manipulator, like his mother and that girl. Well, her days of manipulation were over. She was done playing with him, lying to him. The gag in her mouth kept her from screaming, but she was screaming silently with her eyes as they followed him while he doused her room with gasoline. Then, her pupils grew wider with terror as he lit the match. Such a beautiful sight. It took every ounce of strength he had to exit that room before the fire consumed her and melted her skin like a porcelain doll. The flames climbed the curtains, and he knew he must hurry. Running through the rooms, leaving a trail of gasoline. Now, it was time for him to go. His heart ached with the beauty of it all as he looked back one last time. He wished he could take her one last time as he studied her lovely naked breasts. This woman was special. She looked like an American movie idol. The cords in her neck stood out as she struggled to break free of the handcuffs. *Time to go.* He sighed and whispered, "Goodbye, my sweet Aryan goddess. You were such fun tonight. I shall always remember you as you are right now. But your time has come. It's time for you to die. You see, my dear, you should never have lied to me. Women who lie to men deserve to die. My mother lied to my father; she used her lies to control him, just like you. And because she made him hate her, he hated me too. The bitch was never punished for her actions. Did I ever tell you that she looked just like you, goddess? Well, she did." Then he smiled at her. It was a maniacal smile. And then he turned and walked out of the room, closing the door softly as the fire consumed the small writing table. Quickly, he left the woman's room and ran down the boarding house stairs, pouring more gasoline as he went. Soon, the windows would explode from the intense heat. He wanted to be out of the building before that occurred. It was late at night, and he was alone as he left the boarding house. He looked up at her window for a second and saw the lovely orange flames. *Everyone in this building must be asleep.* No one smelled the smoke. At least not yet.

Once he was safely outside, he poured the remainder of the contents of the gas can around the perimeter of the entire building. *The fire should be well underway before any chance of saving the residents inside.*

The man smiled, and then he turned and walked away. He was heading towards his home but had to stop briefly to observe his handiwork. Proudly, he looked up and was excited to see the orange flames licking the sky. By morning, his crimes would be untraceable.

Whistling softly, he turned the corner, and as he did, he heard the sound of a fire alarm. Loud voices came from the area where the fire was raging. But he couldn't make out what they were saying. Still, he wasn't worried. He was quite certain that it was too late.

CHAPTER 1

Margot sat on the bed in her room and opened the package her landlady delivered. It had arrived earlier that afternoon, but Margot had been out, so her landlady had kept it for her until she returned home. It was a large and beautiful box, all wrapped in blue paper with a large blue bow. But Margot was nervous. She was not expecting anything from anyone. And since she was hiding from her past, and no one she had previously known knew where she was or where to send anything, the gift came as a surprise. The only person who this gift could be from was Kurtis, a Nazi officer she'd been forced to have dinner with the night before. Margot had given him as little encouragement as possible, hoping he would lose interest in her. The last thing she needed was a member of Hitler's SS pursuing her. This could only cause her more problems, considering she had recently learned that she had been adopted as an infant and that her mother was Jewish. If this man became seriously interested in her, he might try to find out everything he could about her. And that would be very dangerous.

Her hands trembled as she tore the blue paper and matching

ribbon off the box and opened it. Inside, she found a magnificent royal blue velvet dress. It was exactly her size. With her fingers still trembling, she touched the fabric. She'd never owned anything so lovely, yet she wished it had never arrived. Terrified, she read the card. "Blue is your color." Instantly, she knew that her fears were warranted. When she and Kurtis were having dinner the previous night, he had said those exact words. Now, she was certain that this dress was from him. Her shoulders slumped. *He hasn't lost interest at all. In fact, he is trying hard to woo me. This dress had to be very expensive. I'm sure he thinks spending this much money on a girl will guarantee him a night in her bed. And I'm afraid that saying no to him will only cause him to try harder. Sometimes, when you reject a fellow, especially this kind of fellow, he becomes obsessed with you. And that's the last thing I need. I don't know what I will do to discourage his attention, but I must find a way.*

She was feeling overwhelmed. There was nothing she could do right now, and sitting in her room dwelling on her fears only made things worse. Margot decided that she desperately needed a distraction. Since she had recently purchased a book from the bookseller, she took it from the shelf in her room. For a moment, she thought about the bookseller. He was a kind old man. Margot met him when she was looking for work. She had gone into his shop and asked if he needed any help. He told her he didn't have enough business to hire an employee. Desperate, she asked him if he knew anyone looking for help, and he had recommended the restaurant where she had been hired and was now working. She opened the used book carefully because of its weak spine and began to read. Since she didn't have to be at work until four that afternoon, she planned to stay in her small, rented room and relax all day. But because of Kurtis and his gift, she was too anxious to concentrate on her book. She leaned against the bedpost and closed her eyes. *What am I going to do now?* And then there was a knock on the door. Margot's heart raced. "Yes?" Margot said in a small voice after a long pause.

"It looks to me like someone has found a suitor," the old landlady said slyly.

Margot reluctantly opened her door.

The old woman carried another box. This one, like the other one, was wrapped in blue paper. Then she smiled and winked. "You are a pretty one. Even so, I must say that it was quick. You haven't been in town very long."

If she only knew. "Thank you," Margot said, taking the box and closing the door in the woman's face.

Margot tore the paper off the box and opened it. Inside, there was a lovely leather handbag. The card read, "I would have sent matching shoes, but I didn't know your size. Kurtis."

CHAPTER 2

It began to rain later that afternoon as Margot walked to work at the restaurant. By the time she arrived at work, her hair was damp, and a light dew had settled on her skin. Before she entered the restaurant, she shook out her hair so as not to wet the floor. Then she went to the back area by the kitchen, grabbed a towel, and began to dry off. Tilly, one of the waitresses who worked with Margot, came to the kitchen to see her. "Well, well, it looks like someone has a boyfriend," she said, smiling. But it wasn't a sincere smile. It was spiteful.

"What are you talking about?" Margot asked, but she already knew the answer. *Kurtis must have come here looking for me already.*

"The *Kommandoführer* was here earlier this afternoon. He is very handsome. But aren't you married?"

When Margot started working at this job, she met two girls. Tilly and Marie. Marie had proved to be a friend. But Tilly reminded her of her sister, Trudy. She was deceitful, conniving, and jealous. Consequently, Margot knew she must be careful of everything she said and did when Tilly was around.

"My husband was killed serving the fatherland," Margot lied. She had no idea where her husband, Max, might be. But this was the story

Ben, her Jewish lover, now dead, had created for her before he died, and she trusted his judgment completely.

"You never told us that," Tilly said.

"You never asked." Margot snapped at Tilly. She slipped on a black apron. Then, putting a notepad and pen in her pocket, she left Tilly in the kitchen and went into the dining room to serve the customers.

When Klaus, the restaurant owner, saw Margot working, he immediately walked over to her. "I promised *Kommandoführer* Richter that you would be available for dinner tonight. He came by to see me this afternoon. I told him that you would be here at eight o'clock to meet him. So, you'd better go home and change. He said I should expect you here at eight wearing a blue dress."

Margot was fuming. This Nazi who had taken an interest in her had too much control over her life. Her boss was subtly letting her know that he expected her to entertain this SS officer as long as he was in Frankfurt. She had no idea how long he planned to stay, but she knew he was supposed to return to work at a place called Dachau. The very idea that she might lose her job if she didn't comply with Kurtis's desire to spend time with her was infuriating. But she knew that finding work had been almost impossible. And she needed the money. If she spent everything Ben had left her when he died, she would be in trouble. *I need to save as much as I can. So, I must work at this restaurant until I find something else. For right now, I must do what Klaus tells me to do. So, I'll go home and put on that blue dress.*

Margot walked back to the boardinghouse where she was staying and changed her clothes. Then she waited. By seven-thirty, the rain had stopped, and she made her way back to the restaurant.

Kurtis was already there. He sat at the bar, waiting anxiously for her. When he looked up at the door and saw Margot enter, a big smile came over his face. She walked up to him.

"I was right," he said. "You really do look stunning in blue."

Her lips trembled as she smiled at him. She was trying hard to hide her real feelings. *The Nazis have taken so much from me, and now this one thinks he can win my affection. He must be crazy.* "Thank you," she whispered, looking down at the table.

He didn't realize she was not meeting his gaze because she was hiding something. He thought it was because she was shy, and he found that charming. "Let's go eat. Yes?" he said.

"Sure, of course." She nodded. Out of the corner of her eye, she saw Tilly watching her with envy. A cold chill ran down Margot's spine. *My sister was jealous like that, and it cost me the life of my son and the separation from my husband. Indirectly, it even caused Ben's death. That kind of jealousy is dangerous, and I am very afraid of Tilly. Women like that will do whatever they can to get what they want. They don't care about the trouble they cause or other people's feelings.*

Kurtis didn't notice that Margot was lost in thought. He took her hand and wrapped it around his arm. Then he led her outside. It had started to rain again. She cursed under her breath. He thought she cursed because she was afraid the rain would ruin her new dress. But she was really cursing out of frustration. Margot was sick and tired of having to accommodate Nazis just to survive.

"Oh dear, oh dear," Kurtis said with a smile. "It's been a wet day today, hasn't it?"

She nodded.

"Well, no need to worry. We'll take my auto. That way, you won't get wet. And you won't ruin your lovely dress." He winked at her. "I'll see to that."

She wanted to protest. The last thing she wanted to do was be in a car alone with this man. But she was tired of fighting. So, she just agreed. To her surprise, Kurtis was a gentleman. He didn't even try to kiss her, and she was relieved when, at the end of the evening, he stopped in front of the door of her building and didn't even try to force his way inside. "I had a wonderful evening," he said.

"Yes, me too."

"I would love to stay here in Frankfurt forever, but I must return to work. I have an important job, you see."

"Oh, what is it that you do?"

"I work at a facility in a little town called Dachau. Do you know where that is?"

"No. I don't think so," Margot admitted.

"Right outside of Munich. It's a quiet place. The concentration camp where I work used to be a training site for the *Waffen SS*." He looked at her proudly, and she knew he was waiting for her to say something.

"Oh?" she said.

"Yes, and in case you didn't know, I am a member of the Waffen SS. You see. It just so happens that I did my training at the camp where I am now working," he said, puffing his chest out ever so slightly. "But because there are so many criminals in our country, we were forced to convert the facility from a training site to, well, let's call it, a detention camp of sorts."

"You mean like a prison?" she blurted out the question and was immediately sorry she had asked. The last thing she wanted to do was anger him. But he wasn't angry. Instead, he was delighted to tell her more about his work.

"Exactly. My dear, there are a lot of dangerous people out on the streets these days. People who would try to destroy everything our *Führer* is working so hard to build for the future of our precious fatherland. Therefore, they must be stopped, and so there is a great need for their containment. If you understand."

She stared at him but said nothing.

"I was selected to help rebuild this camp. It's a dangerous job, working with criminals like that. However, I am not afraid. I am strong." He smiled. "And I am proud to say that the work I am doing will help to keep Germany safe for the good Aryan people."

"I see," she said, a shiver running down her back as Ben's face flashed in her mind.

"Anyway, that's one of the reasons why I must return to work so quickly. But I like you, Margot. And I promise I will come back on my next day off, and we will see each other again, yes?"

She nodded, hoping he would lose interest before then. It was a long train ride, and she thought he would probably find another girl rather than make the trip. "Well, goodnight. And thank you for dinner," she said, smiling.

"Margot. Please wait."

She stopped, hoping he wasn't going to kiss her. He didn't. He just smiled and said, "The blue is really lovely against your skin tone."

She nodded. "Thank you for the gifts."

"You deserve them. You're a beautiful woman."

There was a long silence. She swallowed hard. Then she said, "Well, I should be going."

"I'll call you when I get home. Do you have a phone here?"

"I don't have a phone of my own. But there is one in the boarding house."

"I'm sure the landlady will get my calls through to you. Especially if I send her some money."

"Oh yes, she's like that. So, I'm sure of it, too."

CHAPTER 3

The following morning, when Margot awakened, she felt sick to her stomach. She quickly climbed out of bed and ran to the bathroom, where she vomited. *It must have been all that rich food and beer last night. I feel so nauseated.*

It was a few hours before the nausea subsided, and she felt better. As soon as she did, she went down the hall, showered, and washed her hair. A half-hour later, her landlady delivered a large box to her room. "Look at this, Margot. It seems that your boyfriend sent you another gift. This time, it appears to be chocolates. He must have money or connections to buy an expensive box this big," she said slyly.

Margot nodded, not looking at the old woman. Her landlady had a way of getting on her nerves.

"Thank you," she said almost curtly to her landlady and then closed the door.

She had always loved good quality chocolates but couldn't remember the last time she'd had a piece. She opened the box and looked inside. A small laugh escaped her lips as she shook her head. A piece was missing, and she knew that her obnoxious landlady had helped herself. But as the sweet fragrance of the chocolate wafted up to her nose, she found that it made her sick to her stomach. *I'm nause-*

ated again. Quickly, she put the cover back on the box and set it on the night table. For a moment, she was tempted to go downstairs and tell the landlady she could have the candy. But she really didn't like her. Instead, she decided to give it to Marie, the waitress at work who had trained her and become her only friend in Frankfurt.

Margot sat down on the bed, but she was still nauseated. Strangely, she imagined that she could still smell the chocolate. Her senses seemed so heightened, and she couldn't bear the smell. Standing up, Margot took the box of chocolates and put it on a high shelf far away from her bed. Then she sat down and closed her eyes. A thought that she had been suppressing burst through to the forefront of her mind. *What if I am pregnant? I felt like this when I was pregnant with Erik.* Her hand flew up to her mouth. *The last time Ben and I made love was the night when he went to try to find Max to help us, right before he left. We were both in such a hurry and so nervous because he was leaving the safety of the attic that he forgot to use a condom. So, it's very possible that I am having a baby. If it turns out that I am pregnant, what am I going to tell everyone here? Klaus? Kurtis? Tilly? Everyone. Everyone except Marie. She is so kind that I don't think she will ask me any questions. But the others will, and they all think my husband was away at war and that he died in battle. So, he could not have made me pregnant. They will all ask me who the father of my baby is. I dare not tell them the truth, that this child's father was dead and that he was Jewish. That would be suicide. No, no, no. But if I am pregnant, God has given me a wonderful gift. He has given it to me, so I will always remember and honor my sweet Ben for the rest of my life. I refuse to let these Nazis kill this baby the way they killed my other son. I will protect this child with my life. But how?* She stood up and began to pace the room. Walking back and forth several times until she had an idea.

CHAPTER 4

Kommandoführer Kurtis Richter was packing to return to work the day after his date with Margot. He had one more night in Frankfurt before he had to take the train back to his job at Dachau, and he could have waited to pack, but he liked to be organized and ready. He had learned this when he joined the *Waffen SS*. Kurtis had excelled in his army training. And because he did, he was awarded the job he now had. It was a job he enjoyed because it gave him power. He loved the very idea of knowing that men's lives were in his hands. Kurtis thought about his childhood and how his father had never believed he would amount to anything. His father had been an intellectual snob. He was an educator who spent countless wasted hours discussing the existence of God with his close friends and coworkers. And he was a strong disciplinarian who punished Kurtis severely when he disappointed him, which was often. Kurtis had no interest in philosophical discussions. He thought they were pointless. However, his father tried to pique Kurtis's interest by sharing his views with his son. He explained to Kurtis that he was certain that a higher force existed. He believed that God was not good or kind and that he doled out punishments to those whose behavior he did not condone.

Fredrick, Kurtis's brother, was so much like his father that it was almost as if his father had produced a twin of himself. The two of them would often get lost for hours in discussion in his father's study, while Kurtis, who was like his mother, preferred to be outside playing sports with the local boys. Once, Kurtis overheard his father tell his mother that he was ashamed of Kurtis, who he found to be superficial and ignorant. He often lashed out at his son in front of friends or neighbors. This made Kurtis feel small and inferior. But for some odd reason, Kurtis couldn't give up on his father. He longed to win the man's favor. Several times, he tried to read his father's books by philosophers Kant or Nietzsche but could not comprehend what he was reading. When his father asked him what he thought of the books, he told his father that he couldn't understand them. Instead of offering to help him, his father laughed at his son. It took everything Kurtis could do to hold back his tears. But he refused to let his father see him cry. And try as he might, he couldn't bring himself to hate his father. However, he found that he was able to blame God for his father's vicious outbursts. And he began to see this God his father told him about as his enemy. He started to see God as something that kept him from living his life fully. But then, like a miracle, when he was old enough and became a member of the Hitler Youth, things began to change for Kurtis. The Hitler youth told him that he didn't need his father's God. They told Kurtis that Adolf Hitler was his new higher power. It wasn't difficult for Kurtis to accept this.

Hitler respected and admired men with athletic abilities, which he had. The leaders of his youth group told him that he could take pride in himself because he was a pure German, part of a superior race. Also, Kurtis was admired by the rest of his Hitler youth group for his blonde hair and blue eyes. They loved his Aryan good looks. When he graduated from school, he joined the army. By the time he became a part of Hitler's *Waffen SS*, he had completely forgotten about the angry, judgmental God his father had warned him about. Kurtis replaced him with the great and mighty *Führer*. There was no doubt that both of these higher powers were equally mean and heartless, but the difference was his father's God was mean to him, while Hitler loved him and gave him the power to rule over others.

Kurtis wouldn't have minded returning to work. He enjoyed his time off, but in Frankfurt, he was just another officer. At his position in Dachau, he was feared and respected. He might have returned to work early if not for his fascination with Margot. But she had stirred something within him. Kurtis couldn't decide if it was because he could not possess her entirely the way he did with other women or if it was something deeper. She was attractive, but not in a conventional way, and he found her to be a good conversationalist. And, more importantly, a very good listener. *I'll be back in a month or so. I'll see her when I return.* He thought, but even as he thought this, he was sorry to be leaving. Just then, his telephone rang. He picked up the receiver, annoyed at being disturbed during his thought process.

"Kurtis? It's Margot," she said in a soft voice.

"Margot?" his entire demeanor changed. He was no longer annoyed. He was utterly intrigued. *I can't believe it. She telephoned me. I would never have expected this.*

"I know you are leaving Frankfurt soon, but if you have a little time before you go…well…" She hesitated, then in a seductive voice, she added, "You see, I've been thinking about you…and I would love to see you."

"Of course. I would love to see you. I'll make time. My train leaves early tomorrow morning. But we can have dinner tonight if that would be all right."

"I would like that very much. However, I am supposed to work tonight. I hate to ask this, but is it possible that you can telephone Klaus and let him know that I need the night off?" she said. *I hate to take time off because I desperately need the money, but this man is leaving tomorrow, and this might be my only opportunity to do what I must do to protect my unborn child.*

"Of course. I'll call him right away. Don't you worry. I'll take care of everything. How soon shall I pick you up?"

"An hour?"

"I'll be there," he said.

CHAPTER 5

Trudy hardly gave a thought to Max's arrest as she unpacked her things into the new luxury apartment Peter had rented for her. Max was no longer important to her. He was little more than a part of her past. A messy part that had to be gotten rid of if she and Peter were to have the affair she was planning. So, she decided to feel no guilt about having asked Peter to see to it that Max was arrested and sent to a concentration camp. Now, she would never have to see Max again. Chances were good he would not survive, and as long as she would never have to face him, she found no need to contemplate the suffering that she had caused him. Trudy was the type of person who put her own happiness first. And she was happy now. Max had failed to provide for her. He had no money and no ambition, two things she could not tolerate. That cheap, run-down apartment where she'd lived with Max disgusted her. A luxury apartment like the one she was in now was where she belonged. It would have been better if Peter had not been married, but she felt no sympathy for his wife or family. They quite simply didn't matter to her.

As time passed, she planned to find a way to win his love and devotion. Then, she would force him to leave his wife and marry her. Peter was everything she wanted in a husband, far more handsome than Rudy, Trudy's first husband, but equally successful and ambitious. She sighed. *Life is good. For so long, I believed that Max was the man for me because he was handsome. I was a fool. It's true he had good looks, but other than that, he was worthless. He hated the Nazi party and refused to try to build any kind of financially successful life for himself. Money was not important to him. Max never minded living in poverty. Neither did Margot. They really did belong together. She had no ambition either. However, she's a Jew, and they both deserve to be in that camp.* Trudy smiled, feeling self-righteous. She knew she could justify anything.

A few days after Trudy moved in, Peter called and told her that he planned to come to Berlin next week to see the apartment. She was very excited and wanted to have everything clean and perfect before he arrived. There was a lot to do. Moving in was a daunting task. She had so many items from her home with Rudy that she had not unpacked when she moved in with Max due to a lack of space. But she worked harder than she ever had, and by the time Peter knocked on the door a little over a week later, Trudy was ready for his arrival. Her hair was perfectly coiffed, her nails newly manicured, and her makeup expertly applied. She wore an emerald green silk negligee that Rudy had brought back from France for her.

"Don't you look inviting?" Peter said as he entered the apartment in his clean-pressed black uniform.

Trudy smiled. "Come in. I want to show you the apartment."

"I can't wait."

She took his arm and began to lead him through the rooms, but when they got to the bedroom, he stopped her and turned her around to face him. Then he took her into his arms. "I'll see the rest later," he whispered in her ear.

Sexual electricity ran through her as he kissed her ardently. They made love. When it was over, he sighed. "I certainly have missed you."

"I missed you too. How long can you stay?"

"A few days."

"I'm glad. But quite honestly, I wish you could stay forever."

He smiled in the darkness, and even though she couldn't see his face, she somehow knew he was smiling. "I'd like to stay with you. It's peaceful here."

"Yes, and I promise this apartment will always be your sanctuary." She reached up, touched his chest, and curled the hairs around her fingers. "You've never told me exactly, but I believe you have children, right?"

"I do. I am a good Aryan man. I've done what our *Führer* asked of me. I spread my good Aryan seed. It's important that we bring plenty of pure Aryan children into this world for the future of our country." He waited a few moments, then asked, "And you? Do you have any children?"

"Me? No. I had a daughter with my husband, but she died."

"Oh, I am sorry. You've never told me about your husband or your child."

"My husband was an important man in the party. He was always getting promoted. By the time he died, he was an officer in Hitler's death squad."

"Very impressive."

"Yes, he was a good husband, too. He pampered me. When our daughter was born, he decided I needed help in the house. So, he brought home a Jewish maid from one of those camps to care for the child. Unfortunately, Jews are irresponsible. And just like a Jew, she neglected to do her job. My daughter died in a terrible accident when the maid was supposed to be watching her. Of course, my husband was overcome with grief, so he shot the maid."

"I see," Peter said. "Well, I am sorry to hear about it."

There was a long silence. Trudy stopped toying with Peter's chest hair. She wondered if she had said the wrong thing. But then he said, "Enough about sad things. Why don't we go and get some food? I'm starving."

"I'll get dressed."

———

THE NEXT THREE days were a whirlwind of romance. Peter and Trudy went out to lovely restaurants for expensive dinners. Then, they returned to the apartment, where they made love until the wee hours of the night.

Not once did Trudy ask Peter anything about Max. And Peter never mentioned him.

Early in the morning, a few days later, Peter packed his things, got into his automobile, and headed home. But before he departed, he left a pile of Reichsmarks on the nightstand beside Trudy's bed.

When Trudy awakened, she saw the empty bed and felt abandoned, but only for a moment because as she got up, she noticed the money. Counting the bills, she giggled. Peter had left a nice amount. *Since I have plenty of money right now, the first I must do is find an unethical doctor who will fix me up inside so I don't get pregnant again. I'm terrified of having this done, but I am afraid that if I get pregnant, Peter will lose interest in me. He has a house full of children at home. This apartment must always be his sanctuary.*

By the end of the month, Trudy was sterile.

CHAPTER 6

Margot was not surprised that Kurtis was enthusiastic about seeing her, even though he had plans to leave Frankfurt in the morning. She felt sick to her stomach. But she would do whatever she must do to secure a safe future for her unborn child, Ben's child.

She dressed quickly, then, as an afterthought, she went downstairs and walked a few steps down the street to a general store where she purchased a tube of red lipstick. With the lipstick in hand, Margot ran back to her room, where she carefully applied the lipstick to her full lips, then she smeared a little on her cheeks to brighten up her color. By the time she was finished, Kurtis was knocking at her door.

They went to a quiet German restaurant where they had schnitzel and dark beer in big decorative mugs. Kurtis told her how happy he was that she had telephoned. "I thought I was going to have to wait for a month before I could see you again. And that made me sad," he admitted. "I would have missed you."

"I quite agree. I couldn't wait either," Margot said, trying to sound sincere. "I wanted to see you."

His eyes lit up, and a big smile came over his face. "Really? I didn't think you cared too much for me."

"Oh, I'm sorry. It's not that I don't care for you. I must admit, I am shy that way. I mean, I haven't dated anyone since the death of my husband. I suppose you might say it's difficult for me to show my feelings," she said demurely.

He was sold on her lie because it was what he wanted to hear.

After they finished eating, they got into the car that Kurtis had borrowed from the Nazi headquarters for this holiday. "I hate to say goodbye," he said. Then he drove quietly towards her apartment. She smiled at him, but inside, she was cringing. *I can't do this, but I must. I must force myself to do it.*

When they arrived at her rooming house, Margot said, "Kurtis, are you tired, or would you like to go back to your hotel room where we could have a drink or something?"

"Yes, I would like that," he stammered nervously. "And, no, I'm not tired at all. Let me stop and buy a bottle. Do you like schnapps? Whiskey? What do you like?"

"Schnapps," she said.

"All right, all right," he said nervously.

In the darkness, she could see that he was trembling. A shiver ran down her spine. *How am I going to get through this?* Then she thought of Erik, her son who had died a miserable death. And she knew she would do anything to protect the tiny life growing in her womb.

Kurtis stopped the automobile in front of a small liquor store. Margot waited in the car while he went inside to purchase a bottle of good schnapps. When he got back into the car, he showed her what he had bought. Margot nodded at him. "That's a nice schnapps," she said, knowing the brand because of the restaurant where she worked and knowing it was expensive.

"Only the best for you," he said.

"That's very nice of you," she answered, smiling.

They drove to his hotel in silence. When they arrived, he took her arm and escorted her to his room. Margot gathered up all the courage she had inside of her. She thought of Max, of Ben, and of Erik. Then she looked up at Kurtis. He was handing her a glass of schnapps. It was unusual for her to drink. But she gulped this down. *I need this for courage.* Then she stood up and walked over to Kurtis and kissed him. His face could not hide his shock at how bold she was. He never expected this from her. But that was why he was so intrigued by her. She never stopped surprising him.

Once Kurtis was overcome by his desire, he was no longer nervous or embarrassed. He turned the light off and then led Margot to his bed, where he made love to her. Kurtis was so caught up in his desire for her that he didn't notice her crying the entire time.

Even though it was late when Margot returned to her room at the boarding house, she still took the time to take a long shower. She scrubbed her skin until it was so raw that it hurt. She washed her hair with the only soap she had, which was far too harsh, and it stripped the oils, leaving her hair feeling brittle. Margot knew that it was against the rules to shower this late at night. Her landlady had made that clear to her. But she had to break the rules. It would have been unbearable for her to try to sleep with the scent of that Nazi on her body. She thought as the warm water spilled over her, washing her clean like summer rain. *Well, at least it's done. I have his seed now, and he will believe me when I tell him I am pregnant. He won't deny that this child is his.*

What she didn't know was that Kurtis would never want to deny that this child was his because he was already falling in love with Margot.

CHAPTER 7

"*Kommandoführer* Kurtis Richter is back. I saw him this afternoon," Adrien said gloomily. Then he turned to Kaz and added, "You were right. Didn't you say the worst ones always come back?"

"Yes, I did say that. And I am not surprised he has returned. Of course, the louse is back. I only hoped he would maybe get into a train wreck or something equally terrible," Kaz said.

Max was silent. He just shrugged. Unlike his Jewish friends, he'd seen life on the other side of the equation. *I'm glad that they don't know that I was once a member of the Nazi Party. Not that I ever believed in the doctrine. They fooled me. They made me believe that I could help Erik. My poor son, Erik. He was so sick. And Margot, my wife, and I were so worried about him. Margot's school friend, Ben, who was Jewish, did all he could. He was a good and qualified doctor, but he had no way of getting his hands on the right medications or equipment. Our little boy's epileptic seizures were more and more frequent. My sweet Margot was terrified. So was I. And the only people who had access to good medical care were the Nazis. Margot's* sister Trudy, who I later found out was a monster, was married to Rudy, an SS officer. He tricked me into joining the party in hopes of getting Erik the help he needed. I did it. I still feel sick about it, but I did it. They gave me a job working at the postal service. I was glad it wasn't a very important job. But it offered a steady income, and Margot and I believed we might be able to get Erik some help. I am still angry with myself for believing that doctor who came to our house with a promise that they would cure Erik if we sent him away to a special hospital. He rubbed his temples. They didn't cure him. They murdered him. They murdered our son. Our precious little boy and it was my fault for believing them. I will never be able to forgive myself for what happened to Erik. I was his father. I should have been there to protect him. But I was dumb enough to be tricked into sending my own child into a program that the Nazis created to murder anyone who was physically or mentally handicapped. I will never forgive myself. Although I would like to kill Trudy, she isn't foremost in my mind. My heart aches with worry about Margot. Is she alive? Is our child alive? The last time I saw her, Margot was pregnant. I know if she is alive, she needs me, and it is killing me to know I can't be there to help her.

"So deep in thought? What are you thinking about?" Kaz asked Max as he looked over at him.

"My wife. What am I always thinking about?" Max answered. "I wish I could protect her, but I can't. I am here, stuck in here, locked up."

"Yes, I know how that can be." Kaz nodded and patted Max's shoulder. "Sometimes it's good to remember. Other times, it almost kills you."

Max nodded.

CHAPTER 8

Before Kurtis had sex with Margot, he believed that once he slept with her, the challenge would be gone, and he would be able to forget her. Now, he knew he had been wrong. All he could think about on the train back to Dachau from Frankfurt was the delicate girl he'd made love to the night before. His heart ached to return to her and spend more time getting to know her better. But even so, he felt he knew enough about her to know he was in love. She was his type in so many ways. Not the dark hair, of course. It would have been better had she been a blonde, but it didn't distract from her beauty. She was such a quiet, gentle person, yet she seemed to have an inner strength that he admired.

Although Kurtis didn't want to seem overly eager, he couldn't help himself. He telephoned Margot the same day he arrived at his home in the officer's quarters adjacent to the camp. She didn't answer, so he assumed that she was at work. He put the phone down and decided to call the next day. But he couldn't wait. A half-hour later, he called the restaurant. Klaus answered. "*Allo*," he said.

"Klaus, my friend. How are you?"

"Who is this?"

"You don't recognize my voice? It's Richter."

"Kurt. Hello," Klaus said. "Sorry, I didn't recognize you. I have my hands full. I hired a new waitress this afternoon. I'm trying to get her situated here."

"Understandable," Kurtis said. Then he added, "Listen, I was wondering if I could talk to Margot for a minute. Is she there?"

"She just got in. Her shift is about to start. But for you, of course, you can talk to her. Hold the phone. I'll go and get her for you," Klaus said.

When Klaus walked in, Margot was in the kitchen, tying the belt on her black apron. "Get on the phone. You have a call from Kurt."

"Oh?" Margot said. She was glad he called. This was all part of her plan. "All right."

As she walked to the front of the restaurant to answer her phone call, Margot saw a young blonde girl, tall and slender, with a touch of arrogance, standing there. She was tapping her fingers on the counter. "Can I help you?" Margot asked the girl.

"No," she said, dismissing Margot. "I'm Alice. I'm the new waitress."

"Hello, Alice. I'm Margot." Then Margot pointed to Tilly, who looked strangely disheveled across the room. "That's Tilly," Margot said, then she pointed to Marie, "and that's Marie."

Alice just nodded. "Klaus said to wait here for him."

"I'm sure he'll be right back." Margot smiled. Then she walked over and picked up the telephone. "*Allo.*"

"Margot," Kurtis said, his voice was breathless. "I was hoping you were there."

"Yes, Kurtis. Of course, I'm here. What did you want?"

He sounded suddenly shy. "I just wanted to let you know I returned home safely."

"Well, that's good," she said.

There was a long silence. "I'm sorry if I bothered you."

She laughed a little. "No bother. I'm glad you called to let me know that you returned safely. But I do have to get back to work."

"Yes, of course. Of course you do," he said. "Well, goodbye for now."

"Goodbye," she said.

He hung up the phone. Disappointed. He thought she would be gushing with enthusiasm to hear from him. But, strangely enough, she didn't seem to care. *I don't care anymore, either. I've had her, and I am done with her now. There are women everywhere. This one is nothing special.*

Kurtis was determined to put Margot out of his mind. He was furious with her for her indifference towards him. But the more his anger towards her grew, the more he found her in his thoughts. In fact, he was obsessed with her. *I will not call her again. I am going out to meet someone new.* He thought as he got dressed. Then, he went to a *Biergarten* nearby to have a beer that evening. Although the restaurant was crowded with available women, he was not interested in any of them. So, he returned to his apartment alone, with thoughts of Margot dancing through his mind. *How is it possible that I can hate and love her at the same time? I thought she was falling for me. Now, I think she doesn't care at all. She's by far the strangest woman I've ever known. I should forget all about her. That would be the wise thing to do. But the harder I try, the more I want to see her again. Perhaps I can find a reason to go to Frankfurt early next month.*

CHAPTER 9

When Kurtis didn't telephone Margot for a week following their first conversation, Margot was afraid that her aloof attitude might have been too hard and pushed him away. When she was younger, just a teenager still in school, she learned that when she gave a boy a little attention and took it away, he would chase her like a dog chasing anything that ran in front of him. So, she hoped this strategy would have the same effect on Kurtis. She knew she needed him, so she had to be very careful. After all, he was the lifeline to safety for the baby she carried. And a few days later, just when she began to wonder if she should telephone him and show him some interest, he called again.

"Margot, it's Kurtis."

"Kurtis, how are you?" She forced herself to sound calm and not concerned that it had been a week since his last telephone call to her.

"I'm all right. How are you?"

"I'm doing fine," she said as casually as she could. Of course, she was not doing fine at all. The morning sickness had gotten worse, and she found herself running outside to vomit in the evening when she was at work.

"I'll be coming to Frankfurt at the beginning of the month. I'd like to see you."

Don't jump at his offer. It took him a week to telephone, but he did. And now he is coming to see you. Be calm. Let him do the chasing. "Oh, how nice of you. Is it business this time?"

"Sort of. I made arrangements to come. I had to do a little finagling. But my superior officer finally agreed." He laughed a little, then added in a shaky voice, "So, can I see you?"

"Oh, of course," she said in a voice as nonchalantly as she could manage. "I'd love to see you."

"I should be arriving on the fifth. Can we have dinner?"

"I'll have to ask Klaus for the time off from work."

"I'll arrange it. Don't worry."

CHAPTER 10

When Margot arrived at the restaurant the following evening, Marie grabbed Margot's arm. Then she pulled Margot out of the building and a few steps away from the front door so Klaus wouldn't see them.

Marie was shaking.

"What is it? What's wrong with you?" Margot asked. "Are you all right?"

"Tilly is gone. But listen to this: her stuff is still in the cabinet under the sink. If she had quit, she would have taken her things. Klaus didn't say what happened. All he said was that Tilly won't be back. This has happened before with waitresses. The ones who disappear are always a certain type of girl. They are blonde with blue eyes, tall and slender. Just like the new girl."

"You mean Alice, right?"

"Yes, that's her name."

"So, what does all this mean? People quit jobs when they move away. They find other work. It's not unusual."

"Oh, but you don't understand. The last two girls who fit this description and left the restaurant this way were found dead. Both of them were found dead. And both in the same way. Their bodies were found mutilated in the park."

"What?" Margot asked, stunned. "What are you saying?"

"I am saying I think Klaus is killing them."

Margot stared at Marie in disbelief.

"Think about it, Margot. Klaus is too friendly with the SS officers for them to investigate him. He's almost like a pimp for them, and they enjoy coming here to the restaurant where they can find anything they are looking for. But if you ask me, Klaus is killing these girls."

"That's crazy. Why would he do that?"

"Helga was the girl who was here before Tilly. She had blonde hair, blue eyes, and a tall, slender body. All of it, right? Well, anyway, Helga and I became good friends. We spent some time going out on our days off together."

"All right, and?" Margot asked. "What happened?"

"Once, when Helga was drunk, she told me that Klaus liked to have sex with her. He paid her. Plenty. She told me all about it. But the thing is, it was not just sex. She said he liked to do sadistic things. He paid her so much money because he enjoyed hurting her. That's what she told me. She said it was the only sexual outlet he enjoyed. Then, poof, just like that, she was found dead. Now Tilly is gone. And I have a feeling that Alice is next."

"Oh, my goodness. This is horrible."

"Yes, it is. I agree with you. But I am telling you to be careful around him."

"I'm not his type," Margot whispered softly, "and I am glad about that."

"No, you're not. And you're right, that is good. But he is a killer and would think nothing of murdering you if you anger him in any way."

Just then, Klaus came outside. "What's this? What's going on here? You two should be in here working, not outside talking. Come on. Let's go. There are men waiting for food and beer in there. Get to work."

As they walked inside the restaurant, Marie whispered in Margot's ear. "Let's walk home together tonight. We can talk more then."

"All right."

CHAPTER 11

Marie and Margot, whose boardinghouses were only a street away from each other, walked back together after the restaurant closed. Margot felt a chill as they walked side by side.

"I have known Klaus for a long time, and I truly believe that he is a dangerous man," Marie said as she lit a cigarette.

"I've always known that," Margot agreed. "I could tell. He has a lot of influence in the neighborhood with other businesses as well as with the SS. But aren't all the men who come into this restaurant at least a little dangerous. At least Klaus is not in the SS."

"Oh, he may not be in the SS, but he has many connections. He does whatever he pleases, and there are no repercussions for him. I've heard from the other girls before they disappeared that he often goes to secret SS parties where the Nazis bring Jewish women from the camps. They are all sexual sadists. They torture and kill these women."

"Oh, that's terrifying." Margot trembled. "That's absolutely horrific."

"And that's not all…"

"As you know, he uses all of us girls who work for him to make an impression on the Nazis. We have to go out with them if we want to keep our jobs. And if we don't…well…who knows what Klaus would do to us?"

"You're right. I agree with you. I wish we could quit our jobs and the restaurant and find new jobs. But when I arrived in Frankfurt, I had a very hard time finding any kind of work. There simply were no other jobs available. We both have bills to pay, so we have to stay where we are, at least for now. What else can we do?"

"Yes, I know that right now, there are no other jobs. Many times, I've gone out during my time off and tried to find one. But I found nothing. So, all we can do is just keep our guard up and be very careful all the time. We can never fully trust Klaus and never go anywhere alone with him."

"This is kind of scary," Margot admitted.

"It's more than just kind of scary. It's very scary. I realize that you think you know how bad he is. But you don't. Not really. I've been working here for quite a while, and I have learned plenty about him. Just so you know, if we did find other jobs, I am afraid he would hunt us down and kill us for leaving him. Besides being a sexual sadist, he's also a very vindictive man."

"So, what can we do? What does all of this mean exactly? How are we going to get through this? How will we get away from him?"

"Well, first, as I said before, be careful, stay out of his way, and don't go anywhere deserted with him. The good thing is that at least you aren't his type, sexually, I mean. As for Alice, the new girl, the little blond he had just hired. I know she doesn't realize it, but she is in real trouble."

"Should we do something? Should we tell her what we know?" Margot asked.

"No, we don't dare do that. If she doesn't believe us and she talks to Klaus, he will target us. We have to just sit back and stay out of it."

"But I feel sorry for her. She seems so innocent."

"She's very young. She knows she's pretty. And she is flattered by Klaus' attention. I feel sorry for her, too. But not sorry enough to risk our lives. And besides, I must admit she acts a little arrogant." Marie shook her head. "Even so, no one deserves to be murdered by their boss."

"I wish we could help her."

"Yes, so do I, but we can't. Unfortunately for her, she is very typically his type. All the girls that disappeared were like her, very Aryan-looking. He likes that. Now, I can't say that I am sure he wouldn't torture other women if he had the opportunity. Who can say what he would do? But he has a special place in his sick, perverted heart for Aryan blondes."

"Hmmm." Margot shook her head. "This really is terrible. I can't believe I am going to stand by and watch this thing play out."

"Well, yes. I know it's terrible. And I know you feel bad. But that is not the reason that I told you all of this. We can't protect Alice, but I am trying to protect you. Be careful of everything you say and do, even when you go out with those Nazis because they will tell him if you say anything bad about him. They all love him."

"I've noticed that. It's because he gives them anything they want."

"Exactly right. Now, there is only one thing that could protect you from Klaus. And that would be if you had a high-ranking SS officer as your serious boyfriend. That would make you valuable to Klaus because he will never do anything to anger one of the SS. So, if you feel in danger, try to make one of those fellows your steady boyfriend."

Margot nodded. She had already planned this with Kurtis but for a different reason. However, now that Marie had told her this, she had another reason to marry Kurtis. He could be her ticket to safety.

"Anyway, for now, just remember what I am telling you and try your very best not to attract his attention to you, good or bad."

"Well, at least I am not blonde, and I don't look Aryan," Margot said, breathing deeply, then quickly added, "but I am Aryan, of course."

Her friend smiled at her as if she knew the truth. "Of course you are. And it's a good thing, at least in this situation, that you're not blonde. But that still doesn't mean you're safe. He could turn on you at any time, and then you would be in trouble. Stay away from him as much as possible. Take my advice. I am your friend."

Margot shook her head. "I'll do my best. But I can't imagine he is that dangerous. He runs this business. Everyone knows him. I don't understand how he gets away with this sort of thing."

"I know you don't understand my warning. At least not entirely. Not yet, anyway," Marie said. Then she added, "But if you stay here long enough, you will."

CHAPTER 12

K urtis was like a schoolboy in love. He was excited to see Margot again when he got off the train in Frankfurt. Never before had any girl had such a strong effect on him. Usually, after he won the battle of getting them to his bed, he lost interest. It always seemed that the challenge of winning them attracted him far more than a need for true intimacy. And he'd been happy with his social life going on that way. In fact, that was how he had expected things to go with Margot. But she was different. This girl was so aloof. Even after intimacy, she remained aloof. The others he'd known had always become clingy after he took them to bed. Not Margot. When he first met Margot, he found her cool demeanor challenging. And after their first date, he found it intriguing. But he found it infuriating when she didn't take his calls or call him back. However, now that he had bedded her, he was quite certain that he was in love with her.

He borrowed an automobile to use for the next few days from the Nazi headquarters. Then he returned to his hotel room and dressed carefully for his dinner date that evening. He checked out his appearance in the mirror but was unsatisfied. So, he combed his hair three times to make sure not a single hair was out of place. Before he left Dachau, he'd secured a gift for Margot. It was a pearl necklace with a diamond clasp that he'd acquired by trading stolen goods with one of his friends, a guard who was visiting Dachau but worked at another camp. His friend had seen the pearls lying on the top of the bag of an old Jewish woman who had been gassed upon her arrival. He said he had quickly slipped them into his pocket before the other guards noticed. This was not unusual. Kurtis had stolen plenty from the prisoners. In fact, Kurtis had traded the other guard some diamond cufflinks that he'd taken from the suitcase of one of Dachau's Jewish prisoners. Kurtis liked the cufflinks well enough; he would have kept them for himself. But he needed a gift that would impress Margot. Something beautiful. Something that she could see was expensive.

Whistling softly to himself, Kurtis put the gift box into the pocket of his uniform and then left his hotel room. He climbed into his borrowed auto and drove to the restaurant where Margot was supposed to be waiting for him. She wasn't. Once again, she was late. This time, over an hour. By the time she arrived, he was so angry that he'd considered leaving more than once. However, when she walked in, wearing the blue dress he'd given her with her hair combed away from her lovely, delicate face and caught up in a twist that showed off her alabaster neck, Kurtis melted. A smile spread over his face. He wasn't leaving. He wasn't going anywhere without her.

"I'm so sorry, I'm late. The first bus that came was too crowded. There was no room. So, I had to wait for the next bus to arrive."

He thought she could have pushed her way in to be on time, but he said, "Of course, I completely understand. But next time, you should allow me to pick you up at your home. There's no need for you to wait for a bus when I have an auto right outside at my disposal."

"I'm sorry," she said, and her voice was so sincere that he wanted to kiss her.

"It's all right. Come, let's go, and we'll have a nice dinner." He took her hand. "I'm so glad to see you. You look stunning tonight."

She smiled.

They drove almost fifteen minutes before arriving at a quaint little restaurant. Kurtis opened the door for Margot and helped her out of the car. Then she slipped her hand into his arm, and they entered.

He had telephoned earlier that afternoon to ensure they would have a nice table. And when the host seated them, he was not disappointed. It was a quiet table in the back where he and Margot could speak privately.

As they were about to sit down, she looked into his eyes and smiled at him. He felt a shiver run down his back, and his knees felt weak. Then he waved the host away and pulled out the chair for Margot himself.

"This is a lovely restaurant," she said. "I've never been here."

"Yes, it is. I was hoping you'd like it."

"I do." She sat down and opened the menu.

"Would you like me to order for you?" he asked.

She looked directly into his eyes. "No, thank you. I can order for myself."

He was offended. But once again, intrigued. Why was this girl so different from any other he'd ever known? She didn't fall at his feet or act as if she was lucky to have a man of his caliber at her side.

Margot ordered the second most expensive thing on the menu. Kurtis was surprised. Most of the girls he knew tried to show him how frugal they could be so he would consider them good prospects for future wives. However, he didn't care how much she spent because he was so happy to be with her. During dinner, she was very attentive. Not once did she look at any other man in the room. And with her attention focused on his every word, Kurtis felt royal, like a king.

After they finished eating, Kurtis suggested he and Margot return to his room for a nightcap.

"Oh, Kurtis, I'd love to," she said, "but I'm exhausted."

"Just one drink," he pleaded.

"I'm sorry. Not tonight."

He was disappointed and angry. He didn't speak the entire drive from the restaurant to her boardinghouse. Then he got out of the car and opened her door. But he didn't walk her up to the door of her building. He was trembling with anger, but he still had to force himself not to ask to see her again and not to try to kiss her goodnight.

Kurtis turned and was about to get back into the car when she casually thanked him for dinner. He was enraged as he watched her go up the walkway to the house where she lived. She didn't turn around once. She just walked inside.

Kurtis watched as she entered the house. He swore that he was quite done with her for good this time. *She's arrogant. She thinks she is more important than she is. But in fact, she is just a waitress at a restaurant, a restaurant where I could have her fired in an instant if I chose to. And besides all of that, she is dark-haired and dark-eyed. Not exactly a classic beauty. So, what makes her so haughty? Why does she think she can treat me the way she does?* He huffed out loud. Then he pulled the auto away from the curb so quickly that the tires screeched. Driving back to his hotel room, he cursed her and tried to entertain thoughts of the other girls he'd met recently. But the harder he tried to push her out of his mind, the stronger his desire for her became.

CHAPTER 13

Margot turned the key in the lock on the door to her room. It was late. Her landlady didn't like her roomers to stay out late. So, rather than being confronted by the landlady, Margot tried to be very quiet. But once she was inside her room with the door locked behind her, she began to cry. She was unnerved. She knew she was playing a dangerous game with Kurtis. And she was terrified by her behavior. She knew she was making him angry. And if this cat-and-mouse game she was playing with him backfired, she might be in trouble. If he lost interest, she would be pregnant and alone in Frankfurt with no one to claim her unborn child. "Oh, Ben," she whispered softly under her breath as if he could hear her. "I am so afraid for our baby. I might make Kurtis so angry that not only might he give up on me, but he might take revenge and get me fired." *Then what would I do? What could I do to survive? Leave Frankfurt. But where would I go?*

After hanging her dress in the closet, she slipped off her shoes. Then she sat down on the bed in her slip. Her entire body was trembling. She missed the men she loved, Ben and Max. She wished she could talk to Ben and unburden herself, sharing her fears. He would be excited about the baby but worried, too, like she was. She closed her eyes and tried to envision his face. If she tried hard enough, she could see him clearly. How kind and gentle he had always been. Then she thought of Max and could see him smiling at her in her mind's eye. His heart was so good, and he, too, was so kind. He had been dragged into this terrible situation because he wanted to do right by their son. If it hadn't been for Erik, Max would never have joined the Nazi party. She would never, could never, blame him for that. She knew she couldn't tell him she was having Ben's baby if he was with her now. That was her secret. *If I am ever blessed to find Max again, I will take that secret to my grave.*

I know he will think the child is his because I was pregnant the last time we were together. She closed her eyes and remembered how Max told her to run, and she ran through the streets after Rudy's murder. Margot tried not to think of Max's reaction to knowing that she and Ben had been lovers. Instead, she thought of his strong arms around her. If she tried hard enough, she could feel his lips on hers. Could feel the warmth of his skin when she touched his face and the comfort of his strong hand holding hers. But when Margot opened her eyes, she was alone in this little room in a woman's boarding house in a strange city.

CHAPTER 14

K urtis resisted telephoning Margot the following day. He decided he was going to enjoy the city without her. But by evening, he had changed his mind and was on his way to the restaurant where he knew she would be working. When he arrived, he saw Klaus sitting at the bar with a new waitress, a young blonde he didn't recognize. The blonde was sitting on a stool beside Klaus, and they were giggling about something. Kurtis looked around nervously. He did not see Margot, so he assumed she had not arrived for work yet. Kurtis walked over to Klaus. "*Allo*, my friend," he said.

"Good to see you."

"Yes, as always," Kurtis said, nodding but anxiously watching the door.

"Let me buy you a beer." Klaus motioned for the bartender to come over and bring the three of them beers. "This is the new girl I recently hired. Her name is Alice."

"*Allo*, Alice," Kurtis said. He smiled when he looked at her. She was a typical Aryan beauty. "Business must be good. You must be plenty busy to need another waitress."

"Yes, we are busy, but I'm afraid Tilly left us. She had to return home to Hamburg. Her father is sick," Klaus said sympathetically.

"Oh, I am sorry to hear that."

"Yes, I was sorry to see her go. She was a very good waitress."

"Perhaps she'll return."

"Yes, perhaps," Klaus said, nodding.

The beers came, and they toasted the *Führer*. Then Klaus asked, "How are things progressing with you and Margot? I'm assuming they are going well, or you would not have returned to Frankfurt so soon."

"Yes, yes, they are going well," Kurtis lied. He would have liked to tell Klaus the truth, that Margot was too free, too unattainable, and although it intrigued him, it also drove him crazy. But he decided it was better to keep his feelings to himself.

Kurtis sat with Klaus and Alice for the next fifteen minutes. They talked and laughed, but he had no idea what they were saying because his eyes were focused on the door. He was waiting impatiently for Margot to arrive. When she finally opened the door and entered the restaurant, his heart skipped a beat, and he was suddenly self-conscious, afraid she might be angry that he had gone to her job to find her. Kurtis was also worried that she might tell him she was no longer interested in him. *Why do I care so much? She is just an insignificant little waitress. There are a million girls like her. There is nothing about her that is special. So, what is it that is compelling me to pursue her?* He tried to make sense of his feelings, but he couldn't as he watched her enter the room. *Any other Aryan man would find Alice to be far more attractive. And yet, there is just something about Margot that draws me like a magnet.*

CHAPTER 15

Margot did not notice Kurtis when she first arrived at the restaurant. She was on time for work, but just barely. There was no time to waste looking around the room before she began her shift. Quickly, she entered the kitchen and slipped on her apron. Then she waved to Marie as she walked out into the dining room. Marie waved back, then motioned to Margot to look at the bar where Klaus sat with Alice and Kurtis. Margot was relieved to see Kurtis sitting there. She knew he'd come to see her. And she had been concerned that she might have been too distant the previous night. *I'm glad I haven't lost his interest, but I'd better act quickly if I am going to carry out this plan.*

Margot began taking orders, pretending not to notice Kurtis, but she could feel him staring at her. *I must proceed carefully.* She made a point of not looking in Kurtis' direction. Finally, he walked over to her.

"Margot," he said, but his voice cracked. Clearing his throat and trying to sound strong and confident even though she could see he wasn't, he said, "I tried to telephone you."

"Oh?" she said as casually as she could manage. *I never got the* message. "I was out all day," she lied. *I wonder why my landlady didn't tell me he was on the telephone.*

"Are you angry with me for last night? Did I offend you somehow?" he asked, looking at her with eyes wide like a young boy.

She hesitated for a long moment. One of the customers, a fat red-faced Nazi, slammed his fist on the wooden table and called out to Margot, "Waitress, waitress, we need another round of beer over here."

Margot nodded her head to the customer, and then she turned to Kurtis. "I can't talk here. I have to do my work," she said. "I'm sorry." Then, she began to walk away from him.

Kurtis grabbed her arm, perhaps a little too hard. He immediately apologized. "I'm sorry. I got a little carried away. I didn't mean to grab you so hard. But I must speak with you. Can we talk after you finish work tonight? I'll take you to dinner wherever you want to go."

She pretended to consider his offer.

"Waitress, come on, I said we need another round." The red-faced Nazi was growing impatient.

"I can't see you tonight."

"But why?"

"Because it will be too late. My landlady gets mad when I am out late at night."

That's an absurd answer. She just doesn't want to see me. Why? What have I done? I can't let her go just like that. I can't get her off my mind. "Tomorrow then. I'll even pay you whatever you earn for working tomorrow night, and I'll see to it that Klaus gives you the night off."

"Yes, all right. We can have dinner tomorrow," she said, "but I am sorry, I must go now and take care of that table. Klaus will get mad if I keep those customers waiting. I'll see you tomorrow night."

"What time?" He stood watching her as he clenched and unclenched his fists in frustration.

"Eight?"

"I'll pick you up at your boarding house at eight."

"No, I'll meet you at the restaurant," she said, and then she turned away from him. A small smile crept over her face. *My plan is working. My baby will be safe.*

CHAPTER 16

Margot did not sleep well that night. She was far too nervous. So many things could go wrong with her plan. *I have to be very careful. Kurtis was a powerful man, and I am just a woman and secretly a Jewish woman. If he somehow learned that I am Jewish, he could have me arrested in a second. But what if he discovered that I am pregnant with another man's child and that I lied to him? He would probably kill the baby and me.* She shivered.

The following day, she awakened with a headache. But she knew she must see him that night and look her best. Margot hated to spend money needlessly, but knowing that her appearance would make all the difference in whether her plan worked or failed, she stuffed a few Reichsmarks into her pocketbook and walked to the secondhand store to find a dress. It had to be a special dress that made her look alluring but innocent. There was nothing at the secondhand store that fit her properly. It was freezing outside, and she wanted to return to her room and lie down, but she needed a dress and a few cosmetics, so she walked three streets to another thrift store. Again, nothing. It seemed that people were salvaging every bit of fabric as this war raged on. There was less and less at the used clothing stores. She purchased a pot of black mascara and then was going to head back home when she had another idea. After looking at a clock in the window of a restaurant she passed, Margot realized that it was ten in the morning. This was early, but not too early to go and see Marie. Marie's room was not far from hers, so she quickly walked there and knocked on the door.

Marie answered in a tattered nightdress, with her hair in pin curls.

"I woke you up. I'm so sorry. I was hoping you'd be awake," Margot said.

"It's all right. Come in," Marie said. "What's the matter? Why did you come? Are you all right?"

"I'm all right," Margot said. "I have a date with Kurtis tonight. I need to borrow a dress. Do you have something I can borrow?"

"I have a few things. Have a look. They're over there in the closet." Marie pointed.

Margot walked over to the closet and began going through the dresses. When she took a dark blue dress out of the closet, she saw Marie watching her. "I thought you didn't like him," she said.

"I don't," Margot admitted. "But…" Then, Margot decided she needed to trust someone, so she told Marie a half-truth. "I'm pregnant. He's the father."

"What? I never knew you let things get that far."

Margot shrugged. "Sometimes we do things for a meal or a little comfort."

"A meal? A little comfort? You hated him," Marie said in disbelief. Margot wanted to tell her the truth, but she couldn't. She liked Marie very much, but it was impossible to trust anyone completely during these terrible times.

"Can I borrow this one?"

"Of course. Try it on."

It was warmer in Marie's room than outside, but it was still chilly. Margot shivered as she removed her clothes and stood in her undergarments in the middle of the room.

"Sorry, it's so darn cold in here," Marie said. "My landlord doesn't turn the heat up high enough. It's always like this."

"It's all right. My landlady is the same," Margot said, still shivering as she slipped on the dress. It was a little too large, but it was flattering. "What do you think?" she asked Marie.

"It looks good on you. But I have a better one." She got up, went into the closet, and pulled out a red dress. It looked very small. "It's too small for me," Marie said. "But it should fit you just right."

Margot looked at the dress. It was more revealing and sexier than what she had been looking for, but to satisfy Marie, she tried it on. It fit like it was made for her.

"Well, well, you look beautiful," Marie said. "This dress has your name all over it. And you can keep it. I'll never be that small. So, it will never fit me." Marie hesitated, then looking at the dress, she touched the fabric and added, "It was my sister's."

"I didn't know you had a sister," Margot said as she looked at the dress in the full-length mirror. *I have to admit, this dress is very flattering. I don't look innocent by any means. But it is really lovely. I'll wear it.*

"Yes, I had a sister. She was my best friend. But she died."

Marie's words pulled Margot out of her own thoughts. She approached Marie and put her hand on her friend's shoulder. "I'm so sorry," Margot said.

"Yes, me too. I miss her."

Margot didn't want to ask what had happened. Instead, she just held Marie's hand tightly. "I've lost people who were close to me, too."

"Your husband was a soldier, yes?"

"Yes." Margot hated lying to Marie but was afraid to tell her the truth.

There was a long silence. "I don't believe you," Marie said.

Margot was shocked and suddenly nervous. "What? Why don't you believe me?"

"I think you might have a secret you don't want to tell me."

"I don't know what you're talking about." Margot was suddenly shaken.

"It's all right. I don't need to know everything about you to love you. You are my best friend now that my sister is gone. And that's all I need to know."

Margot looked at Marie. "I have a feeling you have secrets, too."

"Yes."

Margot hugged Marie. "I don't need to know them either."

There was a brief silence. Then, in a cheery voice, Marie said, "Why don't you take my sister's clothes? I have a few dresses and things that belonged to her. I believe they will all fit you very nicely."

"That's very kind of you. But I couldn't."

"Why not? I won't sell them to a thrift store. And I would never give them to someone I didn't feel close to. Take them, Margot. They don't do me any good here. I can't wear them."

Margot hugged Marie again. "You are such a good friend." *There is so much I wish I could talk to you about. Maybe someday I will feel safe enough to tell you everything.*

CHAPTER 17

Kurtis was already at the restaurant waiting for Margot to arrive. He was sitting at a table talking with Klaus, trying to pretend he was interested in the conversation. But his mind was on Margot, and his eyes lit up when she arrived, wearing her red dress. The admiration and desire she saw in his face told her that he was falling for her, and tonight was the night she must put her plan into action.

They drove to a restaurant located a mile or so outside the center of town. It was a quiet place with five tables adorned with white table-cloths. The food was exquisite. But Margot could hardly eat; her pregnancy left her far too nauseated. Even the smell of food made her want to vomit. When she felt bile rising in her throat, she quickly excused herself and almost ran to the bathroom. This pregnancy, she realized, was different from her first one. She'd never experienced anything like this when she was pregnant with Erik. Still, she had heard that many girls got sick to their stomachs when they were having babies. Once she was alone in the bathroom, Margot leaned against the wall. It was cool on her forehead, and she felt hot all over. She was dizzy, and then she gagged and vomited. Afterward, she leaned against the wall again. Now, she was cold and shivering. *I'm feeling wretched.* She thought as she went to the sink and splashed water on her face. *How will I be convincing and seductive when I feel this way?* She stayed in the bathroom for almost ten minutes, and her stomach had settled a little by the time she left. When she returned to the table, she was glad Kurtis hadn't waited for her to eat. *He has bad manners. But I'm glad because I want the waiter to take this food away as quickly as possible.*

"Are you all right?" he asked. There was genuine concern in his voice.

She nodded. "I have something to tell you," she said.

"Yes? What is it, darling? Are you ill?"

She ignored his questions. Clearing her throat, she said, "I think we made a mistake last time you were here."

"A mistake?"

"Yes." She looked down at her hands. Her stomach lurched again, and she wished the waiter would come and clear the table. But even though her nausea was returning, she couldn't stop what she had put into motion. She had to continue with her plan. "Well, I was thinking about what happened last time you were here. And I realized that we should not have been intimate. It was just too soon. And I don't do things like that so quickly. I just don't know what came over me."

"I don't understand why you feel that way. I thought it was wonderful. And believe me, Margot, I care deeply about you. In fact, I must tell you that you are all I can think about," he said.

She looked away. He saw her gag. She was embarrassed and couldn't look directly at him.

"You haven't eaten a thing. I can see that you aren't feeling well," Kurtis said.

"I'm not," she admitted.

"Don't worry, I'll get you the best medical care available. Just tell me what is wrong. We can go to the hospital right now."

It's working. Tell him. Tell him now. "I'm not sick."

"Then what is it? You aren't eating, and now you say you feel we should not have been intimate? Don't you care for me? Is that why you are ill?"

"No, it's not that. In fact, I do. I care for you very much. But I must admit that I am afraid to tell you what is wrong with me."

"Afraid? You are afraid of me? How can you fear me? I've been nothing but generous and kind towards you."

"It's not you that I fear. It's how you will respond to what I must say."

"Margot, darling." He took her hand in both of his. "You're talking in circles, and I don't understand. Please, just tell me what it is that you want to say."

She sighed. Then she began to cry and shook her head.

Kurtis reached out and touched her cheek. "You can tell me anything. I will understand. Please, darling. Just talk to me."

"I'm pregnant," she said. "I am going to have your child."

He looked into her eyes. His entire body tingled. It was as if he was hit with a lightning bolt of joy. He let out a loud laugh. Then he got up and went over to her chair, crouching so his face was leveled with hers. She looked away, but he turned her chin towards him gently. "That's wonderful news," he said in a soft but very delighted tone. "Are you sure?"

"I'm sure. I feel terrible. And I missed my period."

"Oh, Margot. This is wonderful." He was smiling broadly. "I've never felt the way I feel about you, about any girl before. I want to marry you and raise our child together. That is if you will marry me."

She finally looked into his eyes. "Are you sure that's what you really want?" she asked gingerly. "Because I don't want you to feel forced."

"It's everything I want," he said. "I'll make all the arrangements for us to have our wedding at the restaurant where you work. I'm sure Klaus will accommodate us. Then, you will move to Dachau with me after we are married. You won't need to keep this job. I earn plenty of money to take good care of you and our baby." He touched her chin. "I'll come back with a ring for you."

She placed a soft kiss on his lips. Then he put his arms around her and kissed her more deeply. "Perhaps you should come and move in with me. You can quit your job. I will support you," he said.

"I would like that very much," she said carefully. "However, since we are going to be newlyweds, I think it's wise for me to continue to work until we are married. I can save money for us. It's a good idea, don't you agree?"

"If that's what you want," he said.

"Well, it would be nice to have some money saved. And I would like to feel I had contributed something to our marriage."

He laughed a little. "You are contributing plenty to our lives. You are having my baby. And a child is more valuable than anything."

She smiled at him. "Indulge me? Please? Let me stay here in Frankfurt and work. Just until we are married. I'll save everything I can." Margot didn't want to move in with Kurtis any sooner than she had to. Here in Frankfurt, she had Marie, and it was good to have a best friend who was like a sister. She knew she would have to leave Frankfurt soon enough, but at least she might still have a few months.

"Very well," he said, smiling. "How could I ever deny you anything?"

When Margot returned to her room, she lay on her bed and sighed. It had gone exactly as she had hoped it would. Her child would be safe because the world would think it was the offspring of a Nazi officer. She rubbed her belly. "We're going to all right, little one," she whispered.

CHAPTER 18

The following day, Kurtis went to the restaurant early. He spoke to Klaus and told him that he and Margot were getting married. Klaus patted Kurtis on the back and said he was happy for them. When Margot arrived a few hours later, Klaus brought her and Kurtis a glass of schnapps. First, they toasted to the *Führer*, but their second toast was to the couple's engagement. Kurtis explained that he would like to have the wedding at the restaurant, and Klaus was more than agreeable. He was enthusiastic. It was to be a small wedding, but Kurtis said he planned to invite everyone he knew that was important to him in the Nazi party. They scheduled the wedding for early July. Even though Margot would have preferred it to be sooner. But Kurtis said his important coworkers would need time to arrange their schedules so they could attend. Not wanting to seem overly eager, Margot agreed. Kurtis told Klaus that he was willing to pay whatever it cost to have the perfect wedding. Sunflowers were to be ordered for each table because they were the official flowers of the Reich. When Klaus heard that Kurtis was willing to spare no expense, his eyes lit up.

A few days later, Kurtis returned to work at Dachau. The first thing he did was inform his superior officer that while he was in

Frankfurt, he'd gotten engaged. He invited his superior officer to the wedding. His superior officer made it known that he would make sure Kurtis and his new bride received a decorative copy of *Mein Kampf.* This was a gift of honor given to all SS officers and their brides. It was bestowed upon them by the Nazi party.

Margot asked Marie to help her with the wedding. Marie agreed although she looked at Margot skeptically. "Are you sure you know what you're doing?" she asked.

Margot nodded.

"You don't want me to ask you any questions, do you?" Marie asked.

Margot shook her head. "Please don't."

Marie nodded. "You know that if you ever want to talk about this, I'm here to listen."

"I know," Margot said, then she forced a smile. "Will you help me find a band?"

"Of course. What kind of music are you looking for?"

"Well, you know it must be Wagner or German folk music."

"Yes, I do know that," Marie said. "But I know of some good bands."

As Margot and Marie were discussing music for the wedding, followed by an intense discussion of which foods should be served, Tilly's mutilated body was found in a field on the outskirts of town. The police arrived at the restaurant that afternoon. Marie was closest to the door when they walked in. "Can I help you?" she asked.

The officer asked to speak with Klaus.

"Of course. Wait here. I'll get him for you," she said, but as she walked towards the back of the restaurant, Marie glanced at Margot, who looked at her puzzled. Since Klaus was Tilly's boss and technically the last person to see her alive, he was taken to the police station.

"I'll be back in a little while," Klaus said as he walked out with the two policemen.

After Klaus and the officer drove away, Marie motioned for Margot to meet her outside.

"Did you hear what the policeman said?" Marie asked breathlessly.

"No, I couldn't hear, I was too far away. What did he say?"

"He said Tilly has been found dead."

"Really? That's horrible."

"I know. It is. And I am sure it was Klaus who killed her. The police should know it too because she's not the first girl who worked here who was found murdered. And yet, you just watch. Klaus will return to work as if nothing happened. They won't convict him even though I can't believe they don't know he's the one who is doing this."

"Poor Alice. She's still here and still alive. She's the same type as Tilly," Margot said, but even though she felt sorry for Tilly and the other girls Klaus had killed, she had problems of her own. She was always worried that somehow Kurtis would find out that the baby she carried was not his.

Klaus did not return to the restaurant that evening after questioning at the police station.

"Do you think they know he's been killing these girls?" Margot asked.

"I think they know, but I must admit I am surprised he hasn't returned. They always take him in and question him, but he always comes back without a care in the world."

"Who knows? Maybe this time they will arrest him."

"We'll have to wait and see. But if they do, I think they'll close the restaurant. Then what are we going to do for work?" Marie said.

"I have no idea. We'll have to wait and see what happens."

CHAPTER 19

BERLIN

At first, when Trudy became Peter's mistress, he was very attentive. He came to see her every few weeks. Often, he brought her gifts of flowers and chocolates, and once, he gave her a pair of silk stockings. She was happy with him. Much happier than when she had been with Max. Even though he was married, he took her to several parties where she met and mingled with other Nazi officer's wives and girlfriends. Trudy loved dressing up, and it had been a while since she had the opportunity. In fact, it had been since Rudy's death.

Peter and Trudy never chatted about anything of importance. He told stories in which he was the hero, and she listened intently, always smiling, always encouraging him. There was no mention of his wife or children. His other life, as he called it, was not up for discussion. But she didn't mind. In fact, she preferred not to talk about his family. If there was no mention of his wife, Trudy could pretend that no wife existed. And that was exactly what she did. In her mind, she pretended that Peter was her husband, and she pretended that when he was gone, he was not living another life. He was just away on business. For a while, this worked out well. But by the beginning of March, Peter seemed to be losing interest in Trudy. He was still telephoning, but now, instead of three or four times a week, he only called once a week. And he was making excuses for why he was unable to come to Berlin to see her. This made Trudy edgy, as she had no job or income and was afraid that Peter might have found another girl. It was difficult for her to sleep as she had begun to have dreams of being abandoned and left out on the street. *What would I do? Would I have to move into a brothel? I have no skills. I can't type or take shorthand.*

But then, one Sunday afternoon, Peter telephoned. He was in high spirits when he called. "How are you, dear?" he asked.

"I'm alright. But I miss you. When are you coming to see me?" she asked.

"I have a surprise for you. I am going to be attending a party for the Führer in April. It's not exactly a birthday party, but his girlfriend Eva Braun is giving it, and since the Führer's birthday is on the 20th of April, I will bring him a lovely gift."

"Oh?" she said, wondering what the surprise was.

"And…" he paused for effect, "I would like for you to join me."

She gasped excitedly. "Really?"

"Yes, actually. It will be in a very special place. You may have heard of it. It's called the Eagle's Nest. And it's supposed to be the most beautiful place in all of Europe. I'd like you to take a train to Munich. I'll send you money for a ticket. Then we'll drive to the Eagle's Nest together. That is, of course, if you would like to accompany me."

Trudy breathed a sigh of relief. *He's still interested in me. And I am going to a party where I will meet the Führer.* "Of course, I would love to," she said.

"I'll wire you some money for the train and also for something special to wear to the party. Go out and purchase a very lovely, expensive dress. I need to make a good impression on everyone there," he said.

"Of course, I will do as you ask," she agreed.

This was the best news that Trudy had received in a long time, and she was uplifted, hoping Peter had a change of heart. If there had been another girl, she was sure he'd broken up with her. Whatever it was that had threatened to destroy his relationship with Trudy, it seemed to be gone. And Trudy was certain that after this birthday party, everything would return to how it was before.

CHAPTER 20

Max leaned against the wall in his barracks. Kaz and Adrien stood beside him. "That louse Richter has been in a good mood. I've noticed he hasn't been shooting prisoners as often as usual."

"Who knows what's up with him?" Kaz threw his hands up. "He's probably happy because he's planning something terrible to do to someone."

"That could well be true. But for now, whatever drives him to be less awful is good for me because he's been easier on my crew at work. He used to be quick to shoot. Now, he seems a bit softer," Max said. "He hasn't killed anyone in two whole days."

"It makes me nervous when one of them acts out of character," Adrien said. "I never have to worry about that with Mengele. He's a sadist. Always a sadist. And when he does act kindly, and sometimes he does, I know that his cruelty is waiting just around the corner. I watched him in the hospital. He'll give a child a piece of candy, then operate on the child without any anesthesia. He really enjoys seeing people suffer. I have to say that I can't figure out how he got a medical degree."

"Rich parents," Kaz let out a little laugh.

"Probably right," Max nodded.

"That's one man who should never have been a doctor."

"I'm so hungry, papa," a teenage boy said as he sat beside his father on one of the bunks.

"Poor thing. I wish I had some food to give him." Kaz shook his head.

"I wish we had some food for ourselves, too," Adrien said.

"I know," Max agreed. Then he turned to Kaz. "I hear your stomach singing a song at night." He made a joke.

"My stomach?" Kaz said.

"Yes, yours."

"No. It's not."

"Oh yes, it is. I sleep right beside you, and it's yours."

"Stop bickering, you two," Adrien said. "All of our stomachs are making noise all the time. We're starving. What do you expect?"

"Jews, always making jokes." One of the other inmates said loud enough for Max and his friends to hear. "Everything is funny to them."

"Better to laugh than to cry," Kaz said, smiling. "You know what? When I get out of here, I'm going to be a comedian."

"None of us are ever going to get out of here, you stupid Jew," the man said. "This place is designed to kill us, and it will. You'll see. It will kill us all."

"Shut your mouth, or you won't have to worry about this place killing you. I'll kill you right now," Kaz said.

Max could see that Kaz was getting annoyed. "Come on, let's go and play cards."

Adrien grabbed Kaz by the arm, and the three of them went to the other side of the room, where they sat down to play.

When it was time to sleep, Max lay on his bed of straw and thought about Margot. He closed his eyes and tried to remember the smell of the soap she used to wash her hair. How he had loved to bury his face in her soft brown curls. It seemed like a lifetime since he'd last seen her. And with all the terrible things he'd witnessed since he was sent to this prison, he began to doubt that she was still alive. The Nazis were so cruel. Even the stories that were told by the new prisoners attested to a constant increase in arrests in the world outside the camps. They said that now Jews were being shot and murdered on the streets for no reason at all. One new prisoner mentioned that he had just escaped a mass murder where Jews were lined up and shot and thrown into a mass grave. Then, after his escape, he'd tried to hide in an underground sewer, but the Nazis had found him and sent him here to Dachau. Hatred for the Nazi party burned like a constant flame in Max's heart. But now, he hated Trudy, too. And he knew that if Trudy were right in front of him, he could have easily choked the life out of her with his bare hands. She had been the cause of all of his misery. And someday, if he lived, he promised himself that he would find her and kill her and thereby avenge his family's suffering. With these thoughts blazing in his mind, Max fell asleep.

CHAPTER 21

Margot was sick with guilt over having cheated on Max. But even so, she knew that if she was faced with the opportunity to be Ben's lover again, she would not deny him. It was wrong to cheat on Max, her husband, whom she loved dearly. However, they did not live in normal times. Her love affair with Ben was the last time Ben had ever felt even the tiniest bit of joy in his life. And she was glad that she'd made that possible for him. Because, in truth, she loved them both, her husband Max and Ben. She was more ashamed of the fact that she was about to marry a Nazi than she was about her love affair with Ben.

Sometimes Margot wondered what she would do if she saw Max again. She missed him terribly and wished she could talk to him. However, as she became more entangled in this web of deceit she was creating, she wondered if she could ever face Max again. *I don't know how I could tell him that my baby was Ben's child and not his. Then how could I ever explain that I married a Nazi to keep the baby safe? If this third Reich ever ends, and Max and I find each other again, I will have to live a lie forever to protect him.* She paused for a moment. *Of course, there is always the possibility that Max was arrested for Rudy's murder. I don't know where he is or what's happened to him. I only know that I would be so ashamed to see him now. Ashamed. I don't know how I could explain everything I've done. I couldn't bring myself to tell him the truth. I know he would be appalled at my behavior. Maybe it's best that we never see each other again. Then, he would always remember me as the woman he'd once loved. A good woman. Not a liar. And with the secret my parents kept from me about my Jewish mother, there have been enough lies in our lives already.*

Margot sat down on the bed in her small room. She put her head in her hands and began to cry softly. Then, there was a knock on the door. She wiped her tears away with her forearm and said, "Who is it?"

"It's me. You have a telephone call." It was the landlady, nosey as always. "It's a man."

"All right. Give me a minute. I'll be right there," Margot said, wishing she could go to the bathroom and wash her face before facing the landlady, but there was no chance. The woman stood waiting just outside her door. When Margot opened the door, she glared at the landlady, who was looking at her as if she was trying to figure out why her eyes were red. Margot said nothing. She just walked to the telephone.

As she walked past, the landlady said, "You know that I charge by the minute to use the telephone. I'm sure you understand. I have to charge you because I have to pay for it. So, of course, nothing is for free."

"Yes, I know," Margot said, then picked up the phone. The old woman followed her. Then she stood there, listening. Margot turned to her, "I will pay you for the phone, but I would like some privacy if you don't mind."

"Of course," the old landlady said, and she walked away.

"*Allo,*" Margot said.

"It's Kurtis. I overheard you and your landlady talking. Sounds like she's an old witch."

Margot tried to laugh. "She's a bit difficult."

"Don't worry about using the phone. Just tell her that I said I'll pay the phone bills."

"Oh, thanks so much," she said.

"Of course." He was cheerful. "I have some very good news."

"What is it?" she asked, trying to sound as lighthearted as she could.

"We've been invited to a party for the *Führer*. Can you believe it? This is such an honor. And do you know where it is?" Kurtis paused for a moment of suspense. "It's up at the Kehlsteinhaus; another name for it is the Eagle's Nest."

"What?"

"Eva Braun is giving a party for Hitler. I can't believe I have been invited. And, of course, as my fiancée, you will be my date."

"What is the Eagle's Nest?"

"Oh, it's the most beautiful place in the world. It's located in the Bavarian Alps on this secluded mountain. Only Hitler's top people own homes up the mountain. Then, at the top, there is the most incredible building in the world, with the best view in the whole world. I've never been. But I've heard it's spectacular. You are going to love it."

"When is it?"

"April."

"Oh." She had reacted too fast and had forgotten to hide the disdain in her voice.

"What's wrong?"

"Nothing. I just dropped something on the floor. That's all."

"Oh, what is it?"

She had to think fast. "A bit of bread I bought for dinner. Nothing to worry about." Margot made her voice as cheery as she could.

"So, you will go with me. Yes?"

"Yes," she said, wishing she could come up with some excuse but knowing she dared not try. He must never suspect her true feelings about Hitler and his government.

"I can't wait," he said. "Well, goodbye. I'll telephone again tomorrow."

"Yes," she said. "Goodbye."

"What? Did I hear that you are going to a party with the *Führer*?" the landlady, who had been hiding just behind the door, asked.

"You shouldn't listen to other people's conversations," Margot said rudely as she walked back to her room.

Once she locked the door, she sat on the bed and shivered. She felt trapped, nervous, and frustrated. She was going to be sitting next to Hitler's elite and hiding secrets that she knew would make them turn on her in an instant. If they had an inkling that her mother was Jewish or that she carried Ben's child, they would kill her and her unborn baby. Margot closed her eyes and remembered when she was a girl, perhaps eight or nine, and she had auditioned for a play at school. She had gotten a small part because she was popular and everyone liked her. But even then, she knew she was not much of an actress. Her face was too expressive, and she had difficulty hiding her true feelings. *Well, this party will be the most difficult part any actress has ever played. And the stakes are very high. If I am not convincing, the consequences will be dire.* She rubbed her small, rounded belly and whispered to the tiny life inside, "I'll do my very best for you. I won't fail you, no matter what."

CHAPTER 22

A week after Klaus had gone to the police station, he finally returned to the restaurant. While he was gone, his wife had come in and handled everything. This was the first time either Margot or Marie had met her. In fact, before she came into the restaurant, neither of them knew he was married. Klaus' wife was a gray-haired, heavy-set woman who looked older than her years. Unlike Klaus, she did not drink or smoke. Her expression was stern, and she ran the restaurant like a military organization. The woman allowed for no unnecessary talking between employees or even between employees and guests. She was always watching the workers and always ready to criticize. When Klaus returned, he told them he had been exonerated from wrongdoing. Margot was glad to have him back. It wasn't that she liked him; she didn't. But he was far easier to work for than his wife had been. And that evening, as Marie and Margot walked home after work, they discussed Klaus and his involvement in the death of the former waitress.

"I know he is committing these murders. I'd bet my right arm on

70

it," Marie said. "But we can't say a word, and we don't dare try to investigate."

"And you were right. But let's just be glad we are not his type. From what you told me about his sexual escapades, I am assuming these murders are sexually driven," Margot said. "And since he's attracted to certain types of women, we're sort of safe."

"I overheard the policeman say that the police think it's a sexually motivated crime. They said the same thing when they came to talk to Klaus the other two times as well."

"It's terrifying."

"Yes, it is. All the women were Blonde, Aryan women."

"Yes, just like poor Alice. I feel bad for her," Margot said.

"So do I. But she should be taking notice of what is going on. She should be able to see that Klaus was questioned for this murder, and I'm sure she's heard about the others."

"I'm sure she probably has."

"My conscience is bothering me. So, I've thought about talking to her," Marie said. "But I can't. I just can't afford to anger Klaus and possibly lose this job."

"Or worse. He might kill us," Margot said. Without a thought, her hand went to her belly. She rubbed it gently.

Marie saw her do this. "Do you have a stomachache?"

"No," Margot shook her head. "The baby is kicking."

"That's exciting. What does it feel like?"

"It's actually quite amazing to know that there is a person inside of me who is alive and moving," she said.

"I have always wanted a child," Marie said wistfully. Then she giggled and gently put her hand on Margot's belly. "This is exciting. A new baby! If I can't have my own right now, I'll enjoy yours!"

"Yes. I want you to enjoy the baby. You'll be like an aunt to him or her. But it's also very scary to have a child right now. I mean, with the way the world is."

"I know, but regardless of all the dangers surrounding us, a child is such a blessing," Marie said.

Margot nodded. "I agree with you. But every day, I worry. I just wish we weren't at war."

"Of course. So do I. But you and I are powerless to stop the war. We don't like the way things are going, but there's nothing we can do. But we can take pleasure in this bit of happiness, right? So, let's be happy about the baby."

Margot nodded. She was happy about the child. But the love she already felt for the innocent child in her womb terrified her. It made her vulnerable. She knew she would do anything, anything at all, to protect it.

When they arrived at the front door of the building that housed Margot's rooming house, Margot and Marie said good night. Then Margot hugged her friend. "Thank you for everything."

"For what?"

"Just for being a good friend. A good friend is a gift, too."

"Yes, and I thank you for being a good friend as well."

Margot turned and went inside the building. She wished she could unburden herself by telling Marie the truth about everything. *I believe I can trust her. Eventually, perhaps, I will. But the baby's survival depends on my being very careful, and so, for now, I can't risk it.*

CHAPTER 23

t was late at night, but Margot couldn't sleep. She tried to read but was unable to concentrate. Lying in bed, she glanced out the window at the moon and stars. Then she rubbed her belly and closed her eyes. In her mind's eye, she envisioned Ben's face. Then, she began to talk to her unborn child in a soft whisper.

"My baby, you are always in my thoughts. Your well-being is the most important thing to me and comes first in every decision I make. I know right now, I am making some tough choices. I hope I am doing the right thing. I am robbing you of your heritage because of the man I am choosing to marry. He's a Nazi. I know this and I am sorry it has to be this way, but your survival depends on it. And I already love you more than life itself, so I am willing to marry a man whose ideals I hate to protect you.

"More than anything, no matter how this turns out, I want you to know that you were conceived in love. Your father was a good person with a big heart full of kindness and compassion. If he had the opportunity, he would have been a brilliant doctor. Even without having the proper training or any medical supplies, because both were forbidden to him because he was Jewish, he still saved lives. He would have loved you; he would have been so proud of you. So, I have decided that I will name you for him. The Jewish people name their children after loved ones who have died. Your father's name was Ben. If you are a boy, I plan to name you Barrett because it is a strong name. You will need the strength in this life. It is a difficult world that you are coming into. I am also sorry for this. I wish I could make it better for you. However, I am powerless."

She sighed as a tear rolled down her cheek. "If you are a girl, I will call you Belinda because Belinda means beauty." Margot smiled a knowing smile. Then she rubbed her belly again. "But I am pretty sure you are a boy. I can feel it." Then, in an even softer voice, she added, "I plan to give you a very special Hebrew name, which will be our secret. I've done a lot of research to find this name. It's Baruch, and it means blessed. My sweet baby, my sweet Baruch, may you always be blessed."

CHAPTER 24

K urtis was surprised at how he was feeling. He had never really been in love before. Women attracted him, and they came and went in and out of his life. Sometimes, he cared. Most times, he didn't. But nothing compared to the way he felt about Margot. If anyone asked him, he would have to admit that he finally knew what it meant to be madly in love. They were engaged, and soon, she would be his wife. But somehow, she was still aloof, and that drove him mad. At times, he would telephone her, and she would take his call, but she would seem cold and distant. This cool behavior of hers should have discouraged his love for her. Instead, it seemed to intensify it. Kurtis reminded himself that she had agreed to be his wife, and they would have a child together. That, he thought, should assure him that she was his, yet, somehow, he never felt that she was wholly committed to him. He yearned for absolute devotion on her part. In fact, that longing often drove him crazy. When he traveled to see her, sometimes she would allow him to make love to her. And this was when he was happiest. On those days, she paid him the attention he needed and made him feel like he was the most desirable man in the entire world.

But other times, she would be very distant, and when he tried to make love to her, she would refuse to allow him to touch her, giving him the excuse that she didn't feel well due to her pregnancy. Sometimes, he would surprise her at the restaurant where she worked after taking a long train ride, and she would seem happy to see him. But other times, he would surprise her with a visit, and she would avoid him, only speaking to him briefly. He hated it when she treated him like every other customer, not like the man she was engaged to marry. When she didn't show him any affection, Kurtis fell into a deep depression, not knowing how to win her affection back again. He dared not complain to Klaus about her or anyone else because he feared she might call off the wedding entirely if he upset Margot. And so, he put up with her mood swings and found that his own moods were affected by hers. When his visits to Margot in Frankfurt were disappointing, he would return to Dachau angry and frustrated. Then, needing to lash out, he took his misery out on the prisoners. Especially the weak ones.

If Margot had known that her treatment of Kurtis influenced the lives of others, particularly Max, she would have been kinder to Kurtis. But as it was, she knew she must keep him intrigued, so she kept him confused. This way, he would not get bored with her. One afternoon, Kurtis called from Frankfurt. She was running late to work, so she had been short with Kurtis on the phone. When they hung up, he was down, full of self-doubt, afraid she was losing interest in him. He wanted to jump on the next train to Frankfurt to see her. But he knew he had been taking too much time away from work. The smell of the camp and the sickly starving prisoners disgusted him even more than they usually did. But he knew he must make his rounds, so he began walking through the camp. There was one teenage boy, a Jew, whom Kurtis had a particularly strong hatred for. His name was Harry. In Harry's former life, before the Nazis had taken him and his family away from their modest home in a small town in Poland, he had been a quiet, unpopular student who shied away from girls and sports. If it hadn't been for Max's helping him, Harry would have been killed immediately upon his arrival. But it just so happened that Max was returning from work just as the transport carrying Harry arrived at Dachau.

Max glanced over and saw the boy. He looked away, trying not to feel any pity for the men coming into this terrible place. But he couldn't help himself. Something in him stirred when he saw Harry. There was something about this pathetic boy that tore at his heartstrings. Perhaps it was that Harry reminded him of his son, Erik. Harry, like Erik, was weak and sickly. Max knew he had to do something to help this young man. A frail boy like this was bound to be exterminated within a half hour of his arrival. Instead of heading to get in line for dinner, Max looked around to make sure no one was watching. Then, he quickly grabbed the boy's arm and pulled him out of the inspection line. Before he even said a word to him, he led Harry back to his block, where he asked Adrien, his doctor friend, to take a look at him. Then he turned to Harry, who was stunned and afraid. As gently as he could, Max explained why he had taken Harry out of inspection. He told Harry he looked too weak to pass the first inspection, so he planned to hide him on this block. It would be difficult because Harry did not go through an inspection. Because of that, he would not have any identity. This meant he could not get in line to receive the meager food rations the others would receive. And so as not to stand out, he would also need a uniform, which Max planned to steal a uniform for him.

"You do realize that Harry is going to have to be clever. He'll need to stay hidden during roll call every day," Adrien said to Max.

"Yes, I know. I've explained it to him," Max said. "He doesn't have a number, so he would really stand out. I've mapped out a few hiding places for him. He knows he must avoid the guards at all costs. Especially that sadist Richter."

"You've taken on a responsibility, haven't you?" Kaz said.

Max shrugged. "What else could I do? They would have put him to death. I have no doubt. And he's just a boy."

"A sickly one, too," Kaz said. "Isn't he Adrien?"

"Yes, he is not healthy, not strong," Adrien said.

"I know he's weak. I can see that," Max said.

"He won't be able to work. He'll have to stay hidden all the time," Adrien said. "He would be dead in one day if they put him on one of the crews to build the roads."

Max nodded. "I know."

"How do you plan to feed him?" Kaz asked.

Again, Max shrugged. "I don't know. I don't have a plan. But I just couldn't let them kill him. As soon as I saw him, I knew he would not make it through the first elimination. I don't know what it was, but I felt so much pity for him."

"Trying to protect someone here will get you killed," Kaz said sarcastically. "But, since you felt heroic and have already rescued this young fellow, I'll help you. I'll share my rations with him. You share yours too, and maybe between us, we'll have enough to survive for a little while, anyway."

"You're a good fellow, Kaz."

"Not really. I'm just a human who still has a heart left, even though these monsters have torn it to shreds."

Max patted Kaz's shoulder.

"You do know that Harry is anemic, but then again, who isn't in here?" Adrien said as Harry walked over to them. "But I would say he's fairly healthy, considering. He doesn't seem to have typhus or tuberculosis, so that's good." Adrien patted Harry's shoulder.

"Yes, that's a plus," Kaz said, nodding sarcastically. Then he looked at Max. "How do you plan on stealing a uniform for him?"

"I haven't figured it out yet."

"Ehh, don't try it. I'll help you. I have a friend who works in that section. He'll get a uniform for me," Kaz said. "I'll ask him right before roll call tomorrow."

That was the beginning of Max and his friends pooling their resources to help Harry survive. As he promised, Kaz got Harry a uniform. And the three of them gave him small pieces of their tiny hunks of precious bread. There was hardly enough for the four of them. Still, Max, Kaz, and Adrien agreed that they were preserving their humanity by helping one who was weaker than they were.

Every day that Harry survived became an achievement for the three friends. But what they didn't know was that Kurtis Richter already knew of Harry. They had tried to hide him, but nothing got past Kurtis' watchful eye. For Kurtis, watching these foolish men try to protect a boy who was already sick was puzzling. But he did find it fascinating. It was like observing ants on an ant farm. Kurtis despised Harry for being weak and allowing his friends to protect him. And he was just waiting for the right time to punish him.

As Kurtis made his rounds on the evening after Margot had been short with him on the phone, he walked into the block where Max, Kaz, Adrien, and Harry played cards. They didn't expect the *Kommandoführer* to come into the barracks at such a late hour. He usually was done with his rounds by this time. There were hordes of new prisoners arriving each day at the blocks and crowding them even more. Kaz nudged Max and motioned with his head for Max to look over and see the *Kommandoführer*. Max nodded. "Go on playing. Pretend you don't see him," he warned Harry. But Harry couldn't take his eyes off the *Kommandoführer*. He was terrified.

Kurtis walked through the block, disgusted by the buckets of human excrement overflowing in the corner. He walked until his eyes fell upon Harry. They settled there, and he watched Harry squirm as he stared at him. For a few moments, Kurtis stood in front of the men playing cards and just stared. Between his frustration and hatred for weakness, Kurtis felt an overwhelming desire bubble up inside him. He wanted to hurt Harry. He looked into Harry's eyes. "You. Get up," Kurtis said.

Harry looked from Kaz to Max. He was shaking and did not know what to do next. There was no place to run or hide. "You have to do what he tells you," Kaz said.

Harry looked at Max in panic. But Max just nodded.

Shaking, Harry stood up in front of the Nazi, who stood taping his nightstick on his thigh. "Do you know who I am?" Kurtis asked in a soft but evil-sounding tone.

Harry shook his head.

Kurtis slapped him hard across the face. "I said, do you know who I am?"

"No, sir."

"I am *Kommandoführer* Richter. But to you, boy, I am God. I decide if you live or if you die. So," Kurtis smiled wickedly, "tell me one reason why I should let you live."

Harry was dumbstruck. He could not speak. His whole body was shaking. His knees gave way, and he fell to the ground. Then he began to weep. Max started to stand up and go to him, but Kaz grabbed Max's arm and held him down. "Don't move," Kaz warned. "You can't help him. The *Kommandoführer* will do what he pleases."

Kurtis didn't hear Kaz. He was not paying attention to him. He was fixated on the weak boy, falling apart before his eyes.

"You're not convincing me to keep you alive," Kurtis said. His eyes twinkled with fascination.

"I…I… don't know what to say. But please…" Harry was choking, his nose was running, and his cheeks were covered with dirt-smeared tears. He was a young man, but he looked like a boy.

"Get up. Get up off the ground, you pathetic worthless Jew."

Harry stumbled, but he stood up. He was shaking and looked more like a rag doll than a human being.

Kurtis shook his head. "You are disgusting," he said, then he took his foot and kicked Harry's legs out from under him. Harry fell back down on the floor. His bony body lay on its side. Max saw Harry's wrist. It was the size of a child's wrist and made him sick to his stomach.

Kurtis was relentless. He was hungry to spill some blood. "Is that your whole argument?" he asked Harry sarcastically. "I ask you why I should let you live, and all you can say is, please?"

"I-I will do whatever you ask of me," Harry said. "I didn't do anything wrong. I just came in here without knowing where I was going?"

"What in the hell are you talking about?"

"Oh no," Kaz whispered to Max. "He's about to give you up to the *Kommandoführer*. He's going to tell him that you rescued him. I knew something like this was going to happen. Damn it, man, now you're going to be in trouble."

"I was in the line when I first got here. I meant to follow the other prisoners, but I was walking along, and then I got lost and ended up here on this block," Harry said. Even as he was being terrorized, he hadn't turned on Max.

"So, you never went through inspection?" Kurtis said.

Max knew it didn't really matter. Kurtis was enjoying intimidating the boy.

"No, I am sorry," Harry admitted, thinking this was why he had been called out. When, in fact, it was not the reason at all. Kurtis was looking for the weakest man when he walked into that block. He wanted someone to torture. This information was just a bonus. Another reason to frighten this boy.

Kaz moved closer to Max so he could whisper in his ear undetected. "He's going to kill him," he said. "I'm sure you must realize that. But no matter what happens, you are not going to move. Do you understand me?"

Max stared into Kaz's burning eyes. "But I can't let Richter murder him."

"Quiet. Listen. Either that boy will be dead, or both you and that boy will be dead. You can't save him. So, you must save yourself."

"Do I hear talking?" Kurtis' deep, dark voice reverberated through the block. "Is there someone here who would like to trade their own life for the life of this boy? If there is, I would be happy to hear your case. You know, I was thinking about studying law when I left it all behind to join the army. So, we can have some fun here. I would be happy to play the judge. Is anyone interested?" he said casually as if he were asking if someone wanted to play tennis.

Kaz gripped Max's arm and squeezed hard to let him know that he must not say a word. Max sat silent, but inside, in his heart, he wept.

Then Kurtis began to kick Harry in the stomach and in the back. Blood oozed from Harry's lips. Max's eyes were glued to Harry's face as, in his mind's eye, Harry's face changed to the face of his dead son Erik. The beating seemed to go on forever. Harry's screams filled the room. Max wanted to cover his ears. He wanted to scream, too. But then it was over. The room went silent, and Harry was dead.

"Clean this mess up," Kurtis said to one of the prisoners. Then he left the block. Harry's blood was splashed on his shiny black boots.

"They killed my little boy," Max whispered to Kaz.

"That was not your son. That was Harry. A nice Jewish boy. He didn't deserve to die. But he wasn't your son."

"I know. But I am trying to tell you something. The Nazis killed my son, Erik. They murdered him. They tricked my wife and me into believing they would help him. Then they killed him."

Kaz nodded. "Yes. All of us have a story. All of us have lost our loved ones. But Max, you are still alive. And you must not think about those who you've lost. If you do, you'll give up. And that's the end. Instead, you must concentrate on living another day. Do you understand?"

Max shrugged.

"Listen to me. I am sorry about what just happened to Harry. But his pain and agony are over now. And without him, we will have more food. So, our chances of survival will be better."

"Yes," Max said, but he stood up and went over to the bed of straw where he slept. Then, without another word, he lay down, feeling lost and helpless.

Kaz walked over to Max. "You did what you could," he said. "We can't always save others. We all tried to save Harry, but we failed. Sometimes, we can help, and sometimes, we can't. And sometimes we can't even save ourselves."

Max didn't answer. Kaz patted his shoulder, then got up and walked away.

CHAPTER 25

The beauty salon was unusually busy, especially for a Tuesday. But Trudy had offered to pay extra for an emergency appointment. The pretty young hairdresser had been working on her for over an hour when Trudy sat up after her hair was shampooed. She looked in the mirror. For a moment, she couldn't speak. She stared at her reflection in shock and horror. Then she grabbed her hairdresser's wrist. "I need to be blonder," Trudy said. "My hair isn't light enough."

"I did the best I could. This is as blonde as your hair will go."

"I have an important party to attend next week, and I can't have my hair looking like this. It looks orange, not blonde. Get that red out of it right away, or I swear I'll have this place shut down."

The owner walked over to see what the fuss was about. "What is it Frau Schulze?"

"Look at my hair? I am going to a party for the *Führer* next week. My boyfriend has been invited. He's an important officer. And just look at what this girl has done to me. I can't go with my hair looking like this. I suggest you fire this hairdresser on the spot. She has no idea how to do hair."

"Go in the back and wait for me, Ingrid. I have to fix this mess," the owner said to the young hairdresser, who was almost in tears.

"Yes, ma'am," Ingrid said.

After Ingrid walked away, the owner looked more closely at Trudy's hair. "Don't worry. I'll fix it," she assured her. "That girl is new. But I will take your advice and get rid of her."

Trudy smiled with satisfaction.

The beauty shop owner worked on Trudy for over four hours, but by the time Trudy left the salon, her hair was light blonde. She smiled as she walked down the street. She was heading to the finest dress shop in town. *This party is going to be perfect. I will be the most beautiful woman there.*

CHAPTER 26

Some women look weathered when pregnant. Their skin is lackluster, and so is their hair. The extra weight can be unflattering to their figures. However, not Margot. Her skin glowed, and her hair shined. The tiny baby bump in her lower belly was hardly noticeable, but her slender body was womanlier. Her breasts were larger, and her tiny hips spread just enough to give her an hourglass figure. She was, in fact, more beautiful now than she had ever been. When she told Marie about the party, Marie said she could borrow any of her dresses if she wanted to. But Margot didn't want to stand out. She was always nervous when she was around Nazi officers, and so she said she would prefer to blend in with the crowd rather than to bring attention to herself. She and Marie scrutinized the dresses Marie had given Margot, but none were fancy enough for the occasion. So, Margot and Marie went to the thrift store on their day off together. There Margot bought a long black evening dress. She had contemplated wearing one of her work dresses or one of Marie's sister's dresses even though they weren't as dressy, but Marie had talked her out of it.

"I know you don't want to stand out. But if everyone is wearing long evening dresses and you're not, you'll stand out, anyway."

The dress Margot chose was form-fitted but not tight, with a simple, modest neckline. When they left the store, they began to walk arm in arm. They were headed back to Margot's room, where they planned to have something to eat. Margot said, "I wish I didn't have to go to this party. I am nervous about it."

"I know you are. I don't blame you." They walked quietly for a few moments. "Why are you marrying him?" Marie asked.

"What?"

"I know you don't love Kurtis. I can tell. So, why are you marrying him? Because you are pregnant?"

"Yes."

"But the baby isn't his, is it?"

Margot stopped suddenly and looked at Marie. "Of course it is."

"No, it's not. I knew you were pregnant when you arrived here." Marie let out a short laugh.

"How did you know that?"

"My mother was a midwife. I knew. I could tell. When you've spent your entire youth around pregnant women, you just know."

Margot was stunned. She could hardly speak. "You never said anything."

"We weren't that close of friends yet. But now that we have grown so close, I felt compelled to tell you I know the truth. I know the baby isn't his. But don't worry Margot, your secret is safe with me. I would never tell anyone."

Margot didn't know what to say. "I feel very nervous and very vulnerable now."

"Don't," Marie said gently. "I am going to tell you a secret about me. Would that help? Would it help if you knew a deep, dark secret about me? That way, you could be sure I would never tell on you."

"Yes. I suppose it would."

"I work with a group who does what we can to fight against the Nazis. They are not good for our country, and we secretly hate them. I would like you to join us. I know you. I've been watching you since you arrived at the restaurant, and I can see that you hate the Nazis as much as I do. And I also know there is a reason, a secret reason, as to why you are marrying Kurtis. But you needn't tell me why you are marrying him. I'll be honest, it doesn't matter. But this resistance group I belong to could use your help. You wouldn't have to fight or anything like that. All you need to do is deliver papers inside books to the bookseller. It's not difficult. I have been doing it for quite a while."

"The bookseller is one of you?"

"Yes. I also know that he recommended that you apply for work at the restaurant. I knew all about you before we became friends."

"Marie," Margot said, shocked. "Are you crazy? Why are you telling me this?"

"Because I trust you. I know you are not who you seem to be. I am pretty sure that you don't even like Kurtis, and you don't like the other Nazi officers that come into the restaurant, either. I see how you look at them when they don't know you are looking. That's why I hoped you would have the courage to join our resistance and help us."

Margot was shaking, "I don't know. I don't know," she said. She was thinking about the baby. "You're right. I would join you if I could. I've always wanted to be a part of something that was going to help defeat the Nazis. But I am pregnant now, and I can't take any risks. If I am caught, they will kill me and my unborn child. I love you; you are my best friend. But please try to understand that I just can't do anything to put my child in danger."

"I do understand. Of course I do. But children are dying at the hands of these beasts every day. The only way we have to fight against them is by doing what we can to oppose their control of us."

They started walking again. There was a long silence. Then Margot said, "I can't help you. But please know that your secret is safe with me. I will never tell anyone what you told me."

"I know that. I am a good judge of character. That's how I've stayed alive as long as I have. I trust you. And I believe that one day, you will trust me too and tell me your story."

CHAPTER 27

Peter's wife had been ill for the last several months. If she hadn't been, then he would have considered bringing her to the upcoming bash for Hitler. But even before she became ill, she hardly ever attended anything. He loved her in his own way. She was his strength and his security. There had always been other women in his life. But his shy, introverted wife was a quiet oak tree he could always lean on. He knew he would always have lovers, but as long as he lived, he would never divorce her. Her name was Helga, and she came from good German stock. Her hair was blonde, and her eyes were blue, but he had to admit she wasn't exceptionally pretty. She was wise; sometimes, he thought she knew about the other girls. But she never said a word. In fact, Helga never complained about anything. She never asked him where he went when he went out of town. Helga was a quiet girl who was satisfied staying home and caring for the children. There was something about her, something steady and secure that he always returned to, and he knew that he always would. And now that she was ill, he was worried about how he was going to go on without her. He tried to put the idea out of his mind, but the possibility that she might die haunted him.

Lately, he'd found himself losing interest in Trudy. Her self-indulgent attitude had begun to bore him. In fact, to distract himself from his fears of losing Helga, he'd started looking around for a new female who he found interesting. And he had already met a new woman, Christa. She was a tall blonde, similar in looks to Trudy but less boring. Christa was much younger than Peter and even younger than Trudy, and so far, she had rejected all his advances. When he smiled or winked at her, she didn't respond. The challenge was a good distraction. It kept his mind off Helga and his children.

Christa worked as a secretary at Congress Hall, where he had first seen her when he went to help organize a rally. Finally, he decided to ask her out for dinner. So, he went to her office and walked over to her. "I have been thinking about you since the first time I saw you," he said in his most charming manner. "I think you just might be the prettiest girl in all of Nuremberg."

She answered by saying, "You are a married man. And even though you are an SS officer, which is quite impressive, I don't date married men."

Some men would have been discouraged by her curtness, but not Peter. He was intrigued. He liked this spunky young woman who was more than willing to stand up to him. Even after she turned him down for a date, he'd asked her to go to Hitler's party with him. He was certain she would say yes. *What girl would ever turn down such an offer?* He thought. But to his surprise, Christa refused. And that was why he was taking Trudy. He needed to bring a date who looked Aryan and pure German. It was too close to the date of the gala to try to find another girl, and he knew Trudy would be happy to go. So, even though he was thinking about breaking off his arrangement with Trudy, he decided that he would not do so until after this very important party.

CHAPTER 28

Max was outside toiling with a crew of workers one morning. They were laying the groundwork for a new road when a Nazi arrived in a black automobile. He got out of the back of the car and walked over to the *Arbetsenführer*, who oversaw the work details. He was a very tall man, so he leaned over to speak privately to the *Arbetsenführer*. They conversed for a few moments. Then the *Arbetsenführer* nodded, and the visitor nodded before he turned to the working crew and called out, pointing to Max, "Hey, you. Over there. Come here right now."

Max trembled inwardly. But trying to remain calm, he put down his shovel and obeyed the visitor.

"Take these papers over to the office," the tall Nazi handed Max a stack of papers. "And don't be wasting time. You have work to do. So, return as soon as you've delivered them. Now, go and *Mach Schnell*."

Max took the papers. Then, he began to walk towards the office. But the tall Nazi yelled, "Move, you louse. I told you to *Mach Schnell*. Do I have to shoot you to get you to move faster?"

Hearing this, Max began to run towards the office. He wished he could just keep running all the way out the entrance of the camp and away from this terrible place. But it was impossible to escape; he knew the guards in the tower were watching him, and if he made a move to try to get away, they would shoot him down. When Max arrived at the office, several civilians were working. However, there was also one girl who wore a prisoner's uniform. There were no women in Dachau, which made him wonder who she was and why she was there. No one paid him attention, and he stood in the corner for a few minutes looking around. It was uncomfortable to be in the office.

There were far too many men in Nazi uniforms all around him. Max closed his eyes, and his memory shifted back to when he was one of them, wearing that horrible uniform and working in the postal office surrounded by them. It had never been where he felt at home, but he had somehow managed to make himself believe that the ones he was working with were not so bad. Now that he'd been around more of them, and as a prisoner rather than an equal, he knew better. They were like cardboard men, men without feelings, without sympathy for others. When he was working as one of them, living a lie of his own, he was just as bad because he did nothing to stop their terrible acts of cruelty. I should've cared about other people. I should've tried to help them, tried to be stronger. I was such a fool to believe they would be kind enough to help my son. They hate people who they consider damaged. And that was the way they saw Erik. Damaged. In their minds, his epilepsy was a terrible mental illness he could never recover from. So, they thought he was better off dead. And in my foolishness, I fell for their lies.

Just then, the girl in her prison uniform with a yellow triangle on her chest indicating that she was Jewish interrupted his thoughts. She looked directly at him as she called for him to come forward. "You, over there. What do you want?" She was young, seventeen perhaps. He looked at her and decided that she had probably once been very pretty. But now she was little more than skin and bones. Her cheekbones and jaw were so prominent that they jutted out. Her head was shaved, and her eyes were dark, surrounded by purple and black skin and sunken. However, there was something soft and almost innocent in those eyes.

Looking into her eyes stirred feelings in Max that he had been sure were dead. Months ago, after suffering from terrible yearning, he'd finally forced himself to stop thinking of Margot. It was easier to bear this place if he didn't feel guilty about having someone on the outside who might need his love and protection. And since he'd given up on figuring out what he could do to escape and get to Margot, he'd become almost robotic in his daily attempts to stay alive in this place. However, as he stood in the office looking at this young girl, who was obviously vulnerable, weak, soft, and delicate, a strong desire to protect her overcame him. She was still staring into his eyes. Max looked away. But when he looked back, she had not turned away from him. "So, what do you want? How can I help you?" Her voice was soft, little more than a whisper.

"I was on my work detail when I was told by an officer that I must deliver these papers to the office."

She looked down at the papers. "To whom?"

"The office, that's all he said. He told me to just bring them to the office. So here I am." He felt stupid, awkward, and uncomfortable.

"Oh." She looked flustered. "I don't know who to give them to."

He was staring at her now. "So, I'll just leave them here."

"I can't take them. I don't know what to do with them." Her voice was almost panicked. "I could get into trouble for taking them. I don't need trouble. Please, just go away."

Max saw the anxiety on her face. And he considered leaving. He knew it would be dangerous for him to return to his work detail without delivering the papers. "Well," Max said gently, "maybe you could ask someone?"

She stood there, staring at him. A moment later, a Nazi guard walked over to where they both stood. "What's all this talking over here between you and this prisoner?" he asked the girl.

"Nothing. Nothing at all." Max noticed her hands were shaking, and he felt bad because he had caused her problems. "This fellow brought some papers to the office. He said he was in his work detail, and an officer asked him to deliver them. Now, he wants to leave them. But he doesn't know who they are supposed to be delivered to."

"Give them to me," the guard said.

Max handed him the papers. He thumbed through them quietly.

Then, he nodded. "You go back to work now," he said. "I'll take care of these."

Max nodded and turned to go. When he heard the girl let out a shriek. He whirled around abruptly. The girl he'd been talking with now stood there holding her cheek, which had turned bright red.

"You stole this?" the Nazi asked her, holding up a heel of moldy bread. "We give you a good job, a clean job, working in the office, and you stole this bread from our kitchen. What kind of person are you? Oh yes, why do I bother asking? You're a Jew. You're not a person at all." He pushed the yellow triangle on the chest of her uniform. "You deserve to be punished for this, you ungrateful pig."

"No, please, I swear I didn't steal it." She was crying. "Someone gave it to me. I swear it."

The guard squeezed the heel of moldy bread in his hand. Max looked from the guard's angry face to the face of the terrified girl. He knew he should leave. This was not his problem. But he couldn't watch this and just walk away. "I gave it to her," Max said. "It was mine."

"Yours?" the guard said. "Where did you get it?"

"My evening meal last night. I saved it." Max looked at the guard.

"Why would you do that? Are you a stupid fool?" the Nazi asked.

"She looked hungry, and she reminded me of my sister. I felt bad for her. So, I gave it to her."

There was a long pause. Max could hear his heart beating hard like a caged bird in his chest. Then the Nazi started laughing, "You are a stupid fool. But if you want to give your food away, then give it away. What do I care?" He shook his head. Then he turned back to the girl and said, "Get to work."

She nodded.

One of the other guards came out of a back office and walked over to the guard standing beside Max and the girl. "Hey there, Hans. Let's go and eat lunch," he said.

"Yes, let's go," Hans replied. Then he left the papers Max had brought on the counter before the girl and followed the other guard out the door.

After they were gone, Max turned to the young girl and asked. "Are you all right?"

She nodded. "Thank you. You saved me from a beating. I stole that bread."

"It's all right. I would have done the same thing if the opportunity had presented itself. By the way, what's your name?" Max asked.

"What?" She seemed surprised that he had asked her that.

"Your name? What's your name?"

She shook her head. For a moment, he thought she was not going to answer. But then she said, "Rivka."

"Rivka," he repeated. "I'm Max."

She nodded. Her eyes were almost glued to his. But then another guard walked up and said, "What's going on here?" he indicated to Max. "Why is this prisoner here in the office and not working?"

"Nothing is going on," Rivka said nervously. "This prisoner brought a delivery of some papers that he was instructed to bring by an officer. The other guard was going to take them, but he left them. So, the prisoner didn't know what to do." She handed the guard the pile of papers.

The guard took a moment and looked through the pile of papers. He nodded as a smile of recognition came over his face. "Good. Good. I've been waiting for these," he said. Then he turned to Rivka. "Get back to work." Then, to Max, he said, "Go back to your detail."

Max left the office. As he returned to his work detail on the road right outside the camp, he realized he'd not seen a female since he'd been sent to Dachau. He tried to put Rivka out of his mind but couldn't. Something inside him, a need to nurture and protect, had been activated. He thought of Margot and felt guilty. But his soul ached with hunger for affection, warmth, and kindness. He found that all these things were still within him. In fact, they seemed to have grown stronger since he'd denied their existence.

When the men were back on their block that evening, Max told Kaz what had happened with Rivka that day. "What do you expect from yourself, Max? You are only human. And as humans, we have the need to love."

"But I love Margot. I've never loved anyone else. And yet, this fragile young girl stirred something inside of me. I guess you could say that I am ashamed of the things I am feeling."

"Don't be. We have so little joy in our lives. Take any tiny bit of joy you can get from anywhere you may find it. If you felt good for a moment while speaking with a young woman, there is nothing wrong with it."

"But what is wrong is that I want to see her again. I want to speak to her."

"Then why shouldn't you? Max." Kaz hesitated, "Max, I don't know how to say this. But I am sure you've thought this yourself."

"What?"

"Well, we can't even be certain that Margot is still alive." His voice was kind and gentle. "I am sorry to have to tell you that. But we don't know what has happened to our loved ones outside of here. And this girl, this Rivka, is alive. She is warm and real. She's here now, and she's flesh and blood." He hesitated. "I say, go to the office and wait for her outside after you get back from your detail tomorrow. Then, God willing, you have a chance to talk to her. Just talk. Nothing more."

"Yes, just talk. There is nothing wrong with that. Right?"

"Absolutely."

"So, I'll go tomorrow right after work. You and Adrien get into the soup line; don't wait for me."

CHAPTER 29

Max finished his work detail the following day and followed the other prisoners back to the camp. But when he arrived, instead of searching for Kaz and Adrien to get into the soup line, he made his way to the office. It was important to walk quickly and look as if he knew exactly where he was going and had been sent there by an officer. If any guards suspected he was on a personal mission, he would be punished. Max hurried to the office with his head down so as not to meet the eyes of the guards he passed along the way. *She might have already left for the day.* I don't know much about her. All I know is that she is Jewish because she wears a yellow triangle, and her name is Rivka. For a moment, he thought of Margot and the life they had once shared. Things had not been perfect for the two of them, but he could not recall when their problems were Margot's fault. He knew that any suffering they endured was due to the times. He would give anything to have his life back with his wife and son. However, that was not possible. Erik was dead, and even before his arrest, he'd been unable to find Margot. So, perhaps Kaz was right. Perhaps he should hold tight to any tiny light of joy he found in this dark, horrible place.

Max stood outside the office, hiding on the side of the building so he would not be seen. Crouching down to take a quick look through a window, he scanned the room quickly with his eyes. However, he did not see the girl. A few men walked through the room, but no one noticed him. He was about to leave when he decided to be brave. *What have I got to lose? My life? It's hardly worth much anymore. It's not as if I have Margot to go home to. And who knows what has become of my parents? For all I know, Trudy has turned me in for Rudy's murder, and my parents are suffering the consequences.* The very thought of this made him feel queasy. He hated to think anyone had suffered due to his crime. But he knew Trudy for the horrible person she was, and he realized that she could turn on her own parents if she thought it would benefit her. A chill ran down his spine. She very well might have done just that.

It was getting late. If he didn't leave soon and get into the soup line, he would have nothing but water for dinner. This was a known fact and why he and his friends always hurried to get in line early. Those in the front of the soup line got a little more substance in their soup, not that it was much, a bit of cabbage or a potato peel. They were starving, and even this small addition to their meal made a difference.

Max walked quickly to the food distribution area. His stomach rumbled, but it didn't faze him. He was used to hearing that sound. As he approached the line, he saw Kaz alone, without Adrien standing almost at the front. Max considered cutting the line and walking up to stand beside Kaz. But he couldn't do it. He knew it wasn't fair to the others. So, he went to the end of the line.

Just then, Kaz turned and saw Max. "Come up here. I am holding a place for you," he said.

Max felt guilty about pushing his way into the front of the line, but the hunger in his rumbling stomach fought against any righteousness he felt. With his head down, he walked up to stand beside Kaz.

"*Nu?* Did you see her?" Kaz asked.

"No, I stood outside and waited, but she never came out."

"Hey, you. You!" a middle-aged man with a yellow triangle said as he pointed to Max. "get to the end of the line. It's not right that we are all waiting, and meanwhile, your friend is holding a place for you."

"Mind your business," Kaz said to the man. Even though Kaz had grown thinner, he was still a large and imposing man. Max was tall and big-boned, too.

"It is my business. My son and I are hungry," the man complained.

Max wanted to stay at the front of the line, but when he saw the teenage boy who was little more than a walking skeleton, he said to Kaz, "he's right. I'm going back to the end of the line."

"Are you sure? Because I don't think that man would have the nerve to fight us."

"I know, but this is the right thing to do," Max said.

"Whatever you say, my friend," Kaz answered. "I think you should ignore him. But you must follow your own conscience, I guess."

Max nodded.

When Max reached the end of the line, Adrien stood there. "You're late today," Max said. "Something happened at the hospital?"

"Yes. I'm afraid we currently have a bad bout of typhus going through the camp. I had so many patients die today. But there is something good to be said about this outbreak."

"I can't imagine anything good about a typhus outbreak," Max said.

"Well, The Nazis are scared of catching it, so they stay away from the hospital. Even the Nazi doctors are steering clear. This is good because it gives me an opportunity to actually help the sick people instead of being forced by the doctors to euthanize them."

As was predicted, Max and Adrien had only water and a few insects in their soup that night. When Max first arrived, he'd refused to eat the soup if it had dead insects floating in it. But now, he ate them. He had to learn to eat anything available if he wanted to live.

CHAPTER 30

The following morning, after roll call, Max saw Rivka as he was walking to get into the coffee line. She smiled when she saw him. "I was waiting for you. But I can't stay. I only have a moment," she said. "Here, I brought this for you."

He looked down at her hands. In them, she held an orange. "Where did you ever get this?" Oranges were a tremendous treat and almost impossible to get.

"I guess I have truly become a thief. I stole it."

He held the orange in his hand. It was soft, probably moldy inside. But it was a piece of fruit, and it had been long since he'd tasted anything like it. "This was very kind of you. But I can't accept it. It's yours. You should keep it for yourself."

"I want you to have it," she said simply. "Will you do that for me?"

He smiled at her. She returned the smile. *When she smiles, she is very pretty. Soft, delicate. Pretty.* "I have an idea. Why don't we share it?"

She nodded. "All right."

He peeled it quickly. And much to his surprise, it was not green or moldy inside. He split it in two, insisting she take the larger half. Then they sat down and ate the orange quickly. They spent only a brief time together that morning, but the memory of that time stayed with Max for the rest of the day.

The following morning, Rivka was waiting for Max when he came out of the kitchen carrying his ersatz coffee. It was drizzling lightly, but the sun was shining, and if he squinted just a tiny bit, the raindrops on Rivka's dark hair looked like diamonds.

"*Allo*," she said.

"*Allo*." He smiled broadly. It had been so long since he had looked into a woman's eyes, especially one he was attracted to.

"I have a few minutes before my day starts, so I dropped by. I hope it's all right," she said, blushing.

"It's more than all right. I'm glad you came by."

They sat on the ground side by side. It wasn't a great romance filled with passion. There was no kissing or groping. He was much older than she, and they had little in common. But for a lonely man like Max, it was something to look forward to. They didn't speak much at first. But from then on, she came to see him at the same time every day. By the end of the week, they were talking about their lives before they had been taken prisoner.

"How is it that you came to work here?" he asked. "There are so few women who ever enter Dachau."

"I was at Ravensbrück. That's a woman's camp. Hell on earth, if you ask me. But when Himmler came to see the camp, he was watching us during our roll call. He asked all the prisoners if any of us were good at typing and shorthand skills. I was afraid to say I was. Because sometimes the Nazis would trick us. They would ask a question like that and then shoot the women who answered. But I had been going through some terrible torture at the hands of one of the guards, and I really needed to get away from her. I was sure if I continued to work under her, she was going to kill me. So, I mustered all my courage and admitted that I had the skills they needed."

"Do you?"

"Actually, yes. I was a top secretary for a bank manager before I was arrested."

"So, what happened then?"

"Himmler pulled me out of the line. He took me into the office and made me prove that I could type quickly and accurately. Then he dictated a letter, and I had to write it in perfect shorthand. I had never been so frightened before in my entire life. I knew if I failed to please him, he would kill me on the spot."

"But you did please him?"

"Like I said, my secretarial skills are good. So, yes, he was satisfied with my work. Then, I was taken out of my block and transferred here. I work in the office sometimes. Other times, I am a maid and cook for one of the officers at his home. The SS officers have homes right outside of the camp. I am always very careful of everything I do and say, but it's better here than at Ravensbrück. At least it is for me."

He nodded.

"What about you?" she asked.

"Me?"

"Yes, you. What did you do before you came here? I see you don't have a yellow triangle. That tells me that you are not Jewish, so what crime did you commit?"

He avoided the question. "It's terribly sad that being a Jew is a crime."

"Yes, it is sad. But it's true. My people are hated by most people for no reason other than our religion."

He shook his head. Then his eyes caught her eyes. She was staring at him. He knew she was waiting for an answer to his question. But how could he explain that he had once been a member of the Nazi party? A shiver ran down his spine. Then the buzzer rang, and it was time to report to his work detail.

CHAPTER 31

Rivka came to find Max every morning. They sat together away from the others, where they could be alone until the buzzer sounded, indicating that it was time to start their work. They talked about their childhoods and realized they loved dogs and cats. She admitted to him that she had never had a boyfriend. "My parents thought I was too young," she said. "And my father was so strict. He didn't think I should date anyone until I was ready to get married."

He nodded. "So, you have never been kissed?"

She shook her head. "Never. And I shall probably die here in this place, never having been kissed."

He looked into her eyes. Then he leaned over and took her chin gently into his hand. She did not pull away or resist as he placed a gentle kiss on her lips. As he held her in his arms, he felt her trembling. "Thank you," she whispered.

They were both silent for a moment. Max's thoughts went to Margot, and he felt guilty. But he was so lonely. And besides, Rivka was right. She might not live through this. So many people die in this place every day. *A beautiful young girl deserves to be kissed.*

"Max," she said softly, bringing him back to the present moment.

"Yes?"

"I don't know how to ask you this?"

"What is it?"

"I'm ashamed. But I must try."

"What is it, Rivka? What do you want to know?" he asked gently. He was afraid she had heard something about his past, but he decided that if she asked, he would just tell her the truth. That was all he could do.

"I want you to make love to me."

"What?" He was astonished at first. He was glad for the companionship but had never considered doing such a thing.

"I don't want to die, never having known what it feels like to be loved by a man," she was looking down, but he could see that she was blushing.

"Oh," he said, not sure how to answer.

"Will you do this for me?"

He considered her request for a moment. "I have to be honest with you. I have a wife. Although I don't know what's happened to her."

"I'm sorry for asking,"

She said, suddenly getting up. Then she ran away towards the office, and Max felt terrible.

The following morning, Rivka did not come to see Max. She did not come the day after either. He thought about what she'd asked of him. It wasn't such a terrible request. He needed warmth and comfort, too. And his future, like Rivka's, was uncertain. He would never have considered such a thing if he and Margot were together. But they were not. And he was alone in this place, as was Rivka. She did deserve to feel loved. He decided. Every woman deserved as much. So, the next day, he went into the office after he returned from his work detail. She saw him and went to him immediately. "What are you doing here?"

"I came to see you," he said desperately. "I've changed my mind."

"You have to leave right now. If one of the officers notices you, they will ask questions. If they don't like the answers. They will hurt you. Get out of here now. I'll meet you in the morning," she said. "Go, now."

He did as she asked. And all that night, he was unable to sleep. He was filled with mixed emotions. His body and soul longed for human connection. He desperately needed warmth and tenderness. His skin felt starved for the touch of another person. But even with all of this yearning, it was difficult to overcome the guilt he felt at cheating on Margot. He loved her. He would always love her. And this was not the way he thought his life would be. When he and Margot got married, he believed they would spend every day together until it was time for them to leave the earth. But the Nazis had separated them. They had taken her away from him. They had taken the little boy he loved as well. And now, he was alone in this man-made hell with only his two male friends. Rivka was like a light in the darkness. She wasn't Margot, but she was a young, innocent girl who needed love as much as he did. So, he found that he was glad when he saw Rivka walking up to him the following day. It was April and a little chilly. But it hadn't rained the night before, so although the ground was cold, it was dry.

Max watched Rivka walk towards him, and instead of seeing a sickly thin young person with a shaved head covered by a scarf, in his mind's eye, he saw a beautiful girl, slender and elegant. The dirty cotton scarf became an imported silk. She didn't speak when she got close to him. Instead, she just looked into his eyes. A pang of guilt shot through him. But then she reached up and touched his face. His entire body trembled, and he was lost to the moment and his needs.

He made love to her tenderly, as tenderly as he could manage.

It was a quick, not very romantic, and almost clumsy encounter. But afterward, she lay in his arms for a moment. As soon as he sobered up from the intoxication of sexual desire, he looked around him quickly to be sure they had not been seen. "Thank you," she whispered.

He didn't know what to say. He wished it had been better for her. This was not the way a first time should be for a sweet virgin girl. "You're bleeding a little," he said. "I hope I didn't hurt you."

"No, you didn't," she said.

He kissed her hand.

"I'd better get to work," she whispered, "before they realize I am not there."

"Yes," he said. "I should get back to the group. If we're caught here, the guards won't be kind to us."

She saw the blood running down her leg. Then she took off her scarf, which, in Max's eyes, now returned to the dirty cotton scarf it had been before they made love, and she wiped the blood away. Then she stood up and put the scarf back on her head, and without looking back, she left him sitting in the grass.

Max stood up quickly, shook himself off, and then ran back to where the others were seated, waiting to start their daily work. Rivka never asked him again about what he did before his arrest.

"Where were you?" Kaz asked. "I looked around the corner where you usually take your coffee with that girl. But you weren't there."

Max shook his head. "No. I wasn't."

"That's all you're going to tell me?" Kaz asked.

"Yes."

CHAPTER 32

Kurtis arrived early to pick Margot up for the party. He was in high spirits. "You look radiant," he told her as she entered the auto.

"Thank you," she giggled a little.

"Are you hungry? Do you want something to eat before we get started? It's a long ride."

"No, I'm fine. Really," she said.

"Well, I do have something for you."

"Oh?"

Kurtis pulled a small white box out of the breast pocket of his uniform. He opened it and showed her its contents. She gasped. "My goodness, Kurtis. That's a very large diamond."

"Do you like it?"

She nodded. "Yes, of course. It's beautiful."

If she had known that Kurtis got the diamond by trading some things with another SS officer who stole it from a Jewish woman's hand at Auschwitz before gassing her, Margot would have never been able to accept it. But as it was, she didn't know. So, Kurtis took the ring from the box and placed it on her finger. "We're officially engaged," he said.

"Yes," she answered, looking at the ring. It fit her well.

"We are going to have a wonderful time at this party," Kurtis said. "You can't imagine what an honor it is to be invited to an event like this. I am so excited."

She smiled.

"Have you ever seen Bavaria?"

"No, I haven't."

"You're going to love it. It's the most beautiful place I have ever been," he said. Then he turned on the engine, and they began to drive towards Bavaria.

Margot wasn't happy to be attending a party in honor of Adolf Hitler. Still, she had to admit that Bavaria was quite breathtaking. This was her first time traveling through the mountains, and with the air so clean and the vegetation so rich, she found she loved the countryside. The Alps were more magnificent than she could have imagined. But it saddened her to know that this land belonged to the Reich.

With the windows of the automobile open as Kurtis maneuvered through the mountains, she felt the wind on her face and dancing through her hair as her heart ached with the beauty of the twists and turns in the winding roads. The mountain roads were narrow, and the drop was very steep. She looked down and felt dizzy. *I should be terrified. If Kurtis makes a wrong move with this auto, we could fall to our deaths.* Yet, she wasn't afraid. *If I am meant to die here, at least then the suffering of my life will be over. And I won't have to worry about the future of my child.* A sense of well-being came over her as she sucked in the fresh air and smiled to herself. *At least it isn't raining. It would be even more dangerous if these roads were slippery.* She thought as they made their way up to what seemed like the top of the world.

Kurtis patted her hand. "It's lovely, isn't it, dear?"

"Yes," she said.

"The homes here were previously owned by townspeople. But when Göring came here and saw how magnificent this place is, he declared it the most beautiful place on earth."

She smiled, but she wished he would just be quiet so she could enjoy the scenery rather than hear about his Nazi cohorts.

"Anyway, do you know what Göring did?"

"No idea," she said, sounding more sarcastic than she had meant to.

"Well, he wanted to give the Eagle's Nest to our *Führer* as a birthday gift. So, he confiscated all the land and took it away from the townspeople. Then, he built a beautiful home for the *Führer*. When some of Hitler's top people saw the area, they all wanted to live there. So, now all the houses surrounding the Eagle's Nest are owned by top people in the Nazi Party," Kurtis explained. He pointed to one of the houses. "Göring owns that one," he said. "Speer owns the one over there. In case you don't know, Speer is Hitler's architect. He's quite a genius. Borman has a home here, too. Someday, I hope to own a home up here, too." Kurtis reached over and patted Margot's hand, "With my beautiful wife, of course. And that will be you."

She smiled a shaky smile. *He certainly has a way of ruining things.*

"I'd like to get some time off from work later in the year so we can take a real honeymoon together, not just a few days. I'd love to bring you up here for a week or so. What do you think?"

"Yes, of course," she said.

"You will probably meet Hitler's mistress at the party tonight. Her name is Eva Braun. I met her once. She is quite gay and lovely. I think you will like her."

"Yes, I am sure I will," Margot said. But inside, he had struck a nerve, and now she was no longer calm. She was anxious and frightened. For a short while, she had put the Nazis out of her mind and was just enjoying the pleasant drive. But now she remembered that soon she would be up on the top of a mountain surrounded by enemies. The very idea of it made her feel dizzy and queasy.

"Are you feeling well?" Kurtis asked as he glanced at Margot.

"I am just a little nauseated. I'll be fine. It's pregnancy. It happens sometimes."

"I know. My mother told me. She also said that nausea during pregnancy is a good sign. She said that if you are sick to your stomach when you are pregnant, it means that your baby will be strong."

She managed to smile. "Let's hope so. Because I have really been quite nauseated this whole time."

"I know, darling. I know. Perhaps you should eat something. I did bring some food with us. If you want to get it, there's a little cheese and some bread in my bag in the back seat."

"No, I am afraid to eat. I might vomit. I think it's best if I wait until we get there. I would hate to have to stop on this narrow road. It would be dangerous."

He nodded. "Yes, of course," he said. "Shall I try to get there faster?"

She sucked in her breath. She would have liked to arrive and get out of this car as soon as possible. But she imagined the car tumbling off the edge of the road, flying through the air, and landing with a crash at the bottom. For a moment, she had a strange thought. She wondered how it would feel to fly to her death. *What if I grabbed the wheel and turned it, spinning the car right off the side of the mountain?* The idea was so real in her mind that she shivered. Then she looked away so he couldn't see her face and said, "No, don't go any faster. Let's just get there safely. After all, I am carrying your precious Aryan child."

He smiled broadly. "I am so proud. I will be a father soon."

CHAPTER 33

As Kurtis pulled the car into a space beside a row of similar black cars, Margot felt a sick feeling of foreboding in her stomach. She had never really wanted to go to this party, but now, as she was looking at the other automobiles owned by the Nazis who were up on the mountain, she felt the danger even more strongly. Here, she would be on display as Kurtis' fiancée. These people would observe and probably scrutinize her every move. *Will any of them suspect?* Kurtis was at her side, and she knew he believed he was in love with her. But he didn't know who she really was, and for a second, she wondered what he would do if he ever found out the truth.

Kurtis stepped out of the car, walked around, and opened the car door for Margot. Like a perfect gentleman, he extended his hand and helped her get out. Then he gave her his elbow and escorted her up the incline to the opening of a tunnel that would lead up to their destination. They entered the dark tunnel and began to walk forward. The sound of their heels clicking on the cobblestones and the musty, damp air in the tunnel made Margot uncomfortable. She wished she could run away before she reached the end. She was shivering, but she smiled at Kurtis. She knew she could not leave. She had to go forward.

Besides, if she ran away, there was no place to go. They were isolated in the Bavarian Alps. *I have to go through with this as planned.* She thought. *Once I marry this man, my child will be safe.*

"Are you feeling all right?" Kurtis asked. "I know this is a lot of walking for you, being pregnant, and the air in this tunnel is so musty."

"Yes, I'm fine," she squeezed his arm where she was holding on to him tightly for balance.

At the end of a long corridor stood a strange-looking elevator. It was gold inside with a panel of controls. Margot's heart raced at the sight of it. "I hear the *Führer* is frightened of this elevator," Kurtis said. "He's afraid that he will be struck by lightning or bombed while he is inside. From what everyone says, he's terrified of heights."

"That's rather frightening. I mean the very idea of being stuck when you're in an elevator," Margot admitted, and she trembled as she remembered the damage she'd witnessed when she had seen bombs fall in Berlin.

"I suppose. But I am not worried about it." Kurtis smiled at her. "And you needn't be either." Then he added, "By the way, don't mention that to anyone."

"Mention what?" she asked.

"What I just told you about the *Führer* being afraid of the elevator and heights. These are just rumors, really, and the truth is our *Führer* doesn't like to admit any type of fear."

"Oh, of course. I would never mention anything that you told me in private."

He looked down and smiled at her. "I didn't think so," he said.

When they got off the elevator, they were inside of a building. Kurtis put his hand on Margot's back and led her outside. The temperature here was several degrees colder, and it had started to rain. But the view was magnificent. "Look." Kurtis pointed. "That's Strasberg."

Margot looked down to see a town at the base of the mountain.

They were about to enter the banquet hall when they were greeted by a pretty, vivacious, young blonde woman. She wore a very feminine white dress adorned with a pink rose print. "Kurtis Richter, it's been a long time since I last saw you," she said, hugging him slightly.

He smiled broadly. "I'm surprised you remembered my name," he said, and Margot could see he was very flattered.

"Well, of course, I remember," the pretty blonde said as she smiled again. "And who is the lovely young lady at your side?"

"This is Margot Kraus. She is my fiancée."

"It's a pleasure to meet you. I'm Eva Braun."

"The pleasure is mine," Margot said, making sure her voice sounded warm and sincere. She knew it would be considered rude for her to stare at *Fräulein* Braun. But she did her best to look the woman over quickly. *She's rather pretty. And she seems so carefree, not like the kind of woman I would expect Hitler to be with.*

"Well, please, won't you both come in? Everyone is enjoying cocktails, and dinner will be served shortly."

"Thank you," Kurtis said. Then, he led Margot into a large room. At the front of the room, a fire crackled in a large red brick fireplace. "See that fireplace?" Kurtis whispered to Margot. "It was a gift to the *Führer* from Mussolini. It's rather impressive, no?"

"Yes, especially on such a chilly, rainy evening like this," Margot said.

They walked up to the table that held the place cards. Kurtis searched through the guest cards and found one with his name. It read "*Kommandoführer* Kurtis Richter and guest. Table 10."

He led Margot to the table. It was in the back of the room. He whispered to Margot, "Someday, we'll be sitting in the front. I promise you that."

She nodded but said nothing.

He placed the card between two place settings. Then he escorted Margot up to the bar and ordered a drink from a skinny male bartender who Margot thought had a face like a rat. "Would you like a beer or a glass of wine?" he asked Margot.

"Riesling, please," she answered.

They walked around the room. Kurtis introduced Margot to everyone that he recognized. They were returning to their table to sit down when Margot noticed a tall, very handsome officer walking towards them.

"Kurtis. Well, well, I hardly expected to see you here. It's been a long time," the handsome Nazi said, even before he was close enough to speak to them.

"Oh no, not Peter. I can't stand him. He thinks I don't belong here with the upper echelon. He doesn't think I deserve to be here," Kurtis whispered to Margot.

She didn't have a chance to say anything before Peter stood beside them. "Well, well, my old friend. It certainly is good to see you." Peter smiled, but his smile was insincere.

"Yes, likewise," Kurtis answered unenthusiastically.

"Who's the lovely young lady?" Peter winked. "She's far too beautiful for the likes of you." Looking her up and down, Peter eyed Margot, then added, "Now, I wish my date was as pretty."

Kurtis frowned and didn't answer.

"Oh, Kurtis, you are so thin-skinned. Can't you see? I'm just joking. Don't be so easily offended," he said. Then he turned to Margot and said, "I'm sorry if I overstepped my boundaries. Do forgive me." Then, turning back to Kurtis, he asked, "Now, who is this young lady?"

"This is Margot. She's my fiancée," Kurtis said, and Margot could see by how he introduced her that Kurtis was proud of her.

"Lovely indeed. So, Kurtis, I hear you've been doing well."

"I'm fine. I've been working a lot. But I've put in for a transfer."

"Aren't you working at the camp at Dachau? At least, that's where I thought you were the last time we spoke."

"Yes, I'm still there. But I want to get away from the camps once I am married. I think a different surrounding might be better for my wife."

Peter let out a laugh. Then he spoke to Kurtis as if he were speaking to a child, "We must all do what is necessary if our Reich is to be a success. No one wants to work at those places, but those are important jobs, Kurtis."

"Everyone, please listen." It was Eva Braun. "Come outside. The rain has stopped, and we have such a beautiful view from up here of the sunset, which is about to occur. I wouldn't want any of you to miss this."

Everyone followed Eva Braun outside. Margot was stunned as she looked across the tops of the mountains and down at the village below. It was magnificent. As the sun began to set, the colors in the sky appeared as if God had been doing a watercolor painting of pinks, purples, and oranges. Kurtis gently embraced her waist and squeezed. "It's really incredible, isn't it?" he asked.

"It is," she agreed.

"You can't imagine what an honor it is to be invited to a private party up here," he whispered. "This is such a major achievement in my career."

Margot tried to smile. She was brought back to the reality that although her surroundings were beautiful, the people at this party were not. Looking across the open area at all the Nazi officers and their wives and girlfriends, she noticed that Hitler was not present. "The *Führer* is not here," she whispered to Kurtis.

"I know. I wouldn't tell anyone, but I think it's because he is afraid of heights. Who knows if he'll show up at all?"

She nodded. "It is rather strange that he will have a house up here on this mountain if he is so afraid of high places. Don't you think?"

"The *Führer* is complicated. He had to have a house up here because it's the most beautiful place in the world."

Margot had not seen the world, and she wondered if Kurtis had seen it in its entirety. This place was lovely, but she had a feeling there were other locations just as lovely, if not more so.

Just then, Peter walked back over to Kurtis. "So, I would assume that because you've been invited here, someone must be considering you for a higher position. Unless, of course, you are only treated well due to your uncle's friendship with the *Führer* during the Great War. If I recall correctly, your mother's brother knew the *Führer* during the war. Is that correct?"

Kurtis didn't answer. He frowned at Peter. He squeezed Margot's arm. And she knew Kurtis wished he could get rid of him. But Peter wasn't going anywhere. At least not yet. He was obviously enjoying humiliating Kurtis. Margot didn't want to add to Kurtis' humiliation, so she turned to look out the window, ignoring Peter's slights.

Then, a girl walked up behind Peter. She touched his shoulder. "Well, hello, everyone," she said.

"Here's my date now," Peter said, smiling.

Margot heard Peter's date's voice, and her heart sank. "I'm Trudy," the girl said.

Margot whirled around to see her sister standing right in front of her.

CHAPTER 34

T he short time between roll call and the beginning of the day's work detail, when Max saw Rivka, became the highlight of his day. Sometimes, they made love, but only when they felt certain no one could see them. This was not very often, so they usually just held hands and talked quietly. Rivka told him a little about her life before she'd been arrested. "I was always a shy, introverted girl. I guess I was sort of afraid of boys. Even in our synagogue, boys and girls were seated separately. I attended an all-girls school where I learned about the Jewish way of life."

"Like what?"

"Well, I learned about our holidays and how to keep a Jewish home."

"Weren't there dances where boys and girls met each other?"

"Not really. My father would have chosen my future husband."

"And you would have no say in it?"

"Well, according to Jewish law, my father would have had to ask me if his choice was all right with me. But I knew my father better than that." She laughed a little. "If he chose someone for me to marry, he would have expected me to do what he told me to do."

"He sounds like a tyrant."

"No, not really. He just wanted what was best for me."

"So you had to do what he said? No matter what? What would have happened if you had met someone on your own?"

"Like I said, my father was very strict. He would have killed me if he thought I was talking to a boy without his consent."

"So, what did you do with your days?"

"Well, I was a very good student in school. At least when Jews were still allowed to attend school. But even if the Nazis hadn't forbidden my education, my father would have taken me out of school soon enough. He didn't think education was important for girls. And as soon as he found a suitable husband, I would have had to leave school and marry, anyway. So, after the Nazis forbid Jews to be educated, I spent most of my time helping my mother cook and keep the house."

"And what did you do that you enjoyed? I mean, did you have a hobby? Knitting or sewing?"

She smiled. "I had one vice. I always loved to read. I knew my father would never approve of the books I read. He would only have approved of certain religious texts. But I secretly went to the library and hid the books under my bed. I really enjoyed reading adventure novels. They transported me to places I knew I would never see."

He smiled at her and patted her hand. "You don't know that for sure."

She shrugged. "I know. I know I will never see the world."

"Oh, Rivka. That makes me sad."

"I used to dream that I would somehow grow up to be a teacher. With my father, I knew it was probably impossible. But I loved to fantasize about it. I guess it was my dream. But my reality, at least what I thought would be my reality, was that I would marry a man of my father's choosing and have lots of babies. However, the Nazis had other plans for us Jews."

"You must really like children?"

"I do. I love them. I used to help my mother with my younger brothers and sisters." She sighed. He saw that she was about to cry. "They are probably all dead now."

"Oh, Rivka. Don't think about it. It doesn't do you any good to think about that."

"I think about them often. I wonder if I will ever know what happened to them."

There was a moment of silence. Then he said, "I was married before I was arrested. I had a son."

"Yes," she whispered. "Go on. Please tell me about them."

He proceeded to tell her about what had happened to Erik. Then he told her about Margot and Rudy. "I don't know if she is alive. I don't know anything. But I miss her terribly."

"I know you must still be in love with her, right?"

"Yes. I am. I have been in love with Margot since we were children. We met when we were very young. And well, there was always something about her." There was a long silence. Then he whispered, "I'm sorry. I didn't mean to hurt you by telling you about my wife."

"It's all right," Rivka said. "I understand. You had a life before this place. And you loved someone. I must admit, I feel a little jealous. But it doesn't really matter. I am just happy to have what we have now because I don't know what the future will bring. So, I am just enjoying the present."

Then the siren sounded, and they jumped up from where they were sitting. "*Mach Schnell.* Get in line and to your work details," a Nazi guard said as he walked through the crowd.

"Goodbye," Rivka whispered, and then she turned and ran to the office.

CHAPTER 35

The following morning, Max waited, but Rivka did not show up for their usual meeting. Kaz saw the look on his friend's face and went to him. "What is it?" he asked. "You look even more miserable than usual."

"Yesterday, Rivka and I talked about my wife, and this morning, Rivka didn't come to see me." Max sighed. "I probably shouldn't have told her anything about Margot. But I couldn't help it."

Kaz nodded. "Life here in this hell is very complicated for us. We hold on to the past, yet there's always that little voice in our minds that maybe those people we once loved are gone. Maybe we are holding on to nothing more than a memory. And yet…" he sighed, "if we give up that memory, what do we have left?"

"You've never told me about your past. You've never mentioned a wife or a girlfriend," Max said to Kaz.

"I can't talk about it. It's like a sore, and every time I say a word about it, it's like tearing the scab off a wound and opening it to bleed again."

Max nodded. "I understand."

When Rivka did not come to meet Max the following day or the one after that, Max felt terrible. That evening, when he returned from his work detail, he went into the office to see if he could speak to her. There were only a few minutes after he returned from his work detail before the office closed. He knew that if he took the time to go in, he would miss the opportunity to be in the front of the soup line, and of course, that would diminish his nutrition for the day. But he felt he had hurt her, and this made him unhappy. So, he knew he must find a way to make things right. Max rushed to the door of the office. He shivered, knowing going inside without a valid reason was dangerous. If one of the Nazis asked him why he was there and he didn't have an answer, it could cost him his life. And yet, he opened the door and entered. His eyes scanned the room. There was a girl there. He had not seen her before. She, like Rivka, was a very young woman. She, too, wore the yellow triangle that told him she was Jewish. He walked up to the front and whispered, "*Fräulein. Fräulein*, please, can I ask you something?"

"What do you want?" the girl asked abruptly.

"Rivka, do you know Rivka?"

"Of course," she said, her eyes darting around the room. "What do you want? She asked again nervously."

"Is Rivka here?"

"She's dead. Go away unless you want the same fate to happen to both of us."

"What? What happened? Please, you must tell me." He wanted to jump over the counter and grab the girl by the arm so she couldn't walk away before she explained.

"She came in late for work the other day. We had a surprise visit from *Reichsführer* Himmler. He was surveying everything. And when she came running in, he was livid and started yelling at *Kommandoführer* Richter. 'Do you allow Jews to come in late for work duty? How lax of you, *Kommandoführer* Richter. I would have thought you have control over your staff.'"

The young woman took a deep breath and looked around to assure herself that no one was watching. Then she continued, "*Kommandoführer* Richter was very upset with Rivka. She caused him embarrassment in front of that devil Himmler. I am sure you know Richter. He is a devil, too. That man is horrible. So very cruel."

"I know him well," Max said.

"Himmler was furious. He said belittling things to Richter. Then he glared at Richter and said that if Richter was a strong Aryan man deserving of a promotion, he would take control of these lousy Jews by making an example of Rivka."

"Oh, dear God," Max moaned.

"I won't tell you everything because you should go. I don't want trouble, and I don't want to see you get into trouble. But Richter killed her."

"Is he here? I would like to see him. I don't care what happens to me. I will kill him." Max was furious. His face was the color of fresh blood.

"He's not here. He's gone. I overheard that he went to a party for Hitler. Somewhere in the mountains," she said. "Please, go now. I am begging you. Go. If not for your sake, then for mine. I don't want to die here like poor Rivka."

Max nodded. He turned and left. Tears ran down his cheeks. *Rivka was late because she was with me. It's my fault that she's dead. That bastard Richter. I will kill him someday. I swear I will.*

CHAPTER 36

The Eagle's Nest

A wicked smile crept over Trudy's face as her eyes met Margot's. "And who is this?" she asked Kurtis, pretending she had never met Margot.

"This is Margot, my fiancée," Kurtis answered.

Trudy winked at Margot, and Margot felt dizzy. Her blood ran cold. She shivered as a soft drizzle began to fall.

"And this is Trudy, my very dear friend," Peter said, introducing her to Kurtis and Margot.

For a single second, Trudy glared at him. Margot caught the expression on Trudy's face, and she knew that Trudy was angry with Peter, but she had no idea why. Even so, it didn't matter why. Margot was hoping that whatever was causing Trudy to be upset with Peter was so overwhelming that it kept Trudy's concentration on Peter rather than on Margot.

"Looks like it's starting to rain again," Eva Braun announced. "Let's go inside before we all get wet." Then she giggled. "Dinner will be served now, so please take your seats."

The group followed Eva back inside. Margot was so nervous that she tripped and almost fell. Kurtis caught her. "Be careful, my love. You almost fell off the mountain."

She tried to smile at him to reassure him that nothing was wrong. But her lips were quivering. But she couldn't help but think about Trudy. *If Trudy chooses to tell these people what she knows about me, what will become of me? This is my worst nightmare coming true. Here I am, on this high mountain, surrounded by my enemy and, most importantly, my worst enemy. My terrible, horrible sister, Trudy, is here, and she is watching.*

There was nothing to do but pretend everything was fine and pray that Trudy would find it in her heart not to reveal Margot's secrets. Margot thought about Max. *Trudy is here with Peter, so does that mean she is no longer with Max? If she is not, then where is he? What has become of my dear husband?*

The band leader announced that the *Führer* was about to enter the room. Everyone stood up and saluted. Then, the band began to play a traditional German folk tune as Adolf Hitler entered the room, waving and smiling. Seeing him in the flesh standing right in front of her made Margot feel terrified and light-headed. Margot thought she might faint. *I wish I could sit down.* But she knew better. *I dare not sit down until the Führer is seated, and the rest of the crowd follows suit.*

Finally, the *Führer* stood in front of his chair and smiled at them all. Then, he sat at the head of the long table in front of the room. Once he was seated, the music stopped, and everyone else in the room sat down.

Eva Braun stood up and said, "I want to thank all of you for coming to celebrate our *Führer's* party with us this evening. We are so glad to have you here on Adolf's Mountain, the Eagle's Nest." She smiled her prettiest smile at Hitler. Then she turned back to the guests. "Now, please, won't you all enjoy your dinner?"

The staff began to serve the food, but Margot was too sick to her stomach to eat. She excused herself and went to the bathroom. When she was gone, Trudy, pretending to be concerned about Margot, walked over to Kurtis. "Is your fiancée all right?" she said. "She looks a little pale."

"I hope so. She tends to get nauseated at high altitudes," he lied, not wanting to tell anyone that Margot was pregnant before they were married.

Trudy smiled at him, knowing that this was not true. "Well, I just wanted to say she is such a beautiful girl. Where did you two meet?" she asked, pretending that she was only making casual conversation.

"Oh, there is this friendly little restaurant in Frankfurt that I like to go to whenever I am there. It has the best food I've ever eaten. When I was on holiday, the last time I went there, and would you believe it, Margot was my waitress. Can you imagine? What good luck." He smiled.

"Yes, what good luck." Trudy returned his smile. "I often go to Frankfurt," she lied. "What is the name of the restaurant? I would love to try it the next time I am in town."

"Of course. I highly recommend it. Let me write down the name and address for you," Kurtis said as he pulled a pen and paper out of the pocket of his uniform jacket.

After Kurtis finished writing, Trudy put the paper into her handbag. "Well, I see that Peter is looking over here. He's probably wondering what I am talking to you about. He cares so deeply for me that sometimes he can be so jealous. He's so silly, but of course, he's a man in love," she lied. Then, after a sigh, she added, "Anyway, I must return to my seat for dinner. Please tell Margot that I hope she feels better," Trudy said.

"Of course I will."

CHAPTER 37

t was late that night when the dinner party for Hitler finally ended. Trudy was singing softly to herself as they walked from the car to the door of their hotel. The stars were bright, and the air was cool but not cold. She slid her arm through Peter's, leaning close to him. She felt his body go rigid and assumed he might be exhausted. After all, she told herself, it had been a very long day. They had to get dressed for the evening and then drive up the narrow roads of the mountain. And then, of course, there was the party. She was trying hard to make excuses for him; he had been pulling away, and she hoped this little holiday together would make him feel amorous towards her. When they entered the hotel room, she walked over to him and looked into his eyes as she unbuttoned his trousers. But to her chagrin, he put his hand on hers and stopped her. She looked away; her eyes were glistening with tears. "I'm very tired," he said. His voice was neither soft nor sympathetic. And she knew he wasn't fazed at all by the fact that he had hurt her feelings. She turned and walked away from him, embarrassed. He glanced over at her, and her eyes

125

caught his. There was no affection in his gaze. Peter shook his head and walked out of their hotel room. Trudy followed him and watched as he walked down the stairs and into the lobby. She returned to the room and began to cry. Several hours passed, but he didn't return. *What if he left me here? How will I ever get back to Berlin? I don't have enough money to take a train.* She shivered and put the thought out of her mind. *He'll be back. He's just in one of his moods. That's all it is. I'm sure he'll be fine when he returns.* Trudy was still wearing her party dress. She removed it and decided to take a shower. As the warm water caressed her, she thought about Peter. *I don't want to believe it, but I can tell that I am losing him. I must try my best to seduce him. If I can get him to make love to me, maybe I can change his mind. I must try. If I lose him, I don't know what will become of me. I have no job, and he is paying all of my bills. If he stops, I'll be living on the street. Or worse, I'll have to go home to my parents, who have both been sick and would probably need me to care for them. That's the last thing I want, to be stuck nursing two old people. So I couldn't go there. I suppose I'd have to beg Mattie to let me stay with her. And I would hate to beg her. She and I have been estranged since that trip to Munich we took together, and I don't want to give in to her rigid moral standards. If I lived in her house, she would be in charge, and I would be forced to do whatever she told me. That would be unbearable. No, I must try with Peter again. I know what to do. I'll change into some sexy lingerie and try to excite him.* Trudy put on a short transparent nightgown made of black lace, which she had purchased for this occasion. When she bought it, she had looked at herself in the mirror, and then she had been quite certain it was very sexy, and Peter would not be able to resist her when she wore it. She put it on and then redid her makeup so it was flawless. Then she waited. It was a little over an hour by the time he finally returned to the room. When he walked in, she had been sitting on a chair in the corner, thumbing through a magazine. Seeing him, Trudy stood up. She wanted to make sure he would see her in her lingerie, but he didn't even look at her. He just took off his uniform, threw it on the top of the dresser, and then got into bed. Within minutes, Peter was snoring. *He's asleep, or he's pretending to be.* Trudy thought as she studied him and sighed. The nightgown had no effect on him, and now she had to admit that she was losing him. He came to see her less often these days. And rarely called. When he'd asked her to come to this party, she'd hoped that getting away together would reignite the spark between them. It wasn't working, and she knew it. Trudy couldn't bear to think of him anymore. She closed her eyes and tried to sleep but couldn't rest. As she lay there in the dark, her thoughts went to Margot. *How could she be dating an SS Officer? She has somehow managed to hide her filthy secret. I hate her. No matter what happens, Margot always seems to come out of it all right. Well, if I wanted to destroy her, I could reveal her secret. Her fiancé would be surprised to learn that she had lied to him. I am sure he has no idea she is a Jew. If I tell Peter that I know for sure that Margot is Jewish and living a lie, he will send someone to have her arrested.* She thought about Peter. *But things between Peter and me are bad enough. Who knows what he would think of me if he knew I grew up in the same house as a Jew? Things are just too rocky between us right now for me to let him know such a shady thing. I'd love to hurt Margot, but not at my own expense. So, telling Peter all of this might not be my best choice. But I do have an idea. Margot may just prove useful to me in the future. If Peter breaks things off with me, I am going to need money to keep up my apartment. And I certainly don't want to get a job. So, since I know where Margot is working, I could go there and threaten to tell her employer if she doesn't pay me a monthly fee. She is working, so she has an income, and I am sure she can get some money from Kurtis if she asks him. After all, she is his fiancée. This might just be my best solution. And if Peter breaks up with me, I'll try to get some money from him before he goes. If he refuses to give it to me, I'll threaten to tell his wife about us. He's always been so protective of her and his family. It makes me sick. But it might be to my advantage right now. I don't think I will be able to extort it from him every month. That would be too dangerous. If I push him too hard, he might just find a reason to have me killed. But I am sure he will give me at least a little money when he says goodbye. Once I have it, I'll take that money and travel to Frankfurt to see Margot. I will probably need to move to Frankfurt to collect money from her each month. But if I play this right, I'll be able to get* an apartment that is comparable to the one I have now. She sighed softly. I will miss Peter. *But there are new men in Frankfurt. And I will surely find one.*

CHAPTER 38

Klaus was already growing tired of Alice. He was sitting at the bar in his restaurant. It had been a slow night. Marie was handling things because Alice just couldn't keep up. He thought about Alice. She had resisted all the advances he'd made towards her, and he was yearning to play his little games with a lovely Aryan woman. It had been a while since he'd been forced to murder Tilly. He remembered Tilly and sighed. Then, his thoughts went back to Alice. She certainly was a disappointment. He thought about firing her. Since she wasn't his lover nor a very good waitress, it seemed pointless to keep her on. Klaus was surprised that Alice could be so slow and forgetful as a young woman. Poor sweet Alice was not capable like Margot or Marie, who were both very good waitresses. Klaus was glad that he was not attracted to either of them. It would have been terrible for his business if he had been. Fortunately, one was a redhead, the other a brunette, and Klaus was only attracted to that perfect Aryan blonde.

A beautiful blonde girl like the first girl he'd fallen in love with. He closed his eyes and took a sip of beer as he thought about that first girl who had caught his eye. Her name was Ilsa, and she had been one of those tall, slender blondes with piercing blue eyes. Ilsa lived a few streets away from him when he was a teenager. But unlike Klaus, Ilsa came from a wealthy family. She wore beautiful clothes and was admired by all the boys in the neighborhood where they grew up. He wanted her from the first time he saw her, and he swore he would have her, one way or another. But they were still in school, and although he had a job, he didn't earn enough money to take her to places he thought would impress a girl like her. Klaus couldn't ask his parents for money to help him woo a girl. His family was very poor. Each month, they were scrounging to pay the rent on a dirty, cold-water flat where they lived. Klaus was an only child with no brothers or sisters and was often very lonely. The flat where he lived was located in the basement of an apartment building. But even as poor as they were, Klaus' mother tried her best to shelter her son from the world. She stole food from the market so he would have enough to eat. But even though she loved him fiercely, his mother was overbearing and demanded his complete loyalty. She disapproved of him having friends or showing interest in girls. Many times, his mother told him stories about her own childhood. She had been born under an unlucky star to poor parents who could not afford to keep her. They dropped her at an orphanage when she was just seven years old, telling her they would return in a few hours. But they never came back. His mother spent her life in an orphanage, fighting for every morsel of food, attention, or affection until she met Klaus's father. They met at a school dance. The chance meeting between them wasn't exactly a romance. It was just a quick sexual encounter that same night after the dance. He had asked to walk her back to the orphanage, and she had agreed. On the way, they stopped in the park. He was the first boy to pay her any attention, and she was so flattered that she wanted to please him. He seduced her easily. But after a night of hot sex that made her feel loved, he abandoned her. She was miserable, and then, to make matters worse, she found herself pregnant. She waited for him after school and told him she was going to have his baby. She begged him to marry her, but he said he didn't want to because he didn't love her. And he thought she was ugly. This made her cry and run all the way back to the orphanage.

She studied herself in the mirror when she was alone in the bathroom. Her thick, dark blonde hair hung around her face like a sheet of oily paper. Her tall, thick body was covered in soft fat, and her features were far from delicate. She had a thick, bulbous nose and heavy cater-pillar-like eyebrows. "I was ugly," she told Klaus, "But I wasn't going to give up on your father. I couldn't. Once my pregnancy started to show, I knew that the nuns at the orphanage were going to be angry. They were going to beat me because that was how they handled misbehav-ior. So, I did what I had to do. I found out where your father lived, and then I went to see your father's parents. I held on to your grand-mother's hand and wept at being used so harshly."

Klaus's grandmother felt sorry for the young pregnant girl and insisted that since her son had gotten her pregnant, he should marry her. And so he did. But instead of trying to make the best of a bad situation, Klaus's father was cruel to his mother and him. This anger and frustration on his father's part only made things worse. Klaus remembered that throughout his childhood, his mother worked as the building manager for their apartment building. Klaus never really knew what his father did for a living, if he did anything at all. What Klaus did know was there were constant arguments between his parents about money, and this brought out his father's violent streak. He beat Klaus and his mother, often leaving Klaus bruised and bleed-ing. Klaus never finished school because his father left him with a black eye or a bruised cheek so often that he was embarrassed to attend. His mother was glad to have him at home. She needed his help around the house; besides, she didn't set much store in education. Klaus both loved and hated his mother at the same time. When they were together, she coddled him, but it was because of her that he didn't have any friends. Whenever he became friendly with another boy his age, his mother would find a way to make Klaus look foolish in the other boy's eyes. Then, one spring day, Klaus's father came home after being gone for two nights. He told Klaus and his mother that he had gotten a job working at a tavern as a bartender.

For a few months, things in their home seemed to be getting better. There was a little extra money for an occasional treat, like candy or an afternoon at the cinema. But the good fortune didn't last. One night, his father left the apartment to work and never returned. Klaus' mother took Klaus with her and went to the tavern to look for him the following day. But his boss told them he'd never come in the night before. No one but Klaus knew that it was not because his father had run away. It was because Klaus had secretly reported his father to the Nazis, and his father had been arrested.

From that day on, his mother's attention towards him became even more intense. She would not even allow him to go fishing without her. And sometimes, he had feverish dreams that scared him. Dreams of killing her and finally finding his freedom.

Klaus' mother constantly cautioned him against the evils of women. She warned her son to steer clear of them because they would surely take advantage of his good nature. But Klaus was a young male whose body craved the satisfaction only a woman could bring. Feeling sorry for himself, Klaus often wondered if he would ever have a girl of his own. When his mother was busy working, Klaus sat at the window in his apartment, where he watched the girls walk by on their way home from school. There were community parties where boys and girls met, but his mother forbade him from attending. She was even against him finding a job for fear that he would meet a girl at work and leave her.

Sitting at home all day and night was getting to Klaus. He was depressed. In fact, before Klaus met Ilsa, he often contemplated suicide. There was nothing in his life he felt was worth living for.

Sometimes, when his mother sent him to the market, Klaus would take a walk and pass the neighborhood park. It was there that he saw Ilsa for the first time. She was sitting on a bench talking with her girl-friend. He had stopped at the market on his way home after his walk and was carrying a sack of cabbages that he had purchased. When his eyes caught a glimpse of her, he stood still and stared for a few moments. She was so lovely, more beautiful than any other girl he'd ever seen, at least in his opinion. Klaus stood there looking at her. Mesmerized. He was certain that everything in his life would change if he could just find a way to make her love him. Everything would be perfect. He hid and watched her for a while. Then he followed her home. Now he knew where she lived. From that day on, he made sure to walk and pass by her house daily. He would stay as long as he could, which wasn't long because his mother would be expecting him. But he would stand in front of her home, his heart aching, waiting and hoping she would come outside. One morning, he saw her come out of the house carrying books. He followed her as she walked to the school and learned she was a student. Now he knew where she lived and where she went to school. But he still had not spoken to her. And he knew he had to find a way to speak with her. Every day, his desire for the pretty blonde grew stronger until he became obsessed with thoughts of her. Finally, Klaus could no longer bear the pain of longing for something he could not have. So, he decided that he must be brave. He was mad about Ilsa, and he was going to find a way to ask her to go out with him. *Women love beautiful things. They love gifts.* After all, he'd gone to the cinema where he'd seen plenty of films where handsome men presented expensive gifts to the girls they loved. In these films, girls always responded with excitement and kisses for the man who gave them presents. Klaus decided a fancy gift would make Ilsa fall in love with him. He decided he had to find a way to give Ilsa a gift. Without money or a plan, Klaus stole the bus fare from his mother's handbag and took the bus to a local jewelry store. He walked inside and looked around, intending to steal. It just so happened that this store was owned by a middle-aged Jewish couple. The man was a diamond cutter, and his wife was a salesperson. They had been in business for over ten years. Klaus walked around the shop. Draped over a bust, he noticed a small diamond pendant hanging from a sparkling, delicate gold chain. Both of the owners were busy with other customers. Klaus felt his heart race. He had never stolen anything before. In his mind, this necklace was his one chance to win Ilsa's love. And he was sure he wanted to spend the rest of his life with her. With a trembling hand, Klaus reached up and quickly grabbed the necklace. It fell from his shaking hand onto the floor. The diamond cutter heard the click as the diamond hit the wooden floor. He looked up in time to see Klaus reach down, grab the necklace, and then put it into his pocket. Klaus ran out of the store and down the street with the necklace in his pocket. The jeweler ran after him, yelling, "Thief, stop him. Stop that man. He stole a diamond necklace from me." Klaus kept running. His heart raced with fear, but he did not look behind him. He ran as fast as he could until he was far enough away to assure himself he had gotten away with the theft. He leaned against a building to catch his breath. Then he looked around. No one was coming after him. Klaus let out a long, deep breath. Then he smiled and took the necklace out of his pocket. The diamond sparkled in the sunlight. He was certain that this piece of magnificent jewelry would change his life. And it was about to do just that, but not in the way he had initially hoped.

The following day, Klaus went to stand outside the school where he was waiting for Ilsa to come out. The necklace was in a box in the pocket of his jacket. He was so nervous he had to go to the back of the school and pee where no one could see him. It seemed to take forever until he saw Ilsa. She was walking out the large front door of the school, accompanied by two other girls. The three young girls were talking and laughing. Klaus felt his heart skip a beat as he forced himself to walk towards her. Feeling clumsy and awkward, he had to remind himself of the glittering gift he held in his pocket so he would have the courage to approach her. Shyly, he said, "Hello. I'm Klaus."

"I know. And I know you've been following me," she said confidently. "I'll bet you know my name too, don't you?"

Ilsa's girlfriends all laughed. Klaus almost turned and walked away. But he couldn't. He had to do what he'd originally planned.

He cleared his throat. "Yes, I do know your name. You're Ilsa," he said. "And I don't know how to say this. But I think you are the most beautiful girl I've ever seen."

She let out a loud laugh, and he felt foolish. Then her friends began laughing, too. He felt like running away from this embarrassing moment and hiding forever. But then she said, "Don't be offended. It's just that you sounded so sweet and innocent when you said you thought I was the most beautiful girl that I couldn't help but chuckle."

He smiled, but his lips were quivering. "I feel like a clumsy oaf. But I really think the world of you. And… well, I have a gift for you."

"Oh, really?" she seemed surprised. "A gift for me? What is it?" she said. Now, she was looking at him with a curious expression. "I love presents."

THE LIES WE TOLD

His hand shook as he took the box out of his pocket and presented it to her. She took the box and then smiled at him. Klaus melted. Ilsa opened the box. Her eyes grew wide with surprise. "Oh my. This is really quite wonderful," she said when their eyes met. Klaus felt his confidence grow because now she seemed to look at him in a new light.

"Would you go out with me? For dinner tomorrow night, perhaps," he asked. He had never been out with a girl before.

She smiled broadly. Then she looked down at the necklace in her hand and said, "Yes, of course, I will. I'd like that. You can pick me up at my house. I'll give you my address. Seven o'clock."

"Yes, I'll be there."

They went to dinner at a lesser-known, cheap beer hall the following night because it was all he could afford. From the look on her face, he could see that she wasn't impressed by the restaurant he had chosen. But after dinner, she asked him to come back to her house. He agreed. No one was at home. She took him to her bedroom, and when she took off her dress, he was unable to breathe. He almost fainted. Then she took off his clothes. He stood, pale and shivering in his undershorts. Ilsa smiled at him. Then, she began to make love to him in her own special way. This was not only his first time with a woman, but this was where he learned that he enjoyed sex when it was combined with pain. She tied him up and did the things to him that he now did to other blonde women.

It could have been the beginning of a relationship that he believed would have made him happy had it not been for that old Jew who owned the jewelry store. The old man had made a police report. To make matters worse, he knew who Klaus was and where he lived. He said he recognized Klaus from the neighborhood, and he was sure Klaus was the thief. The following day, the police arrived at Klaus' apartment and took him in for questioning at the police station. The old Jew was there waiting with the police when Klaus arrived. "All I want is my merchandise back," the diamond cutter said. "I don't want to press charges. I don't want to ruin the boy's future."

But how was Klaus going to give him the necklace? He'd already given it to Ilsa. The policeman told Klaus he must return the necklace.

This frightened Klaus. The officer threatened to throw him in jail until Klaus admitted that he'd given the necklace to Ilsa. What followed humiliated Klaus for the rest of his time living with his mother in Hamburg. Since Klaus had given Ilsa stolen goods, the police went to Ilsa's home and demanded the return of the necklace. She gave it to them. But she told everyone at school and everyone in the neighborhood what happened. After this, Klaus went from being the shy, overweight boy no one noticed to being a complete outcast.

The other people in the neighborhood ostracized and made fun of him until he stole money from his mother's purse and left Hamburg. He took a train to Frankfurt, where he found a job working in a restaurant. He was all alone in a new city. He had no friends, no dates, no one at all to take up his time. Sometimes, he missed his mother; other times, he cursed her. But he never wrote to her. And since he had nothing else going on in his life, he devoted himself to his job at the restaurant. The owner, an old man with no family, came to depend on Klaus and appreciated his loyalty and devotion. When the old man passed away, he left Klaus the restaurant. And then Hitler came to power. Klaus listened to the chancellor when he gave speeches ranting about how terrible the Jews were. Klaus never forgot how much he hated that Jewish jeweler he believed had ruined his life. And so Klaus immediately joined the Nazi party. Because he gave the Nazi officers special perks, he made his restaurant the most popular place in Frankfurt for Nazi officers to drink and dine. As the years passed and the clientele changed from local people to all kinds of important government officials and high-ranking party members, few people even remembered the original owner.

Klaus was wealthy now. But he was still ashamed of his childhood. He wanted to escape the embarrassment of his humble and often shameful beginnings. So, he created a new story to share with everyone he met. He began telling people that his family had always owned the restaurant. He lied and told them that his father was a famous restaurateur. No one bothered to question him. They didn't care. They accepted his story as fact, and whenever they were in Frankfurt, they ate at his establishment because not only did it have the finest food and beer, but for young Nazi officers looking for a good time, Klaus was the man to see no matter what you were looking for. If you wanted a girl for the night, Klaus could provide one. If you were in search of a discrete same-sex encounter, Klaus could help you, and he could be counted on to be discreet. Drugs could be acquired from Klaus, and although Absinthe was illegal, Klaus kept a hefty, secret supply at the restaurant for those special guests who chose to embark on a hallucinatory experience. Nothing was impossible for Klaus. For the right amount of money, he would find a way to satisfy their wildest dreams. And that was how Klaus grew even richer, and because he was friendly and known to serve all the high-ranking police officers, he was also above the law.

Klaus leaned his head on his elbow. He was proud of how far he had come from that roach-infested apartment where he had started his life. Then, with his other hand, he lifted his glass and quietly toasted himself, following the toast with a long sip of beer. The bitter, dark beer was satisfying. But he couldn't fully enjoy it. He shook his head and thought about Alice for a moment. Klaus was trying to decide what to do with her. Although he was attracted to how she looked and was sure she would make a perfect playmate, she was always too careful. She never let him get too close to her. It was her way of separating work from pleasure. However, what really discouraged him and made matters worse was that he recently discovered that Alice had an older brother who was an important member of the Waffen SS. This was dangerous because often, the women he played around with turned up dead. And he was certain that if Alice was found dead, her brother would want to have an investigation carried out. Most people didn't have the ability to do this, but because of her brother's position in the Waffen SS, he did. He had the connections to have an investigation conducted.

Alice is a poor choice for me. Quite frankly, she's just not worth it. Klaus thought as he sat at the bar in his restaurant. He was disappointed as he sat at the bar. Marie brought him the bratwurst he'd ordered in a pretzel bun, and he was eating it and washing it down with a beer. *No, he wasn't going to play with Alice. This one was going to get away. What a lucky little girl Alice happens to be.* He laughed aloud softly. *She doesn't even know how lucky she is. She has no idea that she was dancing with death.* "Ahhh…" he sighed aloud. *Well, anyway, little Alice just isn't worth the trouble. When Margot gets back from her trip with Kurtis, I'll just tell Alice that she is too slow as a waitress, so I have to fire her. Then I'll hire a new one. A new Aryan goddess to satisfy my bloodlust.*

CHAPTER 39

Kurtis and Margot lay in bed at the hotel where they were staying after the party. He had not been happy to see Peter at the party. And he was disappointed that Margot had been feeling ill and was on edge the entire evening. But he shouldn't have been surprised. He told himself that, after all, she was pregnant, and his mother had warned him that sometimes pregnant women behaved strangely. Margot was cold and distant that night. In fact, she was not affectionate towards him, and it seemed to him that she didn't enjoy the gala. Kurtis found this odd because any woman should have been floating on air after meeting the *Führer* and Eva Braun like Margot did. But when they got in line to meet the *Führer*, Margot did not gush with admiration for him. In fact, she grew quiet. He thought she was probably intimidated. But Margot's mood grew even darker when they ran into Peter and his date. She didn't smile or laugh at any of his jokes after that, and now Kurtis wondered if Peter's criticism of him had made Margot think less of him. Peter had made Kurtis look small and foolish, and he feared that Margot would be less impressed by him

139

because of Peter. Kurtis felt anger rising in him. His entire body was growing hot with it, and he wished he could kill Peter as easily as he could kill the prisoners who were under his command at Dachau. In fact, if he had been going to work the following day, he would have taken his anger out on the prisoners at Dachau. He would have chosen one, a weak one who he felt was deserving of a miserable death. Then he would have closed his eyes and imagined Peter's face while pounding on that prisoner with his bare hands until he died. *Maybe then I would be able to feel good about myself again.* But he was not going to Dachau the following day. Instead, he and Margot would drive all day until they were back in Frankfurt. Then, he was going to stay in Frankfurt for a couple of days before he was scheduled to board a train back to Dachau. Kurtis grunted softly with disappointment. He would have liked to have an opportunity to let his anger out. Then he remembered that Margot was asleep. He glanced over at her, hoping his grunting hadn't awakened her. But it didn't. She appeared to be still sleeping.

His thoughts returned to Peter. Since joining the SS, he'd met several men like Peter. And he truly hated them because they reminded him of his father. This man took pleasure in making other people feel inferior.

He tried to put Peter out of his mind as he lay beside Margot in bed at the hotel after the party. But even as he pushed the thoughts away and closed his eyes, he saw his father's face in his mind's eye. His father had been dead for over five years, but Kurtis could not forget how he had done everything in his power to please his father to no avail. His father was an academic, and everyone said he was very intelligent. He taught philosophy at the university and wrote essays and published books. Kurtis' brother, Fredrick, took after his father. He was an intellectual who got good grades, loved to read and study, and planned to go to university to study medicine. Kurtis wanted to study law to please his father, but his grades were not good enough to get into the University. His good qualities were that he was very athletic and handsome. In this way, he took after his mother. His father admired her beauty and was impressed by her lean, athletic body, but these were qualities that held no weight in a man as far as his father was concerned. Kurtis admired his mother. She told him she had been one of the best females on the swim team. Even now, she was tall and still pretty. His father was not handsome at all. He was a dark-haired mouse of a man, small and skinny, with a weak chin and thick eyebrows. However, everyone called him brilliant. Fredrick followed in his father's footsteps. His father was ashamed of Kurtis and often disgraced him in front of his friends by calling him stupid. Even though his mother tried to comfort him, Kurtis was an unhappy child.

But then, Kurtis joined the Hitler Youth, and everything miraculously changed. In the Hitler youth, Kurtis, with his strong athletic ability and handsome Aryan looks, was a star. This was how Kurtis came to love the Nazi party. It was here that he was accepted and admired. The leader of his youth group took him on as a surrogate son, and Kurtis responded by embracing every aspect of Nazi doctrine.

Kurtis couldn't compete with his brother, Fredrick, on an intellectual level. When it came to intellectual pursuits, Fredrick always won. But that no longer mattered because Kurtis had a new avenue to shine. He was an Aryan man, tall, blonde, and brave. So, when the opportunity to join the army and fight for the fatherland arose, Kurtis was among the first in his town to sign up. In his training, he excelled at every physical challenge. As soon as he finished his service, he was promoted to the Waffen SS. For the first time in his life, Kurtis felt justified as a man. One Christmas, he returned home on leave to visit with his family. He brought his mother a pair of silk stockings, and she squealed with delight. Kurtis was proud of himself because he could acquire things his father and brother could not. He was part of an organization bigger than their silly intellectual groups. On that visit home, Kurtis walked into the living room, where he found his father and brother discussing a book they'd read. His father looked up and saw Kurtis, who looked handsome in his dark uniform, but instead of welcoming Kurtis home, his father scoffed and said, "Look at you parading around in that ridiculous uniform. I know you're not smart, but you should realize you've joined a group of stupid fanatics."

Kurtis didn't answer. He glared at his father, who ignored him because he didn't realize that his son was no longer the weak child who longed for his love. Kurtis was a strong man with an entire governmental party that shared his hopes and dreams.

"You call me stupid, but it's the two of you who are truly stupid. You waste your time sitting around reading books," Kurtis said. "You don't even realize that Germany is on the brink of a new world order. Our world is changing, *Vater*, and you're worthless to our new government."

"Worthless, but of course. Anyone who thinks for themselves could be called worthless by the Nazis, but the truth is that people like Fredrick and I are dangerous, and you and your group are afraid of us because we see you for what you are."

"Be careful, *Vater*. I will report you. I swear it. I will."

"You can't be that dim. You have to realize that Adolf Hitler is a monster," his father said, "and his followers are fools. Why would you want to be a part of such a group? They are going to bring this country down. You'll see that I am right."

Kurtis was angry. The love he'd once had for this man had now turned to hatred. Kurtis was strong and healthy. He walked over to where his father sat and lifted him by his shirt collar, holding him suspended in the air.

"What are you doing?" his father demanded an answer. But Kurtis could see the fear in his father's eyes, and that fear made him feel good.

"I'm showing you just how ineffective you really are. All you do is sit around and talk. Talking means nothing. It gets you nowhere. I'm about to teach you a lesson, *Vater*. I'm going to show you that power is everything." Kurtis punched his father in the face. Fredrick let out a yelp.

"Stop it, Kurtis," Fredrick yelled. "Please stop it. Dad is not young. You're going to hurt him."

"That's what I had in mind, Fredrick. And if you don't keep that mouth of yours shut, I'll hurt you too."

Kurtis' father's nose was bleeding. But Kurtis punched him one more time for effect. Then he dropped him. His father fell to the ground like a rag doll, broken and bleeding. Kurtis did not look at him. He just turned and walked into the kitchen, where his mother was cutting up cabbage. He leaned down and kissed his mother's cheek. Then he said, "I have to go. I am going back to my platoon."

"But I thought you were going to stay until after Christmas," she whined. "I've missed you so much. I wish you could stay."

"I'm sorry, *Mutti*, I can't. I must get back. But I wanted to drop in and see you just to say hello."

She didn't argue. She hugged him and told him to be careful and stay safe. Satisfied with his encounter with his father for the first time, Kurtis opened the door to his family's apartment and walked outside.

Since Kurtis was not scheduled to return to his troop until after Christmas, he had a few free days. He needed a break, so he went to see his old friend Klaus. Kurtis had come in that very weekend feeling lonely and depressed. He confided in Klaus that he was beginning to feel afraid of dying all alone. Klaus didn't ask him any further questions. He just smiled and introduced Kurtis to a vivacious young prostitute. "This is Heidi," he said. "Don't worry, my friend. Heidi will make you feel loved and wanted."

Klaus smiled. "As always, there will be no ties, no strings attached. When you are ready, you can go, and Heidi will understand."

Kurtis had frolicked in bed with young Heidi for two nights. But he found that it meant nothing. He was unsatisfied. After paying Heidi and sending her on her way, Kurtis returned to the restaurant for a meal and beer, hoping to meet someone else.

CHAPTER 40

Kurtis never spoke to his father or brother again. But sometimes, he would visit his mother when he had time off from work. On one such visit in the spring, they sat at an outdoor café having lunch. Her smile told him that she adored him. And when they spoke, she told him she was proud of him no matter what anyone else thought. They were very much alike. He often wondered what she saw in his father, so he asked her, "Why did you marry *Vater*? The two of you are so different."

"Well," she smiled, the skin surrounding her pretty blue eyes now broke into tiny little wrinkles that showed her age, "I admired him. Just like you used to."

"But I don't anymore. Now, I hate him."

"You hate him because you can't fit into his world. However, you don't realize that even though he is cruel and often hurts your feelings, your father loves you. He just has a different way of showing it."

"I don't believe it."

"And I know that you love him too," she said. "Someday, I hope the two of you can reconcile."

When he was on the train that evening, he thought about what his mother had said, and he realized that he, unlike any of the other fellows he knew, was attracted to dark-haired women with dark eyes. And he wondered if it had something to do with his father being dark-haired. The idea that there was any correlation to this sickened him, and he vowed to date only blondes from then on. Which he did until that day he saw Margot at the restaurant and was immediately smitten.

CHAPTER 41

Kaz always seemed to be watching Max, but he never asked him any questions. One evening, Max was in an exceptionally foul mood when he returned from his work detail. He got into the soup line behind Kaz and Adrien. "Why are you always watching me?" he asked Kaz.

"I see the changes in you since things ended with the girl."

Max gave his friend a look of disgust.

"You've been quiet and sullen. All of your optimism is gone. This affair aged you by ten years."

"Yes. Maybe you're right."

"You can't let a romance do this to you. What happened? Did she break up with you?"

Max turned to glare at Kaz. "No, actually, she didn't, Kaz. She was murdered by Richter. And do you know whose fault it was? It was mine. I caused it."

"Oh," Kaz groaned. "I really am sorry." He patted Max's shoulder. "I had no idea. Is there anything I can do to help you?"

Max didn't speak; he just shook his head. In fact, he didn't say another word throughout the entire meal.

That night, when they were back on their block, Kaz asked Max to join him and Adrien in a game of cards. But Max just shook his head. "Not tonight," he said.

But he didn't join his friends for their nightly card game for the remainder of the week. However, he was keeping an eye on the *Kommandoführer*. Max had made a promise to himself and to Rivka that someday he would find a way to make Richter pay for killing her. He was careful not to step out of line. He did his job to the best of his ability and followed all the rules, but even so, there was something in his eyes, a dark force that kept him watching Richter closely.

Then, one night, after the lights were out and everyone was supposed to go to sleep, Kaz was lying on his bed of straw when he heard Max crying softly. He didn't want to embarrass Max by trying to comfort him. So, he lay in the dark in silence for a long time, just listening. *They've broken him. I can see it. Now that he's been broken, he will either grow stronger, or he will succumb to their torture and die. And there is nothing I can do to help him.* Kaz thought.

CHAPTER 42

Margot was shocked and surprised that she had escaped from the party at the Eagle's Nest without her sister causing her some trouble. When she and Kurtis arrived back in Frankfurt, she thought about Trudy and wondered if it was possible that Trudy had changed. And even though Margot was terrified of seeing her sister again, she wished she could be alone with Trudy for a few minutes to ask her to tell her everything she knew about Max.

Kurtis left to return to work a few days later, and Margot returned to her job at the restaurant. There was no time to spend thinking about Trudy. As soon as Margot returned to work, Klaus told her he had to fire Alice. He lied and said he'd caught Alice stealing and would not tolerate that. But he assured her he had already hired a new girl who he thought would work out just fine. However, he expected Margot and Marie to train her while still doing their regular jobs. It was no surprise to Margot that the new girl was another Aryan beauty. She and Marie discussed it as they walked home from work on the evening of Margot's first day back.

"What do you think really happened to Alice?" Margot asked Marie.

"She's actually fine. I saw her in the market the other day. I think Klaus got rid of her because her brother is in the SS. Unlike the others, she happened to be fortunate. He couldn't kill her. It would have caused him too many problems."

"It's very scary to know that this new girl is in danger from Klaus," Margot said.

"I know, but we can't say anything."

"You're right," Margot said. She thought about telling Marie all about Trudy and Max. She wished she could unburden herself and talk it all out. But although she trusted Marie, she was too afraid. *I shouldn't be afraid to talk to her about this. I know that she is with a group of people who are trying to fight against the Nazi party. She's told me things that could get her arrested. She trusts me. And I would never betray her. Yet, I can't bring myself to trust her or anyone else.*

The new girl's name was Freya. She was a friendly, outgoing type with an easy laugh and a kind spirit. Margot found that she liked Freya and wished she could warn her. Sometimes, in dreams, Margot would tell Freya about Klaus. She wanted to do what she could to keep the young woman safe. But when she was at work with Klaus and the new girl, she said nothing.

Two weeks later, when Margot finally began to believe that Trudy was gone and never going to contact her again, Trudy walked into the restaurant. Klaus was in the back, trying to steal a kiss from Freya, so he didn't immediately see Trudy. But Margot did, and her blood ran cold. She could not imagine how Trudy had found her. She was sure she hadn't told Trudy where she lived or worked. *How did Trudy find me?* Margot was about to run into the kitchen to hide when Trudy called her name, "Margot," Trudy said in a voice that sounded like a long-lost friend and not like someone who had caused so much pain and suffering.

Margot shivered as she walked over to the table where Trudy sat. "Hello, Trudy," she said, resigned. "How did you find me?"

"Oh, I have ways," Trudy winked.

Margot looked into her sister's eyes. "So, why are you here? What is it that you want?"

Trudy laughed. "Is that the way you greet your sister? You don't say hello, how are you, how are *Mutti* and *Vater*. No, instead, you ask me what I want."

"Yes, what do you want?"

"What do you think I want?"

"I don't know," Margot said. She felt the sweat beading under her arms. "I can't play games with you. So, why don't you just tell me."

"Money, my dear sister. What does anyone want? Money."

"How much?"

"Don't be in such a hurry," Trudy smiled. And Margot thought that it appeared that Trudy was enjoying watching her squirm.

"Just tell me what I need to pay you to get you to go away."

"It's not that easy. I have a plan. Now," Trudy smiled. "Family should help each other, don't you agree?"

Margot glared at her but didn't answer. So, Trudy went on, "I expect you to pay me monthly. I am going to move here to Frankfurt, and you are going to help me pay my bills. And in turn, I won't tell anyone what I know about you."

"How can I do that? I can hardly pay my own bills," Margot said honestly.

"Yes, I'm sure you don't earn much. However, I know that you are engaged to an officer. I'm sure he will pay your bills if you ask him nicely. And he'll probably give you a little extra, too. Then, once you are married, you'll move in with him, and then you won't have to rent anymore. So, with all of that going for you, you should have no trouble helping your sister out. In fact, you can tell him the truth, that I am your sister, and because he is family, he needs to help me too."

Margot frowned at Trudy. She hated her, but since she was here, she was going to ask her about Max, and she hoped Trudy could tell her where he was and how she might find him. "I'll help you," Margot said bitterly. "On one condition."

"And now you are setting conditions? One word from me, and you'll be arrested. So, you have no power, my dear sister."

"I want to know where Max is. I don't care if the two of you are having an affair. I just need to know that he is all right."

"What would ever make you think Max and I were lovers?" Trudy scoffed. "He's not successful enough for me. You should know that."

Margot remembered that Frau Danner had said that Trudy had answered the door when she went to Margot's apartment in search of Max. But it might not have been Trudy. After all, Frau Danner had never met Trudy. She only knew what Margot told her about her sister. "Perhaps I am wrong. But, please, just tell me what you know about Max, and I promise I will do what I can to help you."

"I wish I had better news," Trudy sighed. "But I am sorry to have to be the one to tell you that Max is dead. He became ill and died." She was lying.

She sunk down into a chair, paralyzed with grief. "Max, oh dear God. Max." Margot believed her, and her heart shattered into a million pieces.

"Yes, it is quite sad. I really am sorry for you."

Then Klaus walked into the dining room. Several tables were filled with customers, most of them in nazi's uniforms. As Klaus entered, Trudy's back was to him, so he hadn't noticed Trudy. He was walking quickly towards Margot. His face was red, and his fists were clenched because Margot was sitting down at a table rather than serving the waiting customers. Marching up to the table, he slammed his fist down, and in an angry voice, he said, "Margot, let's go. People are waiting for their food."

Margot jumped.

"Get moving. What the hell is the matter with you?" Klaus said.

Margot swallowed her grief and went to work.

When Trudy heard that familiar voice burned into her memory, she felt the hair on her neck bristle. A shiver ran through her as she whirled around. Then, her fears were realized as she stood eye-to-eye with Klaus. Upon seeing Trudy, Klaus forgot the customers for a moment. That same crocked, maniacal smile Trudy remembered came over his face. "What have we here?" he said. "If it isn't my old friend, Trudy."

Her body shook slightly. Being a predator, he saw her tremble.

Then he laughed, "I hope I got your name right. It was Trudy, isn't that correct?"

Trudy didn't answer. Margot was busy, but she saw the interaction between her sister and her boss, and she wondered how they knew each other. *Trudy is his type, blonde, blue-eyed, and Aryan. Could they have once been lovers? The women he chooses to take as lovers don't live to see him again. At least not the ones who've worked here. So, what is this thing between them about?* Margot wondered but couldn't stand around and watch Trudy and Klaus. The restaurant was too busy.

"I hope you remember me," Klaus said. "We met in Munich one very special night and had such a fine evening together."

A bead of sweat ran down Trudy's forehead into her eye. She quickly brushed it away, smearing her mascara. Klaus smiled. "Would you like a beer?"

Trudy shook her head. "I was just leaving."

"No, I must have a few minutes to talk with you. It's been such a long time," Klaus said, then he turned and called Margot over to the table. When she arrived, he said, "Bring us a couple of beers."

Margot went to the bar and poured two beers. She brought them back and laid them in front of Klaus and Trudy. "Thank you, Margot. Now, get back to work."

Margot turned to leave the table, but as she began to walk away, Klaus called her back again. "By the way," he asked, "how do you two know each other?"

"Trudy is my sister," Margot said.

CHAPTER 43

M argot was very busy serving food but not too busy to keep an eye on Klaus and Trudy as they sat together, drinking the beers she'd brought them. She couldn't explain how she knew, but she could tell Trudy was on edge. Whenever Klaus leaned towards her, Trudy moved away quickly. *She seems to be afraid of him. Obviously, she didn't know that Klaus owned this place. But they must have had some kind of relationship in the past that left Trudy frightened. She is his type. The same type he has murdered. I wonder what happened. How is all of this going to affect me? Will Trudy leave tonight and never return? That would be a blessing. Or will she join forces with Klaus, and then will they both turn on me?*

It was over an hour by the time Trudy was ready to leave the restaurant. Margot saw her grab her handbag and hurry towards the front door. Trudy tripped and almost fell before she grabbed onto the wall to regain her balance. This was unlike Trudy, who had always been graceful. Margot stood still and watched as Trudy turned back and looked nervously at Klaus. He was sitting at the table where they had just finished their beers, and now, he was smiling an evil smile. Margot stood there behind the bar, paralyzed by the sight. She couldn't take her eyes off her sister and the murderous man who was her boss.

An SS officer sitting at one of Margot's tables called for her. But Margot could not move. She was mesmerized and glued to the spot on the floor where she stood. Trudy ran out of the restaurant. Then, after just a few minutes, Margot saw Klaus get up and walk out of the front door, jangling his keys in his hand. He was still smiling.

He is going to follow her.

CHAPTER 44

Every time Max looked at *Kommandoführer* Richter, he thought of Rivka. She was just a poor young girl who had lost everything because of the Nazis. Her home, her family, and everyone she loved. And now this horrible man had taken the only thing she had left: her life. This fact gnawed at him, ate at him like a cancer. He had hated the *Kommandoführer* before, but now his hatred for this man consumed him. He sat with Kaz and Adrien in the evenings, trying to play cards, but he could not concentrate. When he spoke to his friends, all he ever spoke of was his burning desire to torture and kill Richter.

"You've changed, Max. You let this place change you," Kaz said one night. "You're becoming just like them. You think of nothing but murder and violence."

"How should I be, Kaz? This man murdered a young girl for no reason. And this girl happened to mean a lot to me. He took her life for no reason. Only because she was a few minutes late for work," Max said. He hesitated before clearing his throat, adding, "And it was my fault she was late. It was all my fault. And now she is dead, and that,

155

too, is my fault. The only way I can ever be whole again is to avenge her death. And the only way I can avenge her death is to kill him."

"If you even try, you will be dead in seconds. He is strong, and he has weapons, and there are Nazis all around us who will help him. You are undernourished and weak. Don't be a fool."

"I will wait, I will bide my time, and when the time is right, I swear to you, I will kill him."

Adrien and Kaz quickly glanced at each other; their eyes were filled with worry.

CHAPTER 45

A week passed, and Trudy did not return to the restaurant. Margot was relieved. She thought whatever happened between Trudy and Klaus had discouraged her from returning.

On the weekend, a few weeks later, Kurtis asked Klaus to give Margot a few days off so she might come to Munich to meet his mother.

"She is going to love you," Kurtis promised. "And you will love her too."

Since Margot and Kurtis were planning to get married, it seemed only right that Margot met her future mother-in-law. *I don't know much about her, and I am worried she might see through my lies. But this meeting cannot be as scary as that night at the eagle's nest.* Margot thought as she packed her things into her small suitcase. Margot was scheduled to take the train to Munich that evening. When she arrived, Kurtis was there to pick her up at the train station, and then they went to get a hotel room. Margot wondered why they were not staying at Kurtis's home. But when she asked him, he said Dachau was too far from his mother's house, and it would be easier for them to meet with his mother if she and Kurtis stayed at a hotel in town. Margot accepted this without question.

———

Kurtis was excited to have Margot meet his mother. And at the same time, he was relieved that his father had passed away a year before he and Margot met. Even though his mother and father weren't together anymore, he was certain that if his father had been alive, his mother would have insisted that he introduce his fiancée to him. Kurtis would have protested, but his mother would have been adamant. She would have said that Kurtis owed it to his father. But Kurtis didn't feel he owed his father anything. In fact, he was certain that if his father had the opportunity, he would have found a way to humiliate Kurtis in front of Margot. And for that reason, Kurtis was glad his father was dead.

Since his father's death, his mother has been thriving. She had many friends and enjoyed dancing, cycling, and outdoor activities. Kurtis's father expressed his dislike for his wife's friends during his life-time. Both of his parents were very different. His father was a strong proponent of equality. He had befriended an American musician who was black, and even though he knew it was against the party rules, he had several Jewish friends. Of this, his mother staunchly disapproved. She didn't like to make waves, and his father was always making waves. Finally, after years of arguing and his father having been reprimanded and almost let go at the University for defending the rights of a Jewish professor who had been fired, the couple separated. It seemed that the couple's two children also separated; they gravitated towards the person they felt closest to. Kurtis towards his mother, Fredrick towards his father. The brothers had never been close, but now they were like strangers. Sometimes, Kurtis thought he should be sad that the family was divided. But the truth was that he was glad to be rid of his judg-mental father and his annoying brother. And then his father became ill and died. His mother went to the funeral, but Kurtis did not. A year had passed, and his mother went on with her life. Now, she was already dating a man with the Waffen SS. Kurtis had recently met him and found that he liked him. In fact, he thought of him as a kindred spirit. He was certain that his mother and this new man would marry.

Margot was to arrive in Munich that evening, and the following night, his mother and her boyfriend were to join Kurtis and Margot at a restaurant for dinner. Kurtis was certain they would both love Margot, and she would love them. This was going to be a wonderful visit. But he had decided to rent a hotel room rather than take Margot back to his apartment at Dachau. He didn't want to risk having her see that place. Instinctively, he just knew that Margot would be appalled at the conditions in Dachau. After they signed the marriage contract, there would be plenty of time for her to see his workplace.

CHAPTER 46

K urtis tapped his fingers on the armrest of the wooden bench inside the train station. Margot was arriving soon, and he was excited to see her. On his lap, he held a small bouquet of yellow sunflowers. *They are lovely. It's no wonder they are the official flower of the Reich.* He marveled as he looked at them. *We will have these flowers at our wedding to honor the Nazi Party.* He had not discussed this with Margot yet, but he was sure she would approve. She never seemed to argue about small things like what they would serve at the wedding or what kind of cake they would have. If he wanted something, she would let him have his way. He thought it was because she loved and admired him because he was a powerful man. This made him feel good. He anticipated having a good life with his future wife. However, Margot was living a lie, and he would have been hurt if he had known the truth. It would have broken his heart to learn that she hated the Reich and she hated anything to do with their power. Her only concern was the safety of her child.

CHAPTER 47

Margot tried to read as the train headed towards Munich, but she couldn't concentrate. When she was busy waiting tables at the restaurant, she could dismiss her thoughts for a while. But as she rode this train alone, in silence, all she could think about was Trudy's recent visit and what she'd said about Max being gone. When Margot heard that Max was dead, she wished she could die too. She'd gone home to her room that night and planned to take her own life. But as she held the razor blade over her arm, Ben's voice came to her. *"Live Margot. Live and bring our child into the world. His very existence is a fight against the Nazis. If you kill yourself, Hitler will have won. Don't do it. Fight…Fight Margot."*

Margot closed her eyes and remembered how she'd felt that night. She'd dropped the razor blade onto the floor and began to cry. Then she thought about Trudy and decided that if Trudy surfaced again, she must get rid of her. But right now, she couldn't figure out how to do it. And to make matters even worse, Trudy knew Klaus.

When Trudy first arrived, things were looking very bad, and Margot had been very worried. But then, as the days and weeks passed, somehow, by some strange miracle, Margot was relieved to find that

Trudy had not returned. *I wonder what happened, why she disappeared. I know it had something to do with Klaus. No matter the reason, I am glad she is gone. Even so, I don't trust her not to come back again. All I can do is hope she doesn't have something even worse in mind for me. It's hard to believe she would go away without getting something from me. Unless…. Is it possible that Klaus has targeted her as his next Aryan goddess victim? Maybe I should talk to Marie about this. I know I can trust her, yet I keep so many secrets. Perhaps she could help me find out what's happened.*

The train whistle blew loudly. The sound brought Margot back to the present moment. She stood up and stretched. Then she rubbed her belly, in an unconscious effort to reassure the fetus growing inside. After she retrieved her small valise, she walked to the door to disembark.

When Kurtis saw Margot, his face lit up like a candle. He ran over to her and took the suitcase from her hand. Then he hugged her tightly and placed a quick kiss on her lips. When he took her hand and led her to his car, she noticed that people around them were looking at the two of them and smiling, and she thought. *They wouldn't be so amicable if they knew the truth. And I would like nothing better than to tell them the truth. But I am living a lie for the sake of this baby. And I will do whatever I must do to protect my child.*

Kurtis opened the car door for Margot, and she slid into the passenger's seat. He ran to the other side, got in, and started the car. They drove for a few minutes, and then he asked, "How are you feeling?"

"I'm all right," she said softly.

"Are you hungry?

"Yes, actually I am."

"Let's stop and have something to eat before we go to the hotel," he said. Then he softly patted her belly. "How's our little man?"

"Fine," she said, then in a worried voice, she added, "I think it's a boy. But it could be a girl, you know? I hope you won't be angry if it is."

"It doesn't matter. It's mine. I mean, it's ours, and as long as it's healthy and pure Aryan, that's all that really matters," he said, smiling.

She let out a breath. "Yes, you're right. Of course, you are. That's what really matters."

They stopped at a lively restaurant right in the center of town. Before entering the restaurant, Kurtis pointed out the famous clock above their heads. "It moves," he said.

"I don't understand. What do you mean?"

"When it chimes at certain hours, all those statues you see inside the clock begin to move around."

"How fascinating."

"Yes, people come from all over the world to see it."

"I'd like to see it."

"We'll come by here tomorrow. The best show is at noon. So, we'll be here," he smiled and took her hand. Then he led her inside the restaurant.

After they finished eating, it was getting late. So, rather than show her around Munich, they returned to the hotel. "I'm sure you're exhausted after a day of traveling. Tomorrow, I'll show you this wonderful city."

She smiled at him. "Yes, I am very tired. It seems that the pregnancy makes me want to sleep."

"I know my mother told me that pregnant women are always tired," he laughed.

"She's quite right." Margot agreed. "I'm going to take a shower. I feel gritty from spending all day on the train."

"Of course. Take your time."

Margot took a long shower, hoping he would fall asleep while she was still in the bathroom. The last thing she wanted to do was have sex with him. But he wasn't sleeping when she returned. He was busy reading a copy of *Der Angriff*. This weekly newspaper was written and published by Dr. Goebbels, Hitler's prime minister of propaganda.

"How are you feeling?" he asked with genuine concern.

"Worn out," she admitted.

"Come, let's get you some rest," he said gently.

She wanted to feel sorry that she didn't love him, but a quick glance at the cover page of *Der Angriff,* which he'd left on the bed, reminded her that he was a Nazi. He saw her looking at the drawing on the cover. It was of a Jewish man sitting on top of mounds of Reichsmarks. His nose was large and over-exaggerated. The caption read, "Jews are rich because they have stolen all of the riches from the good German people."

"Have you ever read this newspaper?" Kurtis asked innocently.

"No," she shook her head.

"Dr. Goebbels is a genius. He really is. You ought to read it. Perhaps you will take a copy to read on the train when you head back to Frankfurt."

"Yes, perhaps," she agreed, but she thought, *I have no desire to read anything by that hypocrite. He's a cripple. I hear he was born with a club foot. Yet, he agrees with that program that murders anyone who is mentally or physically handicapped. Anyone who is like my son, my poor Erik.*

When they got into bed, Kurtis was gentle and considerate. He leaned over and kissed her softly. And to Margot's delight, he didn't try to make love to her. She assumed it was because he was afraid for the child. But as she fell asleep, he reached over and took her into his arms. He held her that way through the night. Margot fell asleep quickly. But she awakened an hour later. Her mind was racing. Talking about Dr. Goebbels had brought on all kinds of new worries. She was suddenly terrified that Erik's condition had been genetic and that the baby she was carrying would have the same medical problems. The thought made her break into a sweat. After the sweat dried, she grew cold, and her body began to tremble. Kurtis awakened; he felt her shiver. "Are you all right? Is something wrong?" He asked.

"Yes, sometimes I get cold at night," she tried to sound casual.

"Don't move, my darling. I'll go down to the front desk and get you another blanket," he said.

"No, it's not necessary. I'm all right, really."

"Are you sure?"

"Quite sure. Go back to sleep," she said, trying to sound as affectionate as possible.

Within minutes, Kurtis was asleep. Margot had never told him about Erik. And she wondered what he would think and what he would do if this child she was now carrying was born with a medical condition. *After all, he is a Nazi, and they hate anyone who they feel is not a perfect specimen. Would Kurtis kill a child he believed was his own? Or would he help her protect it?* Again, she shivered. But this time, Kurtis slept soundly. He did not awaken.

CHAPTER 48

In the morning, Kurtis and Margot went downstairs to the restaurant next door for breakfast. As they sat at a table in the sun, Kurtis brought up their visit to the Eagle's Nest. He mentioned Peter and how Peter was always trying to outdo him. "I've known him for years. He's several years older than I am. But he has always been very competitive with me. We took a sort of training course together once. And I am ashamed to admit it, but he is very athletically superior. He won a lot of the physical challenges we were a part of. I was much younger then; I would like to take him on now. I am sure I could beat him."

She smiled.

Then he hesitated for a moment and looked away. "I love you, Margot. I don't want to lose you. When you met Peter, I was afraid his insults had made you think less of me," he admitted.

"You mustn't feel that way. I didn't think much of him," Margot said. "He's handsome but not nearly as handsome as you are." She knew Kurtis was saying that he was jealous of Peter. She also knew she must make Kurtis feel secure in his relationship with her.

"Do you really think so? Really?"

"I do. You are far more handsome. He's older and has wrinkles around his eyes. His hair is starting to thin."

"But he is so much more successful than I am. Everyone respects him. He has an important job. Better than mine. But I am going to tell you something rather odd."

"Yes. Go on."

"That girl who was with him. Did you see her?"

Trudy, of course, I saw her. "Yes," she tried to sound casual.

"He's married, and that girl who was with him is not his wife. I know his wife. I met her once."

"Oh, is that so strange? I thought it was common with some high-ranking officials," Margot asked.

"Not really, I suppose. Of course, I will never cheat on you. I love you so much that I don't even notice other women."

She reached over and patted his hand. He smiled. Then he said, "But, I thought it was strange when Peter's girlfriend asked me about you. She seemed very curious to know all about you. I wonder why. She wanted to know how we met and where you are working. I think she wants to be friends with us, you know, like couple friends. Perhaps she wants to go out together as two couples. I don't know. But I would rather not have anything to do with Peter."

Margot felt her throat tighten. Now she knew how Trudy had found her working at a restaurant in Frankfurt. "So, you told her all about me?"

"Of course. Why wouldn't I? I am very proud of you, and we have nothing to hide."

"No, of course not." Margot put down her toast. She'd suddenly lost her appetite. Then, in a small voice, she asked, "What did she say about me?"

"Nothing, really. But she was very nice."

What does he know? What did she tell him? And how much should I tell him before she does? "Did she mention that she and I knew each other before?" she asked, feeling stupid.

"You did? No, she didn't mention it."

So, she didn't tell him that I am her sister or that I am Jewish.

Perhaps I should just make light of this and not put too much emphasis on anything that happened. "Oh, yes, well, we know each other."

"You never told me," he said. "Why?"

"I'd rather not talk about it…"

He looked at her skeptically but said nothing.

CHAPTER 49

Dachau

Max stood in line, waiting for his soup. It had been another long, hard, and terrible day. One of the men who worked beside him died early that afternoon. The man was only twenty-five, but he looked like he was eighty. They had been digging a large hole when he just fell over on the street like a rag doll, his body little more than bones covered by thin white skin. At first, the guard yelled at him to get up and keep working. But he didn't move. So, the guard came over to beat him, but he stopped when he saw that the man was dead. Without any emotion at all, the guard turned to Max and another prisoner and said, "Get this body out of our way. There's work to be done here."

Without a word, the two prisoners dragged the body of the dead man to the side of the road, and then they went back to work.

Max knew he must go on working as if nothing had just happened. The Nazis had no respect or sympathy. Showing pity to another person could cause a guard to shoot the sympathetic one. Consequently, Max went back to work, his face expressionless, like a stone statue. He had hardened, but still not enough to stop him from

169

feeling sorry for the loved ones who might be waiting and someday be searching for this poor young man who had died here on the road that day. *If I die here, Margot will search for me. That is, if she is still alive. And my parents too, if they survive. Who knows if any of them will ever learn the truth about what happened to me?*

Holding his bowl and spoon in hand as he stood in the soup line, Max was brought back to the current moment by a conversation he overheard between two guards. Kaz and Adrien had not arrived at the line yet, so he stood alone and listened.

"I got the food and the whiskey," a thick-boned guard said. "I hid them in the back of the office."

"Yeah? So, when should I pick up the girls?" a tall, skinny guard with a pockmarked face and recessed hairline asked.

"After lights out. We must be sure everyone is gone. If we get caught, we'll be punished. You know as well as I do that we aren't supposed to drink or bring girls in here."

"Have you ever done this before?"

"Of course, I have. But I am always careful not to get caught," the thick-boned guard said as he squinted into the setting sun.

"What if the girls don't like the place? It stinks in here. You know that."

"They're whores. They don't care where they do it. All they care about is getting paid. And of course, we are paying them a lot less than usual because we are bringing food and alcohol. They should be happy to have the work."

"Keep them hungry, and they'll do anything."

Both guards laughed. But Max was already devising a plan in his mind. He would sneak out that night and wait for the party to end. Then, when the guards cleaned up and threw away the remainder of the food, he would find it and take the spoils back to his block to share them with Kaz and Adrien.

CHAPTER 50

That afternoon, Margot and Kurtis went sightseeing. They watched the incredible overhead clock in the old city and walked through the beautiful botanical gardens. But much of the old city where the clock was located was in ruins due to the bombings. Kurtis said he wished Margot had seen it before the destruction. She didn't answer, she just squeezed his hand. However, she thought that if Hitler had not been such a tyrant, Germany would not have suffered such destruction.

After walking for several hours, Margot was tired, so they returned to the hotel, and she took a nap while Kurtis went to a beer garden. When he returned, she was ready to meet his mother for dinner. She wore a simple cream-colored dress with her dark hair caught up neatly in a twist. "You look elegant," he said.

Margot laughed. "I wanted to wear something your mother would approve of."

Kurtis freshened up quickly, and then they drove to the restaurant where he and Margot were to meet his mother and her boyfriend. "I think you and my mother will get along beautifully."

"I hope so. I am really looking forward to meeting her."

When they entered the restaurant, Margot saw a good-looking older couple sitting at a table for four. Then Kurtis pointed and said, "That's them, right over there."

Kurtis's mother stood up and hugged her son. Then she shyly said, "Hello. You must be Margot."

"Yes, I am."

"Margot, this is my mother, Frau Richter," Kurtis said proudly.

"Call me Winnie," his mother said, smiling. Her bright blue eyes twinkled.

Margot smiled. "Nice to meet you, Winnie."

"It's short for Winifred," Kurtis chimed in.

"And this is my friend," Winnie said, glancing at the man beside her, "*Obersturmführer* Lehmann."

The man stood up. He was tall and well-built. He reached out and shook Margot's hand, then indicated Frau Richter, and in a teasing tone, he said, "You know we could call her Freddie."

"Not Freddie, dear. That's a man's name," Winnie chided him. But Margot could tell there was easy banter between Winnie and her boyfriend.

"All right, all right, Winnie it is," *Obersturmführer* Lehmann said, patting Winnie's hand. Then he turned to Margot and, in a deep baritone voice, added, "Since we are all family here, you can call me Axel."

"It's a pleasure to meet you, Axel," Margot said politely. These people seemed so normal, kind, and easy to get along with. And yet, she knew better. Her thoughts turned to Ben and how he had suffered, and her heart ached. How terrible his life had been because of people just like this.

Axel interrupted her thoughts. "So, what shall we have for dinner?" he asked.

"Beer. Plenty of beer," Kurtis said, laughing, and the *Obersturmführer* laughed too.

"I couldn't agree more. There's nothing better than German beer in Munich."

"Yes, lots of beer," Winnie agreed.

"How about some pretzels with mustard to get started?" Kurtis suggested.

"Why not," Axel smiled, and he flagged over the waiter.

Four large steins of beer were delivered to the table. Axel passed them around, then stood up, and loud enough for everyone around them to hear, he said, "To our *Führer* and to our Reich, may we reign for a thousand years."

Margot felt a little dizzy as she watched all the people surrounding them raise their glasses and drink to the Nazi party.

After they finished the pretzels, Axel didn't hold back when ordering food. There were plenty of sausages and thick, hearty white bread sandwich rolls. These rolls were soft, crusty, and delicious, not heavy and grainy like the dark bread made with sawdust that the German people were forced to eat due to food shortages. A large bowl of sauerkraut and one of spaetzle arrived at the table, followed by another overflowing bowl of vinegar potato salad. Margot thought of how she and Ben had been starving in the attic while Hitler's elite were eating like royalty. She would have liked to spit in their faces. But she knew she must continue the charade. Besides, the wonderful smell of food reminded Margot that she hadn't eaten since early that afternoon and was very hungry.

They ate until they were so full that they had to stop.

"You were right, Kurtis, the food here is excellent," Axel admitted. Then he turned to Margot and said, "Kurtis suggested this place. I must admit he has good taste. Not only in women but also in food."

"Yes, I must admit that I do," Kurtis agreed.

Then Axel turned his attention to Kurtis. "Are you still working over at the camp at Dachau?"

"Yes," Kurtis said, then he quickly added as if he wanted to change the subject, "and the food here at this restaurant has always been very good."

But Axel wasn't ready to change the subject. He asked, "How is that going? I hear that it's been expanded. No longer just political prisoners. Now you have to put up with some more of the dregs of the earth. Jews, criminals, that sort of thing."

"Yes. That's right."

Margot felt her stomach turn. But she looked down at her plate and did not meet anyone else's eyes at the table. She was afraid her expression would give her away.

"Those Jews are really a problem. I've been stationed at a terrible camp. You would think you were in hell if you were there. It's over-flowing with disgusting, dirty Jews. But at least we are getting rid of them. Eliminating them, if you will. I'm sure you understand what I mean."

Kurtis glanced at Margot, then turned to Axel and said, "Yes, I quite understand, but I am afraid my fiancée is in a delicate way right now. I'm sure my mother told you that we are going to have a baby. And this sort of talk might make her feel ill."

"Yes, that's right. I forgot. I am sorry," Axel said as graciously as he could manage. "No need for unpleasant discussions about the filthy Jews. It's bad enough we must deal with them on a daily basis, isn't that right, Kurtis?"

"Absolutely."

There was a long silence, then, smiling broadly, Axel said, "Anyone for dessert?"

Margot couldn't eat another bite. The words that Axel had used about eliminating the Jews were weighing heavily on her mind. She was tired of acting. The lie she was living made her anxious, and she was ready to leave. But when everyone ordered coffee and strudel, she forced herself to smile and order the same.

The coffee was rich. It was real coffee, made from coffee beans, not the ersatz coffee she had been drinking, made from acorns. And there was real cream and real sugar on the table. Margot was so full that she couldn't eat a single bite of strudel, but she sipped the coffee, and it settled her stomach. They were ready to leave, but the maître d' walked over to the table just before the check arrived. "Excuse me, please. I hate to interrupt your evening. However, I have a telephone call for *Kommandoführer* Richter. The caller says it's an emergency."

Kurtis stood up. His face was deep red with anger and embarrass-ment. "I'm sorry. I am going to have to take this. Are you all right?" he asked Margot.

"Yes, of course," she said.

"Wait for me here, I'll be right back."

Margot trembled inside. *What could this call be about? Is there any chance it has anything to do with Trudy? Oh, dear God, I am in the den of the enemy. I'm pregnant and not feeling well. But how could it be Trudy? How would she know where we are? How would she find me here? I don't have any answers to these questions. All I know is that Trudy has always found a way to do horrible things. She found a way to ask Kurtis where I was working, and I wouldn't put it past her to have found us here at this restaurant.*

"You look pale, my dear," Winnie said. There was genuine concern in her voice.

"I'm all right. I was hungry, and I ate too much."

Winnie smiled, "I understand."

"And I just hope everything is all right with Kurtis," Margot said.

"I'm sure the call is nothing to worry about," Axel said, smiling. But the smile did not reach his eyes, and Margot knew it was not sincere. "These jobs we have are essential. Often, they require a great deal of our attention. But of course, I am sure you understand. Your fiancé is an important man."

But all she said was, "Yes, of course, I know Kurtis has an important job. And I'm sure everything will be all right." Her skin felt hot, and sweat began to bead under her arms. It was only a few minutes before Kurtis returned, but it seemed like hours to Margot.

"It's nothing to worry about," he said. "One of the guards, who works under me, has decided to have a little party in the office. Apparently, he and a friend of his brought in some wayward women." He turned to Margot and his mother. "My apologies for mentioning those types of girls in front of you ladies."

His mother nodded.

"It seems they've brought in all kinds of food and alcohol. I need to go to the camp and put a stop to it right now. Then I have to reprimand him and make sure it doesn't happen again."

"Typical. The guards are lower-class individuals. I have the same problems with the guards where I work," Axel said, trying to reassure Kurtis that he understood.

"Would you like to come to our hotel and wait for Kurtis?" Winnie asked Margot.

"No, thank you. I'll go with him," Margot said.

An odd look passed between Kurtis and Axel. Margot caught a glimpse of it, but it was only there for a second. Then Axel smiled and said, "It was a pleasure to meet you, my dear. Winnie and I will be looking forward to the wedding."

"We certainly will," Winnie said. Then she turned to Kurtis and asked, "Will we be seeing the two of you again before Margot leaves to go back to Frankfurt?"

"I'm not sure we'll have time," Kurtis said as he stood up and hugged his mother. "But we'll try."

Margot could see that Kurtis was nervous.

Then, in a soft voice, his mother asked, "Do the two of you have plans to go to your father's grave before Margot leaves?"

"No, as far as I'm concerned, he was never a father to me," Kurtis said as he took Margot's arm and led her out of the restaurant. They got into the car, and Kurtis turned the key. The engine sprang to life. For a few minutes, they drove without speaking.

"You can wait in the car while I take care of this. I'll only be a minute," Kurtis said.

"Of course," Margot agreed. "But you could drop me off at your apartment, and I could wait there if that's better."

"No," his voice was firm. Margot wondered why he didn't want her to see where he lived. She wondered if he was afraid some of his neighbors might tell her things he didn't want her to know. However, from his tone, she knew she should not question him.

CHAPTER 51

"How are you feeling?" Kurtis asked as he turned off the main road and onto a dirt road. The car bumped along. "Sorry about the bumpy ride."

"I'm all right," Margot said. She was looking around her. There was nothing really to see. Only a guard post with a gate.

Kurtis drove up to it, and the guard inside smiled at him. "Good evening, *Herr Kommandoführer.*"

"Good evening," Kurtis said. Then he drove through the gate. They were surrounded by rows of one-story buildings that looked like horse stables to Margot. It was dark, and she couldn't see much. However, she was certain that this was where the prisoners were kept.

"Can they get out?" Margot asked. She was suddenly afraid of the prisoners. She wondered how many of them were actually criminals. And if they were dangerous. *I don't know what I believe anymore. Desperate people are dangerous. What if someone comes and tries to kill me so he can take the car?*

"No, don't worry. They won't bother us."

"Are they criminals, or are they Jews?"

"Jews are criminals of the Reich, my love. But if you want a break-down, there are Jews here, political prisoners who defy our principles and try to bring down our government, and common criminals like thieves and murderers. Jehovah's Witnesses are fools who just refuse to reject their belief in their God. And then there are the filthy gypsies. I'm sure you have met them. They lie, cheat, steal. That sort of thing."

"I see," she said. Then, something came over her, and for a moment, she felt bold. "Why are Jews considered criminals? I mean, what really have they done?"

"Oh, love. I will explain it all to you later when we get back to the hotel. I am in a bit of a hurry right now. But I promise I will make it all clear to you so you understand better," he said as he pulled the automobile to a stop in front of one of the buildings. Then he turned to her. "Keep the doors locked. I'll be back very soon and don't worry, you should be just fine."

Margot felt nervous as she watched Kurtis walk away. She had heard about these camps but had no idea what really went on inside one. It was dark, but she could see the light shining from a tower. It was hard to tell, but she was fairly certain that she saw an armed guard inside. *I am living in constant fear. Right now, the danger is coming from the prisoners. If, somehow, they can get to me before Kurtis returns, I would be in mortal danger, as would my baby. They would not know that I am most probably Jewish and that my child is defi-nitely half-Jewish. No, they would know nothing. They would see me as the enemy. And they would be right because I am sitting in this automobile that is obviously owned by a Nazi.*

The tiny hairs on Margot's arm stood at attention. She began sweating again, and then she became nauseated. It could have been nerves combined with fear and stress, or it might have been the heavy meal she'd consumed. But since she had become pregnant, she vomited easily. And now, no matter what the cause, she had to get out of the car because she felt the bile rising in her throat, and she knew she was about to vomit.

She told herself she had to be careful as she tried to hide in the shadow of the building. But she could not be careful. Instead, she began to throw up, and when she finished, she was so spent that she leaned against the building.

"Who is there?" A man's voice sent a chill down her spine.

CHAPTER 52

DACHAU

Adrien and Kaz tried to convince Max not to go. They told him that it wasn't worth the risk. But he knew that it was. They were starving, and any food they could get their hands on, no matter how small, could be the difference between life and death.

Max had done this before when he'd overheard two guards talking about having a forbidden get-together in one of the buildings. And that time, he'd returned with half a loaf of bread and two chewed-on boiled potatoes. It was brown bread, and it was a bit moldy. But it was extra food, and Max gladly shared it with his friends. "It's a small gesture," he'd said as they gobbled some of the bread and potatoes and then hid the rest, "and so we live another day."

But that time, the guards and their girlfriends had gone to one of the quiet buildings in the back of the camp. This time, they were going to have their little get-together right in the main office. It was easier to get caught there, but the guards were always sloppy. Max assumed they would probably throw the old food into the trash. He just had to make sure that the guards in the overhead tower didn't see him rummage through the garbage.

"I'll be all right. You know how good I am at avoiding the guards. I'm like a ghost," Max smiled at Kaz.

"That's the whole point of why I don't want you to go," Kaz said. "If you get caught, you'll be a real ghost."

"I'm not going to get myself killed," Max promised. "I'll get whatever food I can and be back as soon as possible."

Kaz nodded and then shrugged his shoulders at Adrien. "*Nu?*" he said. "So when has the *boychik* ever listened to anyone else? He has his own mind. Don't you, Max?"

Max nodded.

"You're stubborn, but that's why we love you."

CHAPTER 53

little while after lights out had been called, things grew very quiet in the camp. Max listened for the guards who patrolled the area. As soon as they passed, he knew he would have a short window to get out of his block unseen. It seemed like forever because his body was so exhausted, and it was almost impossible to stay awake. But finally, he heard the guard pass by. After waiting a few additional minutes, Max got up and made his way out of the building. Then he lay on his belly to avoid being noticed by the guard in the tower and crawled towards the office.

As he approached the office, Max heard the guard announce through a microphone, "Who is there?"

Sure that he had been seen, Max felt his panic rise. He lay on the cold, hard ground with his heart beating so hard it felt like it might explode. *So, this is how it ends. This is it. The culmination of a life. I am going to die on the ground, crawling on my belly like a worm. I will never see Margot again. I will never avenge Rivka's death.* And all of a sudden, he realized that it was sadness, as well as fear, that filled him. He closed his eyes and envisioned Margot, and then he saw little Erik playing on the living room rug in their old apartment. Tears fell on his cheeks as he remembered the happier times he'd shared with his little family. And then something very strange happened. He thought he heard Margot's voice. But she wasn't talking to him. She was answering the guard in the tower. *I am hallucinating.* He thought. But he was frozen on the ground as he listened. *I am sure that it's her. Yes, it's Margot's voice. I must have been shot. I must be dying.*

"I'm sorry to have disturbed you," the voice said. "My name is Margot Kraus. I'm here on these grounds with *Kommandoführer* Kurtis Richter. He was called in on business and asked me to wait in the car, but I had to get out because I wasn't feeling well."

"Wait there," the guard said. "I'm coming to check this out."

Could this be possible? Why would Margot be here with Richter? That makes no sense. But there must be a reason. Max crawled behind the office building, where it was dark and he was hidden from sight. But he watched and listened. A few minutes later, the guard called out, "I am not coming down because I spoke with the gate guard. He verified your story. But for your own safety, *Fräulein*, I suggest you get back into the automobile and lock the doors. It's not safe for you to be wandering around here. There are a lot of criminal elements in this camp. You could get hurt."

"I understand, and I will get right back in the car," she answered.

"Good. And I'm sure the *Kommandoführer* will be right back."

"Thank you," she called out.

Max could not believe his ears. It took him every bit of restraint not to run to her. He wasn't sure why she was here or why she was with the *Kommandoführer*. But he was certain she had a reason, and he trusted her implicitly. *I have to see her. I must speak to her. But I can't go over to where she is right now. I am sure the overhead guard is watching. I'll wait for a few minutes.* The guard in the tower was still shining his light on Margot. Careful to remain hidden by darkness, Max inched forward until he could see Margot getting into the car. He would have seen her pregnant belly if he had been just a few seconds earlier. But as fate would have it, the car door blocked his view. For a single moment, he saw her face. His heart melted. Tears flowed from his eyes. *Margot is alive. My wife is alive.* His arms ached to hold her. His lips ached to kiss her. It was everything he could do to keep himself from standing up and running towards her, letting the guards shoot him. At least he would die in her arms. Max was temporarily insane with his need to be close to her. But then he saw the *Kommandoführer* exit the office, followed by two other guards. The same two guards whom he'd seen earlier talking about bringing prostitutes to the camp for the evening. The men were accompanied by two young women, and Max assumed these were the prostitutes that they brought in. The *Kommandoführer* turned to the guards. His voice was stern, and Max knew he was very angry. "You two idiots have caused me to be forced to come here in the middle of a dinner engagement. I should fire both of you. Now, hurry up and get these women out of here. And you had better make sure this doesn't happen again. Do you understand me?"

"Yes, *Kommandoführer*," the guards said in unison.

"Now go, get out of my sight. I don't appreciate being called in to work during my time off. The next time you do something like this, you can kiss your job goodbye."

Max watched as the *Kommandoführer* got into the car with Margot. He turned on the engine. And Max felt his heart pounding in his throat as they drove away. Staying in the shadows, he lay his head down on the hard dirt and wept. *If only I had been able to speak to her, to touch her. If only I could make sure she was real and not just a figment of my tortured mind. Why was she in a car with that terrible Richter? The way the overhead guard spoke to her, I knew she wasn't a prisoner. But what is going on with her and Richter? I can't imagine she actually likes him. He's a monster, an evil, wicked man.* "Margot, my Margot," he whispered. *I wish I had the power to protect and keep her safe. But I am powerless. All I can do is remind myself that Margot is savvy. I must believe that she knows what she is doing.* It was hard to breathe. And he knew it was because he was terribly anxious, worried more about Margot's safety than his own. Max closed his eyes and forced himself to remember that something good came out of this night. At least now he knew that Margot was alive. And if he could just stay alive, someday, he would find a way to be reunited with her.

CHAPTER 54

A strange, unexplainable feeling came over Margot as the car moved slowly out of the camp. It felt as if someone were watching over her. And yet, there was no reason for her to feel this way. She thought about how she had been so sickened by the smell in the camp that she had climbed out of the car to vomit. But then, for some odd reason, she felt a strange peace come over her. Her nausea disappeared, and even though the place was frightening, she felt safe. She felt very calm even now as she and Kurtis were driving away. It was a strange way for her to feel, considering Kurtis was in a foul mood when he got back in the car due to whatever had just happened at his job. And, besides, she thought, she should be reeling with fear and disgust because she had just left this terrible prison.

They drove down the dark streets in the little town, and for a while, Kurtis did not speak. Then he said, "I'm sorry to have been forced to take you inside that place. I know it's horrible. And I really hope you're all right."

"I'm all right," she said.

"Are you sure?"

"Yes, I am sure."

"Shall we stop and get something to eat or drink?" he asked, and he seemed to be so concerned that, for a moment, she was sorry that her feelings towards him were insincere. She had lied to him, told him she loved him, vowed to marry him. And most importantly, told him that the child nestled in her womb was his. But she had to lie. She had to lie to save her baby. And as a mother, she knew she would do anything for that baby.

"I'm not hungry. I'm still full from dinner," Margot said, "but we can stop if you'd like."

"Are you tired?"

"Yes, very. The pregnancy seems to wear me out so quickly."

"Then let's get back to the hotel so you can get some sleep," he said.

CHAPTER 55

Max was confused and overwhelmed. However, he felt he could not return to his block without at least checking the trash in the office for food the guards might have left behind. He knew Kaz and Adrien would be waiting for him. So, although he'd lost his desire to raid the office, he forced himself to do so anyway. His mind was clouded with questions and thoughts about Margot. So, he had to remind himself constantly that he must pay attention and not allow himself to get lost in thought. If he forgot the danger he was in for a moment, he might make a wrong move. Any wrong move could cost him his life.

In the darkness, Max entered the office building by pushing a window in the back until he was able to dislodge and remove it. Earlier that day, he'd quickly assessed the entire structure and saw that the window was not set right. As he had hoped, it turned out to be easy to remove. This was far better than breaking the glass, which would have been too noisy.

Quickly, he slid through the window and entered the office building. Although his eyes were adjusted to the darkness, it was darker inside than it had been outside. However, the moon shined through a window into the room where the guards and their dates had been gathered. Looking around him, Max saw that they had left a mess. It was obvious that *Kommandoführer* had arrived and surprised them. He must have forced them to leave immediately. They had not taken the time to take out the trash; consequently, there was food in the office for Max to take. But he had to hurry. There were two half-eaten loaves of brown bread without mold, a small hunk of cheese, and a few bites of a mostly eaten sausage. For Max and his friends, men who were close to dying of starvation, this was a treasure. Max smiled. *Kaz and Adrien will be so happy to see all this food.* He thought as he stuffed his shirt with all the spoils and left as quickly as he'd come crawling back to his block.

Max forced himself to stay on task and not allow his thoughts to wander as he made his way through the camp, slithering like a snake. The overhead light from the guard station almost spotted him twice as they circled the camp in search of any prisoner out of his bunk. With his heart racing and his mouth dry, he finally arrived back at his block. Still breathing hard, he entered. Kaz raced up to him. "Are you all right? You were gone for a long time. Adrien and I were worried, *boychik.*"

"I'm all right. But something happened. Something I have to tell you about," Max said. Then he took the food out of his shirt. "By the way, there was food. Plenty of food. Look at this."

Kaz nodded, his eyes wide in the light from the moon.

"Go on, help yourself. Have some," Max said.

Kaz stuffed the bread into his mouth and chewed slowly. "Adrien," he called out softly, "come here."

One of the other prisoners got out of the cot and headed for Kaz and Max. "Give me some food, or I'll tell on you."

"If you don't go back to your cot right now, I'll kill you," Kaz growled. "Get out of here. And keep your lousy mouth shut if you want to go on living."

The prisoner was young, possibly a teenager. Max couldn't tell because he didn't recognize him.

"This idiot is new here. He came in on a transport tonight," Kaz said, reading Max's mind.

"Eh, give him a little bread," Max said.

Kaz looked at the young man who stood waiting. Then he tore off a bit of bread and handed it to the teenager, "You're an arrogant son of a bitch, but here. Max is right. You're starving like the rest of us."

The boy took the bread. "Thank you," he whispered.

"Now go back to your cot," Kaz said.

Adrien walked over to them. "You found food?" he asked Max.

"Yes," Max said, handing him the cheese, "here."

The three of them ate. Then Max took Kaz to the other side of the block and told him everything that had happened while he was gone. Kaz listened quietly until Max finished his story.

"I'm confused," Max admitted in a whisper. "Margot was here at Dachau with that louse Richter. What would she possibly be doing with him? How did she meet him, and what is his relationship with her. And…Oh, Kaz, how I wish I had just been able to speak to her." His heart ached as his voice trailed off.

Kaz cleared his throat. Then softly, he said, "Do you think maybe you might have been hallucinating? Maybe you just want to see or hear her so badly that you imagined it was her, but it was just a woman's voice…"

"No, I didn't imagine anything. It was her voice. I know her voice. Margot is the love of my life. We were married. We had a child together. For all I know, we have another one. She was pregnant when I last saw her…"

"Yes, I know all of this," Kaz said sympathetically, "but the mind works in strange ways. Do you know what I am trying to say?"

"Yes, I know what you are trying to tell me. But I promise you it wasn't just in my mind. I am sure it was Margot. I am sure of it. As sure of it as I am that we are sitting here together right now."

Kaz was silent for a few minutes. They sat together, looking out the window at the moon and the stars. Then Kaz patted Max's shoulder. "Well, *boychik*, you can look at it this way. At least now you have a reason to live. Now you know she is alive, and you will find her again when this is over."

"I thought of that. But who knows if this will ever be over," Max said.

"It will be. It will be," Kaz promised, but he didn't sound convincing. "I heard from one of the newer prisoners; he had a radio before coming here and heard that the Americans have been sending military supplies to England. This help from America could turn out to be life-changing for us."

"Do you think America will enter the war?" Max asked hopefully.

"We can only pray."

CHAPTER 56

T he night Trudy had walked into Klaus' restaurant had been exciting for him. After their night of wild sex in Munich, he was quite certain that he would never see her again. It was the first and only time they had been to bed together, and he had gotten carried away and scared her. When Klaus took a new lover, he usually slowly built up to the level of violence that he had achieved that night with Trudy. It was too much for most girls the first time. But she was just his type, and he was so attracted to her, and because they were both on holiday in Munich, he figured there would be no way to continue their affair. Otherwise, he would have controlled himself better. After he returned to Frankfurt, he often thought about her, but he didn't think he would ever see her again. Still, he had always regretted letting her get away. And now, what luck to find out that she was Margot's sister. He had to admit that they didn't look like sisters at all. Trudy was an Aryan goddess, the type that made his blood stir. And Margot? She was little more than a little brown sister with dark hair, dark eyes, and small breasts. He laughed aloud at the title. Little brown sister was the name given to women of Aryan blood at the homes for the Lebensborn, who were unfortunate enough to have the wrong coloring.

Margot was not his type in any way, and he wondered what a handsome SS officer like Kurtis could possibly see in her. She was far too skinny and nothing to look at, really. He had kept her at the restaurant because she was a good waitress like Marie, who he also didn't find attractive. But then, when Kurtis Richter took a liking to her, he knew she would make a good bargaining tool. Kurtis was not a top official, but he was high enough to have plenty of friends, and Klaus had heard that Kurtis spoke very highly of him and the restaurant. Besides that, Kurtis had used his connections to ensure Klaus could purchase some of the finest German beer. It was difficult for Klaus to understand why Richter was attracted to Margot. He couldn't see it. But as long as Richter was, Klaus planned to make the most of it. In fact, it had been Klaus's idea that they would have the wedding at his restaurant.

That first night when Trudy had appeared out of nowhere, he'd followed her home. Klaus hoped she had moved to Frankfurt to be closer to her sister. He figured if she had, he would do his best to convince her that he was sorry for how he had behaved that night in Munich, and then he would be able to pick things up where they left off. However, he was disappointed to find she was probably just visiting. He followed her to a reputable hotel where he assumed she was staying. And to his chagrin, it was far too nice of a place for him to try to force his way into her room. So, he'd left that night, hoping she would return to the restaurant soon to see her sister again. When she didn't, he hoped she would at least come to the wedding. And since it was only a couple of months away, he decided not to try and find her. He would just sit back like a spider on its web and wait.

But he needn't have worried about Trudy escaping him because the week after Margot returned from meeting her future mother-in-law, Trudy walked back into the restaurant. She did not look directly at Klaus, but he could not take his eyes off her. He walked over to her and said, "Trudy, I'm so glad you've returned. Would you like something to eat or drink? It's on me, of course. You see, I was hoping we could still be friends." He sensed she was afraid of him, so he lied, "I'm sorry for what happened in Munich. I didn't mean it. I don't know what came over me. I've never done anything like that before."

"I don't want anything to eat or drink. I've come to see my sister," Trudy said coldly.

"Of course. Let me get her for you," Klaus smiled warmly.

A few minutes later, Margot walked over to the table where Trudy waited.

"Will you please excuse us?" Trudy asked Klaus not looking directly at him.

"But of course," he said in his most gentlemanly voice and manner.

Klaus walked away. Trudy glanced up and saw him go into the kitchen. Then she turned to Margot and said, "I need to speak to you." Her face was lined with desperation. Her eyes were red from crying or not sleeping.

Margot frowned. "What do you want?"

"The same thing I wanted when I came here before. I told you then that I need money, Margot. But since then, things have gotten worse for me. My boyfriend left me without a dime. I lost my apartment because I couldn't pay my rent. I took the last of the money I had saved and came here. I'm staying in Frankfurt, living at a woman's hotel. I arrived yesterday and couldn't afford to stay in a nice place. So, you can just imagine that it's a terrible hotel. It's not clean, and the other women there are not the kind you want to associate with." She was almost in tears. "You are my sister. I need your help."

"You can't be serious. After all you have done to me, you want me to consider you a sister? Don't you remember? You said I wasn't your real sister. Now, you want me to help you?"

"Yes, I do. I need your help. Besides, I was wrong. You are my sister. Even if you are not my blood. We were raised together."

"Oh please, don't give me your crap. You were the one who broke all ties between us. That's how this started. Or wait, maybe not. I think it started when you allowed my son, my only child, to die at the hands of the Nazis. Yes, I think that was when we became estranged. Or perhaps we always were, and I just never realized it. But, let me tell you, I realize it now, Trudy. I see you for what you are." Margot's voice was low but mean and sarcastic. "You are the reason Max and I are not together. You are the reason my Max is dead. And now, you ask me to help you. I would rather spit in your face."

"If you don't help me out of the goodness of your heart, then I'll tell everyone the truth about you. I'll tell them your mother was a Jewish whore and that my parents adopted you. When the Gestapo hears about your Jewish blood, they will put you away or kill you all together. You're pregnant, Margot. Think of your unborn child. That little Jew inside of you will never see the light of day. It will die in your womb. Is your hatred for me so strong that you will allow that to happen?"

"And who says they'll believe you." Margot trembled with fear and rage. "You are a rat, a beast. You certainly are one of those Nazis, aren't you?"

"Just look at you and look at me. I'm an Aryan, pure Aryan. Anyone can see that. My blonde hair, my blue eyes. I am German through and through. But you, my dear, are dark like a Jew. Don't think they won't believe me because they will."

Margot glared at her, "What about Mattie? Have you asked her for help? I don't have much money to give you. But you two have always been so close. Why didn't you go to her?"

"Because we don't speak anymore. She has stupid ideas about right and wrong and tries to judge me. I don't take that from anyone."

There was a moment of silence. "You ruined my life," Margot said, "I hate you."

"I know, but you also fear me," Trudy said. "And you should. Because I haven't begun to ruin your life as much as I could. If you don't help me, you will see just how far I will go."

Margot sighed. She knew she had no choice but to do as Trudy asked. She was ready to die if need be. She was tired. So very tired of fighting. But at the same time, she could not help but feel a fierce need to protect her child. "Give me your address. I will come to your room tomorrow when I am off work and bring you some money."

Trudy smiled. "I thought so. It's a shame we had to get so ugly with each other." She reached into her handbag and took a piece of paper and a pencil. Then, she wrote down her address. "I'll see you tomorrow morning," Trudy said, then got up and left the restaurant.

Margot put the paper into her pocket. Tears were running down her cheeks. She didn't want the customers to see her crying, so she went into the kitchen, where she washed her face with cold water. Then, before she returned to the dining room, she put Trudy's address into her handbag. Meanwhile, Klaus had been watching Margot the entire time. And as soon as Margot returned to the dining room floor to serve the customers, Klaus took the paper out of her handbag.

When Klaus saw the address, he smiled, happy that he knew where Trudy lived. This gave him the edge he had been hoping for. Then he looked around the dining room. Margot was very busy. So, he quickly copied down the address and stuffed the paper into his jacket pocket. Then he placed the original back in Margot's handbag so she would not know he'd taken it.

CHAPTER 57

Margot didn't sleep at all that night. She lay in bed tossing and turning. She wondered if Kurtis would stick by her if Trudy tried to have her arrested or if he would believe Trudy and turn on her. At first light, she got out of bed and got dressed. The sun rose as she walked to the woman's hotel where Trudy was staying.

Trudy opened the door in a pink chiffon nightgown. Her hair was set in pin curls, and she had some white cream on her face. "You're early," she said as she looked at Margot. "I didn't expect you to come so early. I thought you'd drop by much later in the day."

"Yes, well. I thought I would get the unpleasantness of seeing you out of the way early, so I might enjoy the rest of my day off."

Trudy laughed. "Come in."

Margot walked into the room. It was no worse or better than the room she had been staying in. But she knew how Trudy was addicted to luxury, which was far from luxurious.

"I don't earn a lot of money, I'm afraid," Margot said, hating that she had to bow down to this miserable sister. "I'll give you what I can,"

196

she handed Trudy a few Reichsmarks. "This is all I have been able to save since I started working. I have bills to pay, too."

"But of course. However, this isn't much," Trudy said, counting the money. "You could ask that boyfriend of yours. He must be the father of that baby you are carrying. He wouldn't want you to live in poverty now, would he?"

"I don't like to do that, Trudy."

"Of course not. But you will. Because you wouldn't want him to find out that he poured his precious Aryan seed into a Jew, now, would you? I'd bet that if he learned the truth about you, he would want to destroy you and that half-Jew you are carrying."

"I'll see what I can do," Margot said, defeated. She wished she could kill Trudy. She wished it was in her nature to bring a knife with her the next time she came and to cut her sister's throat. But it wasn't.

"When will you be back? I need money as soon as possible."

"I'm getting married next month. Let Kurtis and I get married first. Then it will be easier for me to ask him for money for you."

"Hmmm, that is a rather good idea," Trudy said, "and of course, I will be coming to the wedding. I'm sure that Kurtis will be inviting plenty of his important friends. Plenty of handsome SS officers. I could possibly meet someone new at your wedding."

"Yes, I suppose so," Margot said.

"Where and when is the wedding?"

Margot told her.

"You must get along quite well with your boss to have the wedding at his restaurant," Trudy said.

"Klaus? He's all right," Margot said.

"I don't care for him. But I suppose I can put up with him for now," Trudy said.

Margot stood up to leave.

Trudy looked down at the money in her hand. "This should hold me until the wedding, but after that, I expect you to come through with a lot more. I don't want to stay in this terrible place any longer than I have to."

CHAPTER 58

K laus left the restaurant and walked to the address he'd written down on the paper. Trudy's address. He watched carefully to ensure he was not seen by Trudy or the man she had introduced to him in Munich as her husband. But when he arrived, he was pleasantly surprised to see that the location was a woman's hotel, and this one was not as nice as the one she'd stayed in when she visited. The fact that Trudy was rooming at a woman's hotel meant she was in Frankfurt without her husband. He wondered for how long? Was she here visiting Margot on holiday? Perhaps she had come for the wedding. Margot could answer all his questions, and he intended to ask her everything the following day. But at least he knew Trudy was here in Frankfurt, and she was unescorted. This would leave her vulnerable to his advances. He crunched the paper with the address in his hand and smiled. *At least for now, I know where to find her. I'll keep a good watch on her and prey upon her like a lion prays on a gazelle. And when the time is right, I will spring. She had tried to run from me, but she wouldn't get away this time.*

CHAPTER 59

When Margot arrived at work the following day, Klaus asked her to have a beer with him. Marie saw this and frowned. Margot shrugged her shoulders at Marie as if to say she did not know what Klaus wanted. Her hands trembled, and she was nervous as she poured the two beers. Then she sat across from Klaus at a table in the back of the dining room.

"Your sister was here yesterday," he said.

"Yes. That's right. She was."

"She must be excited about the wedding, no?"

"Yes, of course," Margot said. *The less he knows, the better.*

"So that's why she came to Frankfurt?" He was fishing for information. She could feel it.

"Yes, that's why," she said.

"And her husband? Is he coming to the wedding too?"

Margot studied this man who was her boss. She knew he was a dangerous man. And she was keenly aware of what he was capable of. She bit her lip and considered him. He was interested in Trudy; Margot could see it, and she wasn't surprised. Trudy was his type. However, Margot knew there was a good possibility that Klaus might murder Trudy. She shuddered at the thought and just how far she was

199

willing to go to rid herself of her sister. In the past, Margot had never been a cruel or vindictive person. But Trudy had backed her into a corner. She had not slept all night because she was busy worrying about what Trudy might do if she could not give her the money she wanted. She despised Trudy, but if Klaus had not dropped this opportunity directly into her lap, she would never have conceived of such a heartless plan. At that moment, she realized that Klaus could be manipulated into helping her finally rid herself of her terrible sister. "I don't know where you got the idea that Trudy has a husband," Margot said innocently. "She's not married. But she did have a boyfriend. Sadly, he broke up with her recently. She's moved here to Frankfurt by herself. She's all alone."

"Alone," he said, stroking his chin.

"Yes, poor Trudy. She has nowhere else to go, so she will stay here in Frankfurt."

"Well, well. I'm glad to hear that she is going to be living here. You see, Trudy and I are old friends," he said. "But I thought she was married."

"No, she's single. Very single. And I assumed you were old friends," Margot said. Then she whispered softly, "I probably shouldn't tell you this little secret."

He leaned forward. It was obvious she'd piqued his curiosity. "Tell me…" His voice was soft, endearing. It was so strange how his whole demeanor could change in an instant. Sometimes, his personality would change so drastically that he even looked like someone else. And that was how it was right now. His facial features were different than normal. They had softened, and his eyes looked warm and kind. "Go on, Margot. You can tell me. You can trust me." He patted her hand.

"She would be very upset if she knew I told you. But you did say that the two of you are good friends. That's right, isn't it?"

He nodded and patted her hand. "Yes, of course we are. We are very good friends. And I will help Trudy in any way I can." A chill ran up her hand where he touched her, then traveled through her wrist, and then made its way through her body. "It's all right. You can tell me anything."

"I'm sorry to say that Trudy has no money. Her boyfriend left her without anything. She's come here to Frankfurt hoping I can give her financial help. This is very unlike Trudy. She's always been so proud," Margot said as she looked down at the table. "I will do what I can for her. But, if I don't have enough money to help her, she will probably leave Frankfurt and return to Berlin to live with our other sister."

"Oh, I see," he said. He leaned back in his chair and took a long sip of beer. Then he took a cigar out of his pocket and lit it. Margot watched him. She was worried that now that she had told him that Trudy was broke, he might think Trudy was too problematic and lose interest in her. He could easily find another victim, another young, innocent waitress with blonde hair and blue eyes. Margot saw Marie standing by the door to the kitchen. She was watching Margot talk to Klaus. Margot could see that Marie was worried about her, but she couldn't wave or smile to let Marie know she was all right. She had to keep her focus on Klaus.

There were several moments of silence. Then Klaus said, "I'll give you some extra money each week to give to Trudy, so she will stay here in Frankfurt. But I don't want to embarrass her, so please make sure that you don't tell her it's from me," he smiled gently, but the smile was cold. It did not reach his eyes.

"Of course, I wouldn't say a word because I don't want to make her feel ashamed," Margot said. "It's very kind of you to help my sister out."

Klaus reached over, and once again, he patted Margot's small hand with his thick red one. When he moved his hand away, her own hand felt dirty. "It's getting busy in here. You go on and get off to work now. Everything is going to be just fine."

"Thank you," Margot said.

He smiled, but this time, his smile was different. She was mesmerized by how quickly his appearance could change. Right now, there was something terribly frightening and strange about his eyes. She looked directly into them for a second and swore to herself that he was completely insane.

CHAPTER 60

On the way home that night, Marie and Margot walked down the familiar streets together towards their apartments. "What were you and Klaus talking about today?" Marie asked.

"Me and Klaus?" Margot asked as if she was thinking about something else, and Marie had distracted her.

"Yes, Klaus. Who else? What's wrong with you, Margot. You're in another world."

Margot didn't answer that question. She said, "Klaus wants to date my sister."

"Your sister?"

"Trudy."

"Oh no. You must tell her what we know. You must save her from him. It's important. Her life is at stake. She should know the truth about him."

"I know what you are trying to tell me, but you don't know the truth about my sister, Trudy. It's time you did. When we get to my apartment tonight. Can you come in for a while? I'll make us some coffee, then tell you everything there is to know about my sister. You'll learn that she is not a good sister to me."

Marie nodded. "All right. I'll come in for a while."

When they arrived at Margot's rooming house, the two women entered and then immediately went upstairs to Margot's room. Margot made a pot of ersatz coffee. She took two mismatched cups down from a shelf and poured them both a cup. Then she sat on the bed beside Marie and told her the entire story of her marriage and her life with Trudy. Margot left nothing out, not even the fact that she was probably half-Jewish and that Ben was the father of the baby she now carried. Margot teared up when she explained how Trudy had destroyed her marriage to Max and how, even though she had the opportunity to help Margot protect her son Erik, she didn't. "She let my little boy die at the hands of those Nazi doctors," Margot was sobbing.

Tears fell down Marie's cheeks. She took Margot's hand and squeezed it, "You poor thing. I'm so sorry to hear this about your own sister."

"And now, Trudy tells me that Max is dead, and I am sure his death was her fault."

Marie shook her head. "Trudy may be your sister, but she is also your worst enemy."

"Yes, she is. I hate to say it, but she is."

"Klaus, it turns out, in this case, may just be your savior."

"I know," Margot said. "I don't like to think of what could be in store for Trudy if she gets involved with him."

"Do you think she will get involved with him? He's older, and he's fat. Besides that, he's sort of disgusting."

"She will, Trudy loves money. And Klaus has money."

"There's a good chance he will kill her," Marie said in a whisper.

"I know. I realize it. But at least without Trudy around to cause me all kinds of problems, it will be easier to keep my child safe once it is born."

"That's true. I bet you didn't realize it, but your sister has always been your enemy. Even when you were young children."

"Yes, I suppose that's right. I would never have believed it when we were children, even though all the signs were there. I loved my family then, and I wanted to love Trudy, too. However, I must admit, thinking back, that she was always doing things to sabotage me. I don't know why she hated me so much. But now, although I feel a little sick to my stomach about turning a blind eye to the danger of her dating Klaus, I don't want to protect her. I see her for what she is."

"Is she your only sibling?" Marie asked.

"No, I have another sister. Her name is Mattie. But Trudy and Mattie were always closer than either of them was to me. And I always knew that Trudy kept Mattie and me from being close. When we were teenagers, Mattie obeyed Trudy's every command, and Trudy forbade her from getting too close to me. Consequently, we never formed any kind of a bond. She ruined any chance of a relationship between Mattie and me and separated me from my husband and my child. I have also not been able to return to Berlin to see my parents. She threatened to tell the authorities about my being Jewish, and so I have been hiding from her here in Frankfurt. That is until I saw her at that party that I went to with Kurtis. I wish I had never gone to that party," she sighed. "I worry about my parents. I don't even know if they are alive or dead." She looked away, wiping the tears from her face with her hand. Then Margot turned back and looked directly into Marie's eyes. "I can't believe I am saying this, but I will be relieved when Trudy's dead. I never thought I would say that about anyone. But it's true. I will be glad."

CHAPTER 61

Klaus truly enjoyed stalking his prey. The hunt made the kill far more interesting. He went to a costume shop where he bought everything. He would need to disguise himself and turn him into a very old man. He purchased a large black overcoat that fit his hefty frame like a tent and a long, untidy gray wig that hung in greasy strands out of an old black fedora. He purchased dark sunglasses, went home, and spent hours perfecting a limp. Then, finally satisfied with his disguise, he left the house to follow Trudy. As he walked through town, Klaus glanced over and saw his reflection in the windows of the local shops. It was impossible to recognize him. Inwardly, he laughed. This outfit made him feel invisible, like he could do or say anything, and no one would ever suspect that the crazy old man in the long black coat was him. For the first few days, he spent all day sitting outside the woman's hotel where Trudy was staying. He kept an eye on the door, waiting and hoping she would come out. When she left the hotel three days later, he followed her. Klaus was certain she would not recognize him, but to be careful, he always stayed far enough behind her so she did not notice him. She made her way to the market, where she stood at the wagon of a vegetable vendor. Klaus watched her and marveled at the beauty of her slender hands and arms as she selected a cabbage and a few potatoes. Then she returned home. The following day, she left the hotel and walked two miles to a very expensive dress shop in a better part of town. This was more walking than Klaus cared to do, and by the time she went into the dress shop, he was exhausted and out of breath. Then, to make matters worse, the windows were dark, and he could not see inside the shop. Now, he was angry and frustrated. Watching her try on different dresses would have given him great pleasure. He thought about leaving, but he didn't. Instead, he waited for her to come out of the shop. When she did an hour later, without a purchase in her hands, he knew it was because she didn't have any money. *What a fool you are, Trudy. If you were my lover, I would buy you plenty of lovely dresses. But since you have decided I am not worthy of your affection, all you can do is try on pretty clothes you will never own.*

Klaus became so obsessed with following Trudy that he told Marie he had business to attend to and needed her to come in early to open the restaurant for him. She had been working for him longer than the rest of his employees, and he trusted her the most. She agreed to come in early.

Klaus was glad to have Marie to lean on. Now, he didn't have to watch the time when he was stalking Trudy. One afternoon a week later, Klaus followed Trudy as she walked through the streets of Frankfurt. She walked for over an hour, then stopped and bought a sausage from a vendor. Sitting down on a bench in the park, Trudy ate her lunch. Klaus hid across the street and eyed her as she nibbled her food. *You would dine so much better if you were mine.* Sometimes, he felt angry when he watched her. Other times, he felt warm and loving. But as the days passed, he found himself looking forward to Margot and Kurtis' wedding when he could actually speak to Trudy again. He had to find a way to convince her not to be afraid of him.

CHAPTER 62

T rudy was bored. Living in that run-down hotel with only women to amuse her was annoying. She had no place to go, no parties, no friends, no money to go to the films or shop. Sometimes, she felt like she was dying, losing her zest for life, living in that hotel each day. The other women she'd met were not the kind of women she enjoyed spending time with. The woman who occupied the room across from hers was working as a maid at a high-priced hotel, and she often lost her train of thought and repeated everything she had just said. Trudy was certain that the woman was mentally ill, and she even considered reporting her to the Gestapo so they could do away with her. But it was too much trouble, so Trudy just avoided her. Another of the borders had a rather sketchy lifestyle. She looked weathered. Prematurely wrinkled, with thin, dirty hair and worn clothes, she was a sight. But what was most telling about her was that she left the hotel when the sun went down and didn't return until morning. Trudy assumed she was probably a low-paid prostitute.

If it had not been for Margot's upcoming wedding, Trudy would be drowning in despair. She hoped she would meet a new man at the wedding, an SS officer who would take her away from this shoddy hotel and back into the lifestyle she was accustomed to. When she first arrived in Frankfurt, she had not been sure she would attend the wedding. That was because she knew it was at Klaus's restaurant, and he would be there. She was still afraid of him. When she closed her eyes, she could still see him standing over her, holding a blade with malice in his eyes. But after a time, Trudy changed her mind about attending the wedding. Even though she didn't like Klaus and would have preferred to avoid him, she felt she had to attend the wedding. There was no doubt that there would be plenty of SS officers in attendance, and she could see no other way of meeting someone who might rescue her from this terrible existence. At first, she was worried about Klaus possibly following her and trying to hurt her again, but as time passed, she began to relax. Since he had not bothered her since she arrived in Frankfurt, she assumed he had lost interest in her. *He's probably found another girl. At least, I hope so.* If he had wanted to find her, she rationalized, he would have asked Margot for her address, and he would have shown up at her hotel. And when she'd first arrived, she had been watching and waiting for this, always worried and afraid. But as the days passed without any problems from Klaus, Trudy began to feel safe.

CHAPTER 63

Kurtis was busy working, but he thought of Margot constantly and telephoned at least three times each week to speak to her. When he called, he always swore his undying love and devotion and told her he could hardly wait for their wedding day. And because he was so happy and excited about his future with his new wife, Kurtis was not as hard on the prisoners at the camp as he had been in the past. However, there were still certain prisoners who had a special way of bringing out his ugly side. Kurtis hated Kaz. He hated him for being so strong and a mountain of a man. It sickened Kurtis that a Jew who had been starved and beaten still stood defiant. Most of the Jews were sick and broken by the time he got them. But not this one. Kurtis was so intrigued by Kaz that he had taken the time to look into Kaz's past. There, he discovered that the Jew's family and his sweetheart had been transported to Auschwitz from the ghetto after Kaz was arrested. So, Kaz did not know what had become of them. Kurtis wondered if perhaps Kaz would weaken and break if he were to tell him that his loved ones were all probably dead. Kurtis made a mental note of this and decided that he would tell the Jew that his family was transported to Auschwitz and that they were most likely all dead. Yes, Kurtis wanted to see how Kaz would react to that. He wondered if it would break him. So, he decided to tell Kaz this as soon as he returned from his honeymoon. After all, it was his job to break these Jews, and this arrogant one needed breaking.

However, for now, Kurtis felt too good to be bothered by the prisoners. His mother and her boyfriend told him that they both liked Margot. And he even considered introducing her to his brother, who he hadn't seen in years. But he decided to wait until after the wedding to think about that. After careful consideration, he chose not to invite his brother to the wedding. There was always a chance he might say something embarrassing that could damage the image he so carefully invented.

CHAPTER 64

Kurtis arrived in Frankfurt two days before the wedding. As he got off the train, he looked handsome in his crisp black uniform. The rays of the sun reflected like a golden halo in his hair. As he walked through town, women of all ages turned to stare at him, and for a moment, he wondered if he should be getting married. There were so many women he could conquer and bed if he stayed single. The idea made him smile. However, he had been lonely for a while now and was certain he would be happy living with Margot. Besides that, being married would be good for his career. The Nazi party liked the idea of its men being family men, with good German hausfraus at home, who produced lots of Aryan children. It would have been better if Margot fit the Aryan beauty standard with blonde hair and blue eyes. However, he was willing to overlook it. Kurtis liked the way she looked. He was very attracted to her. Even so, once they returned from their honeymoon, which was only three days in a nice hotel in Frankfurt, and moved into their new home on the grounds of Dachau, he planned to ask her to go to a beauty shop and have her hair made blonde. He hoped she would not get angry. He would explain that he thought she was quite beautiful, but it would help his career if she were blonde.

A few hours before the wedding, Kurtis arrived at the restaurant. He sat down at the bar and ordered a beer. As he drank it, he noticed that Marie was very helpful in putting everything together for the wedding. She took it upon herself to receive and check several deliveries. Klaus came out of the back and saluted Kurtis. "Heil Hitler," he said, standing at attention with his arm raised high.

"Heil Hitler," Kurtis answered in the same manner. Just as a large box of flowers arrived from the florist. Marie took the box and carried it into the back of the kitchen.

"Get us some pretzels with mustard," Klaus demanded of Marie.

"Yes, I will in just a minute, but I have to check the flowers. I promised Margot I would," Marie said calmly. Then she took the box and opened it where no one could see her. Little did anyone at the restaurant suspect that hidden within the box of sunflowers, secured beneath Margot's bridal bouquet, lay a passport that had been secretly forged for a Jewish man whom the bookseller had been hiding in his basement until the passport was ready. Marie looked around her to be sure no one was watching, and she quickly grabbed the passport and put it into her apron pocket. She looked around again to ensure no one had seen her do it. Everyone was busy. She let out a sigh of relief. Tonight, after the wedding, she was planning to deliver the passport to a nearby safe house. This passport, she knew, might be the very thing that would save a man's life on his perilous journey out of Germany.

"I need two hard pretzels and a bowl of mustard for Klaus," Marie told the cook.

The cook put it together quickly, and Marie delivered the plate.

There was an air of excitement at the restaurant that afternoon. Everyone loved a party. And all the liquor that would be consumed this evening was to be paid for by Kurtis. So, even the employees could drink without worrying. The bartender, an older man who had been with Klaus for years but whom Klaus still didn't completely trust not to steal, sang softly to himself as Marie set up the tables with white tablecloths and vases filled with golden sunflowers.

The Nazi party helped Kurtis to pay for the wedding. They even paid extra to have the restaurant closed to the public that evening, permitting only wedding guests to enter.

The previous evening was Margot's last night of work, and Marie had given her a small goodbye party. She was sad to see her friend leave, but she knew that Margot had to go away to live with her new husband. The two girls had become so close, and things wouldn't be the same. But they had promised each other that they would keep in touch.

CHAPTER 65

Margot and Kurtis had not seen each other for two days before the wedding. But on the day of their marriage, they both arrived at the restaurant dressed for the celebration. Margot wore a simple white dress. And, of course, Kurtis wore a clean, freshly pressed SS uniform. As a gift from the Nazi party, the young Aryan couple were given a copy of Hitler's book, *Mein Kampf,* as a wedding present.

As Margot stood beside her future husband, she could not stop the hot tears that fell down her cheeks. She thought of Ben and his child, who would soon be born. Then she thought of Max and what a good husband he'd been. She remembered how Max had taken care of Erik when he was sick and how he and Ben had done whatever they could for her precious son. All of that had to remain in the back of her mind. Kurtis didn't know her for who she really was, and he must never find out. She had told him so many lies. Her mind whirled in panic. If it had not been for her unborn baby, she would have run out of that room and kept running. She would get as far away as possible from a terrible future where she was married to an SS officer. *If I could, I would run and keep running until I was so far away that Kurtis could never find me.*

But that was not to be. Margot and Kurtis stood side by side at the altar. Bile rose in her throat, and she did not hear Kurtis say his vows. But when Margot's time came to say I do, she trembled but did what was expected of her. Kurtis was looking into her eyes and smiling. She knew he thought that her tears were tears of joy. He bent down and gently kissed his new wife. All the guests cheered.

And then the party began.

Trudy was sitting alone at a table in the back by the bar. She was eyeing three of Kurtis's fellow SS officers, all in uniform. But they weren't paying her any attention.

Margot caught Marie looking at her with sympathy. She managed a smile, trying to let Marie know she was all right. Then, the food was ready, and the drinking began.

Kurtis's friends and colleagues wanted to drink with him, and he drank more beer than usual. But even though he was drunk, he was very careful when he danced with Margot, who only danced a couple of times. Instead, she begged off dancing most of the night, blaming it on her pregnancy.

Then, just before the cake was to be served, a group of green police officers walked into the restaurant. The guests turned to look. "What do you want?" Klaus asked.

The music stopped, and the room grew quiet. Everyone was looking at the police officers who stood just inside the doorway. Margot felt a chill come over her.

"I am here to make an arrest," one of the officers said.

"No, you have the wrong place," Klaus insisted. "This is the wedding of an SS officer."

The policeman looked him directly in his eyes and said, "There is a woman who works here as a waitress by the name of Marie Martin. She has been aiding Jews. She is an enemy of the Reich."

Instead of standing her ground, Marie panicked. She had the fake papers that had arrived in the box of flowers still in her pocket, and she knew that the police would search her. Without a word, she ran outside. But one of the officers saw her run and chased after her. "Stop, halt." He yelled out.

The entire wedding party followed them outside. Margot's hand flew up to her heart. She could hardly breathe. She trembled because she knew Marie was doing things that could get her into trouble. *Someone must have turned her in. It could have been anyone, even someone we don't know.*

Marie was running. She didn't look back; she kept running. The police officer pulled his gun and shot into the air. "Stop, or I will shoot," he yelled. Margot heard the gunshot, and her heart jumped. She felt dizzy, like she might faint. Then she gagged and almost vomited. Kurtis put his arm around her, but he looked stunned and confused. In a desperate voice, she begged her new husband. "Stop them, please stop them," Margot began, fiercely tugging at Kurtis's sleeve and trying to wake him from his daze. He didn't respond. He didn't speak or move. It was as if he was frozen. "Kurtis, please. You must help her. You must. Marie is my friend," Margot begged. "Help her, Kurtis."

But Kurtis did nothing.

The first shot missed Marie. She was still running. Margot could no longer see her. Two of the policemen had already taken off after her. They were young and strong. Margot could not see anything, only the moon and the stars. Then, she heard a woman scream. It was a piercing, terrifying sound. Followed by a gunshot. Then silence.

A few moments later, the police officers returned. One of them carried a few papers in his hand. "We were right. She had a pocket full of falsified papers. And a passport for some man," He showed the papers to Klaus, who looked shocked.

"Well, no matter. It's all over now. She got what she deserved. She's out there lying on the ground, dead," the officer said.

Margot let out a gasp. She gripped her belly and then fainted.

CHAPTER 66

The wedding celebration was cut short. Everyone who had come to help the young couple celebrate left the restaurant, including the bride's sister, Trudy. Trudy was disappointed because the party had just started, and there were so many eligible men. She hadn't had enough time to talk with any of them. On her way home, Trudy stopped at a store and picked up a bottle of schnapps, then she walked slowly back to her miserable room. *Now that Margot and Kurtis are married, my sister will move in with her husband and have access to more money. So she can take care of me while I search for a replacement for Peter.*

Trudy couldn't honestly say she missed Peter or any of the men in her past. But she missed having a man to care for her financial needs. *I am going to go back to my room and get drunk. I can't believe my sister ruined my chances over some waitress.*

Trudy turned the corner and entered the dark alleyway that led to the back entrance to her building. As she walked quickly towards the door to the building, she noticed a black automobile parked on the side of the alley. At first, she didn't think anything of it. Then, for no reason other than it was dark and she was alone in a deserted alley, a cold chill ran up her spine. She shivered, but the fear grew stronger. *I should have taken the long way instead of this shortcut. I am going to turn and go back.* She whirled around and began to run back toward the main street. But before she could return to the light, she heard the car door slam and felt a hand cover her mouth. The bottle of schnapps fell from her hand and shattered on the pavement.

The hand covering her nose and mouth was thick, calloused, and far too big to belong to any woman. It was hard to breathe. Trudy tried to scream, but the hand blocked the sound. Her fears now turned to terror, and she began to kick in an effort to escape. Her entire body strained with the effort. The veins on her neck stood out, and her eyes bulged and burned with tears. Then she heard familiar laughter. "Trudy," It was Klaus. His tone was condescending. "You know we have unfinished business now, don't you?"

Trudy wanted to speak but couldn't because his hand was still covering her mouth. She tried to pry his fingers off her face, but he punched her in the stomach with his other hand. This knocked the wind out of her, and she began to hyperventilate. *I'm either going to faint, or he's going to suffocate me.* She thought.

Klaus leaned his lips close to her ear. He kissed her, then whispered, "If you don't want to die, you will do as I say."

She nodded her head in agreement.

"Now, you and I will go upstairs to your room. You will not make a sound. If anyone sees us, you will act like I am your boyfriend. Do you understand me? If you so much as let on that anything is wrong, I will leave for now, but that will not be the end of it. I promise you, my Aryan goddess, I will find you later, and I will kill you. You will never be safe again. If you cooperate with me, I won't hurt you. In fact, you and I will reach an understanding. And I think you will be quite pleased with what I propose."

She nodded her head.

"Now, before I remove my hand from your sweet, tender lips, I want to make a promise to you."

She nodded nervously.

"We are going to have sex upstairs. I'm sure you must realize that. You know how wildly attracted to you I am. However, I am not going to hurt you again. I will make tender love to you. No more torture.

You see, goddess, I have come to realize that you don't like it rough. And so, I will make love to you sweetly just the way you like it."

Could it be true? Maybe I am not in danger from him anymore. Perhaps Klaus and I will be able to have a normal relationship. If he doesn't hurt me, I would take him as my lover. He would be a very good provider. And I don't mind that he is ugly as long as he doesn't torture me again.

He took his hand away from her lips and smiled at her. It was a warm, sweet smile without a trace of that maniacal smile she feared.

"I'm sorry I had to approach you that way. I knew you wouldn't talk to me if I tried to speak to you. So, I had to silence you to make you listen," he said gently. Then he stopped in front of his automobile and opened the door. Klaus took out a bottle of whiskey and showed it to Trudy. "Let's go up to your room and have a nightcap."

They walked into the boarding house together, looking like a regular couple. However, it was late at night, and no one was in the main room, so no one saw them as they walked upstairs to her room.

She turned the key in the lock, and they both entered.

"Where do you keep the glasses. I'd like to pour us both a drink," he said.

"I don't have any," she admitted. "I don't have much anymore. My husband left me."

"Well, we must fix that. I'll buy you the things you need. And the things you want. You'll see that I am not such a bad fellow."

She smiled at him. This was turning out to be a good night. He wasn't her ideal lover, but as long as he didn't hurt her, she could put up with him.

They drank until the bottle was almost empty. Then, he began to undress her. She didn't resist or move at all. She allowed him to take control. The alcohol made her drowsy. And she lay on the bed naked and waiting for him. "You truly are an Aryan goddess," he said, breathing heavily as he looked at her. Klaus lay down beside Trudy and began to kiss her and touch her. But his manhood did not rise. She reached down and felt that he was soft. For a moment, the effects of the whiskey were gone, and she was lucid and frightened. *I must make sure he can get an erection. This sort of thing makes some men very angry. And I don't want him to get violent again.* Trudy bent down and put his manhood in her mouth. He was repulsive. Rolls of white pasty fat rippled down from his enormous stomach. There was a strong, musty odor of sweat emitting from him. She felt herself gag, but she must not let him know that she found him repugnant. Trudy tried again to raise his manhood with her mouth, but her efforts were unsuccessful. She was very drunk and sick to her stomach from eating too much at the wedding. When the bile rose in her throat, she couldn't stop it. Vomit spewed from her mouth onto the floor. She wiped her lips with the back of her hand. Then she gasped softly when she saw the look in Klaus' eyes. His face was red with embarrassment and anger. He slapped her hard, hard enough to knock her head back onto the pillow. "Do you find me disgusting?" he asked. "Is that why you puked?"

"No, no, I drank too much earlier and ate too much too. I don't usually eat like that. I can't afford it these days. That's all. And sometimes alcohol has that effect on me," she lied.

He knew she was lying. "You are a liar. You've always been a liar. The real truth is that you are afraid of me, so you lie and blame your vomiting on the alcohol. You find me repulsive. I see it in your pretty blue eyes." He shook his head. "I hate liars. I always have. They deserve to be punished, and that is what is about to happen to you, my dear."

"No, oh, no," she said, letting out a short scream, which he immediately stifled with his hand.

"Scream again, and I will break that little neck of yours. If you don't believe me, just try it," Klaus growled. Then he shook his head, "Better yet. Now you can't scream," he said as he stuffed her panties into her mouth. She tried to take them out, but he punched her in the face, and for a moment she couldn't move. Grabbing her bra off the floor, he used it to tie both of her hands to the bedpost. Satisfied for the moment that she could not move, he stood up and walked over to his jacket. He took something out of the inside pocket, but Trudy's vision was too blurred for her to make out what it was. She was struggling again to try to get away, but the knot around her hands was too tight. Then Klaus said in a deep hiss, "Close your eyes. Don't you lay there staring at me, or I will knock you out so you can't stare at me."

She did as he asked. But she felt him fumbling with her hands and tried to escape again. He hit her in the stomach, and her eyes opened. It was then she realized that her hands were in handcuffs, cuffed to the bed.

Trudy prayed to God to help her to get away. More than anything, she wished he would just go and leave her apartment. She was weeping desperately. Her head was heavy, and blood ran down from her nose where Klaus had punched her. The white pillowcase was stained red. Trudy was sick and dizzy from the alcohol. Kicking her feet and rolling around as much as the cuffs would allow, she anxiously tried to break free. But it was impossible. Whenever she moved, the cuffs grew tighter. *Why did I trust him? Why did I believe he wouldn't hurt me this time? I wanted to believe it. That's why. I should have known better. But I thought maybe I could make him happy with regular sex. He said he would be all right that way. I even put him in my mouth.*

Everything was going all right until I vomited. That's what made him turn angry and then violent. He knows he is disgusting. And he blames me for it. Now, he's like a runaway train. I can't stop him. He's too angry, too far gone, and I am terrified. Maybe if I just go along with this torture of his, he will let me go free like he did the last time when we were in Munich. It wasn't pleasant, but at least he didn't kill me. So, if I can just play along, he won't kill me this time. She didn't want to die, and she was afraid that if she continued to try to fight, he might kill her by accident or even on purpose because she'd made him so furious. She closed her eyes tightly and prayed again. But she remembered that he'd promised to break her neck, and she didn't doubt he would keep that promise if she didn't stop fighting back.

It was the same as the first time in Munich. He sliced her skin with a razor blade, just deep enough to draw blood but not deep enough to cause real damage. Klaus slapped her face and called her names until his manhood stood erect. Then he entered her. Her body tensed up against him, but he only pushed more forcefully into her until she could feel hot blood running down her legs. His body was heavy, and the smell of his sweat was growing stronger as he pumped into her. Trudy closed her eyes again so she didn't have to look at his face. It seemed like it took forever, but it was only a few minutes before he was done.

Then he got up and grabbed her dress that lay in a pile on the floor and used it to wipe the sweat from his face and the sperm from his manhood. She felt so much hatred for him that she would have killed him if she could have. *Don't do anything or say anything stupid. It's almost over.* She could hardly wait for him to remove the gag. It was deep in her throat, and it was making her want to vomit. *He's done. His anger and his desire are spent. If I can just hold on for another minute or so, he'll remove the gag and the restraints on my hands. Tomorrow, I will leave Frankfurt. I'll follow Margot and her new husband to Dachau. I'll get an apartment in Munich, which is close to Dachau. Once I am there, I will be far away from Klaus. I can't go through this again. I won't go through this again.*

Klaus didn't remove the cuffs. He left her tied up and ran down the stairs and out to his car, where he had stored a can of gasoline. While he was gone, she struggled again, even though she knew it only tightened the handcuffs. But then he returned carrying the gas can under his coat. Her eyes followed him as soon as he entered the room. She was pleading with him to remove the gag. Klaus ignored her. He began to douse the room with gasoline, and her eyes grew wide with fear. Then he removed the gag.

"Please, Klaus. I don't know what you are going to do, but I am begging you to stop this," she was afraid to scream.

He smiled that maniacal smile, and then he winked. A scream escaped her lips. He shook his head. "We can't have that," he said almost cheerfully. Then he shoved her panties back into her mouth. She gagged again and almost vomited.

But he had no intention of stopping this time. He had made the mistake of letting her live when she was his lover in Munich. This time, she would not be so lucky.

CHAPTER 67

For a few minutes, Klaus was spellbound as he stared at Trudy. He knew her for what she was, a liar and a good-for-nothing whore, like that girl Ilsa who had ruined his reputation when he'd done nothing but try to win her love. Well, he had been a shy boy back in those days, and he'd run away. That girl had never paid for her mistreatment of him. But Trudy would pay for hers. This would be the end of her. Trudy was done playing with him, lying to him, and even as she wept, she was powerless to save herself. The gag in her mouth kept her from screaming as her eyes followed him while he doused her room with gasoline. Then, her eyes grew wide with terror as he lit the match. His heart ached with the beauty of it all as he looked at her lovely naked breasts. She looked like an American movie idol as she struggled to break free. Then he sighed and whispered, "Goodbye, my sweet Aryan goddess. It was a lot of fun, but you know you should never have lied to me. Women who lie to men deserve to die. But that's what women do. They lie. Just like you. Did I ever tell you that my first girlfriend looked just like you, goddess? Well, she did." Then he smiled at Trudy as the fire consumed the table that collapsed in the middle of the room. And he had to admit that it took every ounce of strength he had to leave before he saw the fire consume her and melt her skin like a porcelain doll. However, as the fire burned the curtains and ran through the room on the trail of gasoline, he knew it was time for him to go. Klaus ran down the stairs quickly. Soon, the windows would explode from the intense heat. He knew he had to be out of the building before that occurred. It was late at night, so he was alone as he left the boarding house. There was no one else walking about on the street. It was a warm, quiet night. And the city of Frankfurt slept peacefully. No one smelled the smoke, at least not yet.

Once he was outside, Klaus poured the remainder of the gasoline around the perimeter of the entire building. He assumed that the fire would be well underway before there was any chance of saving the residents inside.

Then he turned to walk away and headed back towards his car. Quickly, he glanced up and was excited to see the orange flames licking the sky. By morning, his crimes would be untraceable. The fire would cleanse them.

Whistling softly, he began to drive away. As he turned the corner, he heard the sound of a fire alarm. Loud voices came from the area where the fire was raging. But he couldn't make out what they were saying. Still, he wasn't worried. He was quite certain that it was too late to save Trudy.

CHAPTER 68

Trudy struggled with all of her strength in an effort to free her hands. *I am going to die here in this fire. I've got to get away. If I could only scream and wake up the rest of the people in this building, I could get help.* She shook her head violently from side to side and pushed at the gag that was choking her with her tongue. But no matter how hard she tried, she couldn't free herself. Her mascara ran down her cheeks as she wept bitterly. Sweat ran into her eyes and down her face and body as the room grew unbearably hot. The smell of gasoline made her cough, but her throat was dry, and the choking gag made bile rise up into her mouth.

The curtains in the room were dancing a macabre dance as they were consumed by fire. Her mind was no longer hazy from the whiskey. Trudy was lucid, and she knew for sure that she was going to die. *This is it. This is how my life ends. But it's not fair. I'm young, and I'm not ready. I don't want to die. I am not ready to die.*

The smoke grew thicker until she couldn't see anything in front of her but a black haze. It felt as if the gag in her mouth had somehow expanded, and it was so hard to breathe. She was coughing and choking on the gag as billows of black, noxious smoke filled the room. Her eyes and throat burned, and now she was gasping, trying to get some air into her lungs. But the air was piping hot, like boiling water, and it hurt to inhale. Pain shot from her throat down through her entire body. The pain was so severe that she felt a silent scream ripple through her entire body. Unable to move, she watched in horror as red and orange flames of fire leaped across the bed, searing into her flesh. And then her eyes closed, and her breath stopped. The pain was over. Trudy was dead.

CHAPTER 69

Margot awakened late the following morning with an aching head. She looked around her to see an unfamiliar room. For the first few moments, she was frightened and confused. But then she saw Kurtis asleep in the chair at the end of the bed and realized that she was safe. Margot took a quick look down at her body and saw she was still wearing her wedding clothes. Kurtis was still in his uniform. *I must be in Kurtis' hotel room.* She realized. Sitting up against the headboard, she rubbed her eyes. *Was last night real, or was it a nightmare? Is Marie really dead? Or did I just have a terrible dream?*

Kurtis must have heard her stirring in bed because his eyes flew open.

"You gave me quite a scare last night," he said. "You passed out. How do you feel now?"

"I'm all right. Please, tell me what happened."

"You fainted at the wedding. You really had me worried."

She looked at him blankly. "Yes, that much I know. But about the wedding. Did I dream it, or did something terrible happen to Marie?" she asked.

He got up, walked over to her, and sat on the edge of the bed. Taking her hand in both of his, he kissed her palm. Then said, "Don't bother yourself about that now. We are on our honeymoon. You and I are married. If you prefer to leave Frankfurt, we can catch a train and stay in Munich for the next few days. I think you might enjoy that. It would be good for you to get out of here. That is if you are feeling up to it. Of course. By the way, I brought you some coffee from the restaurant next door. It's been a couple of hours, so I am sure it's cold by now."

"Thank you. That was very kind. I'm sure it's fine, just the way it is," she tried to smile, but her lips trembled. She had to know the truth. "But, Kurtis, please, I must know what happened to Marie. Tell me, please, tell me. What happened last night? Is Marie dead?"

He sucked in a deep breath. "I was hoping to wait to tell you. But I suppose I should tell you now. I have some rather bad news."

"Yes, go on. Please." She felt chills run through her.

"Early this morning, the police came to the hotel and spoke to me. I am sorry, darling; I am so sorry to have to tell you this. But there was a fire last night at the women's hotel where your Trudy lived. The girl from the Eagle's Nest. The police told me that she was your sister. You should have told me. Even if you and Trudy weren't getting along. You should have told me she was your sister. I am afraid she did not survive." He took her hand and squeezed it.

"You're right, I should have told you. But Trudy and I have never gotten along well. I just didn't want my problems with Trudy to spoil things with us. I didn't want her to spoil our wedding."

"It's all right. It doesn't matter now."

"No, I suppose it doesn't. She's dead."

"I'm so sorry, Margot. I am really so sorry. I am sure that even though you and Trudy had problems, you feel badly about what happened. What a terrible thing to happen on the night of our wedding."

She stared at him in shock and disbelief. *Trudy is dead.* Then she asked again, "And Marie? Did something happen at the wedding with Marie?"

He sighed. "Yes, I am afraid so." He hesitated, not meeting her eyes, instead looking down at the quilt on the bed. "I know she was your friend, love. But you must try to understand that there were things you just didn't know about her. Very bad things. It turns out your friend, Marie, was a traitor. She was a danger to our fatherland."

Margot put her hand on her belly to assure herself that the baby was still all right. She breathed a sigh of relief to see she hadn't lost it. *I am still pregnant. My little one is still all right.* But she was sick in her heart to know that Marie was dead. That terrible thing that happened at the wedding had not been a dream. Still, she needed to hear him say it. She needed to be sure that Marie was really gone. Throwing caution to the wind, she said, "The fatherland be damned. What happened to my friend? Tell me, tell me everything."

"Don't say that about the fatherland, Margot. I know you are hurting at the loss of your friend. But speaking like that is high treason. Marie was not who you thought she was. She was an enemy of the Reich. She had a man's papers in her pocket, including a passport. The police searched her apron and found it. From what I have learned, she has been working with an organization that helps Jews to escape. The police had no choice. They had to kill her."

Margot closed her eyes. Marie was dead. She'd needed to hear Kurtis say it out loud, but once the words were spoken, they sent a pain shooting through her heart and soul. She let out a small cry. Then she began to weep.

Kurtis kissed her hand. "You didn't really know her. The girl who you thought was your friend didn't exist. Marie was a terrible traitor." He hesitated for a moment. "Believe me, darling, I understand why you feel bad about your sister. I was very upset when the police told me about Trudy. I didn't want to have to tell you. But I can't see why you even care at all about Marie. That inconsiderate traitor tried to ruin our wedding."

There was no point in answering him, no point in arguing. Marie was dead, and there was nothing she could say or do that would bring her back to life. So, the tears ran down Margot's cheeks, and she closed her eyes.

I am a Jew, Kurtis. The child I carry in my body is not yours. It is the offspring of a Jew. If you knew this, I am sure you would turn on me, too. You would kill both the baby and me without caring at all. And the worst part of it all is that now you are my husband.

CHAPTER 70

Kurtis took it in stride that Margot was not receptive to his sexual advances that night. After all, she had just lost her sister and a woman she had believed was her friend. Besides all of this, she was overly sensitive because she was pregnant. Although he ached to make love to her, he realized that she was carrying his child, hopefully, his son, and he didn't want to risk the safety of his precious offspring. So, although it took every ounce of self-control he could muster, he didn't make love to her.

He had expected her to be grieving, but he had to admit that he was surprised that she didn't seem to care very much about losing Trudy. But even knowing that Marie was a traitor to the Reich, Margot was miserable about Marie's death. Margot's unconditional devotion to her friend Marie was difficult for Kurtis to understand. He had learned long ago that if the Reich was to remain in power for the next thousand years, all its Aryan citizens had to put their fatherland before any personal attachments. This had not been difficult for him. Everyone he cared about was a pure German who loved Hitler and the Third Reich as much as he did. So, it was hard for him to understand Margot's grief and misery over someone who had betrayed Hitler and Germany.

As Kurtis watched Margot mourn, he found that he was beginning to lose patience with her.

They didn't leave the hotel in Frankfurt for the next two days. But Kurtis could hardly have called the time they spent there a honeymoon. The couple didn't make love, and Margot was sullen, refusing to leave the room. She hardly ate or slept.

When their honeymoon ended, they took the train to Dachau, where Margot moved into the small house Kurtis had received from the Reich. It was located on the grounds just outside of the camp in Dachau. The wives of Kurtis' coworkers, the other SS officers, and the guards welcomed Margot. It was an easy life for Margot, with plenty of food and rest. However, she was always aware that Kurtis witnessed plenty of pain and suffering when he went to work beyond the gate. Sometimes, she wondered if he was the cause of the misery the prisoners endured, but she tried not to think about it. There was nothing she could do to change things, and her belly was growing large, making it difficult for her to move. Kurtis had some very strict rules when it came to their lives in Dachau. He made it very clear that Margot was to stay with the guards' wives. She was never to venture into the camp. Never to pass the entrance into his other life, his other world.

That summer was filled with family barbeques at the homes of the Nazi officers. Margot's pregnancy made her tired, but everyone was very supportive. After all, she was bearing a child for the Reich. Still, she was always aware that she must do whatever Kurtis asked to assure her coming child's safety. So, one morning, she took a bus into town to have her maple-colored hair bleached blonde. It was a long process, and the bleach burned her eyes and scalp, but her hair was a rich golden blonde when she returned home. Kurtis loved it. He said it enhanced her beauty.

But as winter set in with the cold, snow and ice, Margot often refused to leave the house. "I don't want to get sick. Or slip and fall on the ice," she told Kurtis. "This is the last trimester of my pregnancy. I want to ensure that everything goes all right."

He didn't argue. He allowed her to stay at home while he attended parties at the homes of his coworkers.

He talked to his mother once a week and told her how Margot was behaving. She reassured him that sometimes pregnancy made women act strangely and that he should have patience with her. He had to admit that he and Margot were getting along well. They hardly ever fought. But he wasn't as obsessed with her as he had been when she was far away from him in Frankfurt. He told himself that it was because they didn't make love. But soon, the baby would be here. The son he longed for. And then he promised himself that Margot's desire would return. And he and Margot would make love all the time. Then his life would be perfect.

CHAPTER 71

On December 20th, 1941, five days before Christmas, Margot gave birth to a little boy. Kurtis was elated. Although the little boy had Margot's dark hair and eyes, Kurtis never suspected that the child was not his. They named their son Barrett. Barrett was a hearty baby with chubby little arms and legs. But he was active and not a good sleeper. Barrett often woke up in the middle of the night crying. As soon as Margot heard him, she ran to him, but often not before it woke Kurtis. This made things difficult for Kurtis, who had to go to work early in the morning. But even though married life was not proving to be all he had hoped, he constantly reminded himself that he now had a son. This was his child, and if he lost sleep over it, it would all be worthwhile in the end.

CHAPTER 72

achau had always been a terrible place, but then in 1942, the Nazis decided to expand it, and it began to grow. A new crematorium was built beside the old one. This would allow for a large increase in the number of bodies that could be burned daily. They named this crematorium Barrack X. The high-ranking officers, especially Heinrich Himmler, who was in charge of all the camps, were proud of this new addition with its disinfection section and four furnaces. Along with the new crematorium, a gas chamber was added. The crematorium area was set away from the prisoners by a large wall. However, that didn't help. The prisoners knew what was behind that wall, and they were nervous. No one could say for certain, but it began to look as if there might be plans to make Dachau into a systematic killing center. Max, Kaz, and Adrien watched in horror as the changes took place around them. Adrien, still working in the hospital, was witness to additional new horrors. The German physicians he worked under began performing agonizing medical experiments on the patients. They claimed these experiments needed to be conducted to help German pilots who were involved in bombing raids and also those who were drowning in icy water. They tested methods to make seawater potable. They experimented with several drugs, hoping to find cures for malaria and tuberculosis. The results of these experiments left hundreds of previously healthy men dead.

For Adrien, who had spent his entire life as a healer, torturing patients was a living hell. He did what he could to stop their suffering. He stole drugs to ease their pain. But in the end, he was powerless against the Nazi doctors. And often, he was forced to do terrible things to others, which left him feeling worse than if he had died himself. He could no longer be coaxed to play cards with Kaz and Max. When there was free time, he often sat staring out with unseeing eyes, just staring off into the distance.

CHAPTER 73

K urtis was promoted, but along with the promotion came additional responsibilities. He had to spend more time with the prisoners now, and the camp was filled with disease. Kurtis saw how the sick prisoners suffered, and he was terrified of catching one of the diseases that was spreading rapidly. His fears made him anxious and even more difficult.

At home, Kurtis was finding that he was less enthralled with Margot. After Barrett was born, he demanded that they make love. She allowed it, but there was no enthusiasm on her part. They had sex once a week, and it seemed like more of a task for her than a joy. Because of her attitude, Kurtis found little pleasure in it. But what really perplexed him was that he and Margot had gotten pregnant so quickly that first time, but now she did not seem able to get pregnant again. He wondered if perhaps the pregnancy had done something to her that had destroyed her sexual desires and had made her barren. Bored with his marriage, Kurtis began to leave Dachau for a weekend each month, claiming he had to take a trip on business. Margot didn't ask where he was going. And he didn't volunteer any information. However, he went to Steinhöring, the home for the Lebensborn, where he found plenty of young women eager for his seed. They were lovely and young and more than happy to bear a child for Hitler and the Reich. Kurtis justified his visits to the home for the Lebensborn by telling himself that he was a young Aryan man and Hitler needed him to impregnate as many Aryan women as possible. He was, he told himself, doing this task for his country. What he did not know was that he wasn't impregnating anyone. Kurtis was sterile.

Try as she might, Margot could not find it in her heart to be a good wife to Kurtis, even though she knew she needed him for Barrett's sake. As time passed, she could feel that Kurtis was pulling away from her. But as it was, he loved the little boy he believed to be his son, so she was certain he would not divorce her. As he grew older, Barrett became a precocious child, a little too small for his age. But very intelligent. And most of all, he was the greatest joy in Margot's life. She was glad when Kurtis went away for the weekend, even though she thought he might have acquired a mistress. When Kurtis was gone, Margot had time alone with her precious son. And there was nothing she loved more. She told him stories, and the intent look on his little face as he listened reminded her of Ben. His soft, intelligent eyes warmed her heart. However, to Margot's chagrin, when Kurtis was in town, he insisted that Barrett play with the children of the other SS officers. And she often overheard the other children say derogatory things about Jews. She knew they were just children, repeating what they'd heard from their parents. But someday, they would grow up to be like the rest of the Nazis, and it gave her great pain to think that her sweet little Barrett would share their views. But she never contradicted the Nazi propaganda to him for fear that he might repeat the things she told him. That would be dangerous not only for her but also for him. So, although he was learning to be a Nazi, she constantly reminded herself that at least he would live to grow up. If she hadn't married Kurtis and pretended to become one of them, it was hard to say what would have happened to her little boy.

Quite often, when she least expected it, Margot would see hints of Ben in her son, Barrett. Even as a toddler, Barrett was curious and overly smart but always kind. He loved animals. Once, when Kurtis was out of town, Margot and Barrett, along with another child of an SS officer and his mother, visited a farm. Barrett's face lit up when he saw the animals. Margot was so impressed by how gentle he was when he played with them. He was the same towards other children. However, they were not always as gentle with him.

When Margot was able to acquire children's books that didn't have the Nazi propaganda depicting monstrous Jews, she read to Barrett. He, like Margot and Ben, adored books. And he tried to memorize the stories because the books had to be returned often. However, Margot often saw him thumbing through books, trying to teach himself how to read. This made her heart swell. It was as if Ben was still living in some small way.

CHAPTER 74

By 1944, there was little doubt that Germany was losing the war. Secretly, Margot rejoiced. She hoped that all of this would soon be over and that she could divorce Kurtis and take her son far from Germany. But when she heard the other wives talking in secret about how the Allies were bound to torture them because they were the wives of the Nazi elite, she was terrified. Many nights she lay in bed staring at the ceiling, worried about how she was going to explain to the Allies that she was the wife of a Nazi officer in name only. *They will never believe me. How can I hope to convince them?* She was anxious because she had been living so many lies that she was afraid that they would think she was a Nazi. How could she make them believe she had only married Kurtis to protect her son? *And what about Kurtis?* He must not find out the truth about her being Jewish or about Barrett not being his son until she and Barrett are safely in the custody of the Allies. It seemed that no matter what happened in the future, she and Barrett would be walking a tightrope. All of this weighed heavily on her mind.

CHAPTER 75

M ax still thought of Margot every day. However, as time passed, the memory of that night when he heard her speak grew dim, and he wondered if he had imagined her voice that night. He had ached to hear it for so long that he thought perhaps it had not been real. And he found it hard to believe that Margot was somehow entangled with Richter. Max hated all the guards and all the officers, but he hated Richter the most, and he couldn't imagine him and Margot together in any way, not as friends and certainly not as lovers. Since Max had been imprisoned in this camp, he found it hard to believe that he had ever worked alongside anyone who was a member of the Nazi party. Or that he had compromised his own ideals and joined the party himself. Sometimes, the lack of food and the daily misery of his life made him overthink and wonder about many things. There were times when he thought of his parents and wondered if they were alive, and if so, had they ever found out what happened to him? His father had been such a supporter of Hitler. Neither his mother nor Max had ever agreed with his father about Hitler. However, Max wondered what his father thought of Hitler now and if he would ever see his parents again. Sometimes, at night, he would have dreams of Margot. He could see her eyes, feel her touch, and run his fingers through her soft hair. On those nights, he would have liked to sleep forever, even if it meant death. But each morning, he awakened to another heart wrenching day. Sometimes, he would pass a small section of stones; this was where he had sat with Rivka, and he would remember how young she was. She should have been going to school, dancing, and having picnics with her friends. Her life, like the lives of so many other innocent people, had been stolen by the Reich. He often closed his eyes and tried to remember Rivka's face, but he couldn't. In fact, he could no longer remember the face of his son, Erik. And he tried very hard because all he had left were memories. If he lost them, he would have nothing at all.

But there was one person whose face he would have liked to forget and couldn't. It was a face that was burned in his mind. It was Trudy's face. When Max was a boy, his mother told him he would learn something from everyone he met. Well, that had turned out to be true. Trudy taught him to hate. Since then, he had come in contact with a long list of people who he hated. Richter was one of them, but Trudy was still at the top of his list. Someday, he swore to himself that if he lived through this war, he would find her and kill her.

CHAPTER 76

Kurtis met Louisa on a winter day at the home of the Lebensborn. She was a young, vivacious girl with white, blonde hair and pale blue eyes who was as devoted to the fatherland as he was.

"I've had one child for Hitler already," she said proudly. "It was a boy. He was adopted by an SS officer and his wife."

"And now you are planning to have another?" Kurtis asked her as they sat together, eating sausages and potato salad for lunch.

"Yes, actually. I'd like to have as many as I can. It's my duty as an Aryan woman to serve my *Führer*," she said. Then, in a shy voice, she added, blushing slightly, "Perhaps you would like to volunteer to help me?"

He smiled at her. She was gay and charming. Not at all like Margot, who always seemed to be carrying the weight of the world on her shoulders. He had to admit to himself that these were tough times. It was looking like Hitler was going to lose the war. No one spoke of it openly, but there was evidence that things were not going well for Germany. Kurtis, a true patriot, refused to believe it. He was quite certain that his most beloved and respected Fuhrer had a plan that he just had not revealed yet. And in the end, Germany, with its superior race, would defeat the Allies. And, of course, the Reich would last for a thousand years. So, he wanted to donate as much of his seed as he could to the production of Aryan children. Besides all of that, he enjoyed the process of making love to strange women with no strings attached.

"I would love to help you." He winked at her.

She blushed even harder. "Come with me," Lousia said, taking his hand.

Kurtis stood up and followed Louisa upstairs to a small bedroom. It was cozy but could have been warmer.

"I'm sorry it's sort of cold in here," she said. "We must make sacrifices for the war effort. Yeah?"

"Of course," he said. Then he watched her remove her clothes.

When she was naked, he stood up and got undressed quickly.

Louisa giggled. "There's no need to rush. We can stay here all night if you'd like."

He smiled. "Yes, I would like that."

From that day on, Kurtis went to see Louisa every time he visited Steinhöring. At first, he saw only Louisa, but as the weeks passed, he grew bored with just one girl. So, he spent the first day when he arrived with Louisa and the second day with one of the other girls who attracted him. Kurtis loved the idea that he could do no wrong since he was an SS officer. The girls all wanted him to impregnate them, and not one of them tried to force him to commit to them. As far as his being married was concerned, even that was no problem. There was no need to keep that a secret. The girls didn't mind at all. In fact, a great many of the Nazi officers who visited Steinhoring were married. Like the girls they bedded, these officers were honored and respected for their service to the Fatherland's future.

CHAPTER 77

The smell of death was always hanging like a noose in the air above Dachau. And now the death toll was increasing. There was no coal to run the crematoriums, and the piles of dead bodies were growing daily. One morning, after roll call, Kaz and Max, along with a group of other prisoners, were escorted by several armed guards to a hill where they were forced to dig a pit in which to bury the masses of skeletal corpses. The prisoners were forced to load the dead onto carts and then pull the carts as if they were horses all the way to the pit. On one frigid morning, a heavy, soft snow had fallen, covering a plate of ice. This made for treacherous navigation. A man pulling a heavy cart who could not see the ice hiding under the blanket of snow could easily slide and break his leg or his back. And several did. Anyone who fell and was unable to stand and continue to work was shot. Building the roads had been grueling, but this was even worse. And each day, there were more bodies to bury.

Besides the dead and dying prisoners who had been at Dachau, new ones began to arrive. They came from other camps, sick and starving. There was hardly enough food for the current prisoners, and the new arrivals took a heavy toll on the already scant supply. To make matters even worse, the experiments the Nazi doctors had been performing infecting inmates with typhoid had sent the disease running rampant through the camp.

Kurtis was terrified of the disease and asked for a transfer out of Dachau. He was denied. This made him even meaner.

Max, Kaz, and Adrien slept close to each other at night, shivering and trying to stay warm. It was miserably cold on their block, and now that the new prisoners had arrived, it was even more crowded than before. The smell of human excrement, which also increased, wafted through the air from the overflowing slop buckets.

By the time spring finally arrived, Max felt as if he had aged ten years over the previous winter. Then, one night, Kaz whispered to Max and Adrien, "I heard news that the Americans are here in Munich. With any luck, this could all be over soon."

Max looked at Kaz. He didn't realize it, but tears were flowing down his cheeks.

"Don't cry, *boychik*. We just might make it through this after all," Kaz said as he patted Max's cheek.

Kaz looked over at Adrien. He wasn't crying or smiling. He was staring out into space, silent.

"What's the matter with you?" Kaz asked Adrien.

Adrien shrugged.

"*Nu?* Come on, tell me."

"I don't know if it matters to me if I make it or not. Maybe it's better if I don't," Adrien said.

"You shouldn't say that," Kaz said.

"I've done things here that I can never forgive myself for. I'm as bad as the Nazis. Men died in those experiments, and I was responsible."

"You did what you were told to do. You did what you had to do to survive."

"I shouldn't have done it. I should have refused."

"You'd be dead," Kaz said.

"Yes, but at least I wouldn't have to live with myself."

Kaz had no answer. He put his arm around Adrien's shoulder.

CHAPTER 78

There were whispers amongst the prisoners that the guards were considering liquidating the camp. They weren't sure what that meant exactly. So, several men listened to the guards talk. They discovered that the liquidation of the camp would mean killing all the prisoners. The guards contemplated this rather than allowing the Allies to free the inmates. The Nazis' attitudes began to change. They were scared it was beginning to look like the fall of their Reich was inevitable. Kurtis still refused to believe it. When anyone even suggested it, he insisted that somehow Hitler would come through. But as time passed, it became apparent that Hitler was done, and the Nazis were defeated. News arrived at Dachau that the Soviets had invaded Berlin and Hitler had gone into hiding in his underground bunker. The high-ranking officers at Dachau began to destroy any incriminating evidence. They burned all the records they'd kept, and many fled.

Kurtis thought that those of his colleagues who were leaving were cowards who didn't deserve the jobs and titles they'd been given. He was not like them; he would not run away. He was not ashamed of what he'd done. In fact, he was proud of it. Kurtis had been loyal to his fatherland, and he still was. When some of the other SS officers suggested he take Margot and Barrett and get as far away from Dachau as he could. He could not even bear to look at them and stubbornly insisted that Hitler had a plan and, somehow, their great *Führer* would recover his power and be victorious.

Then the Commandant, Eduard Weiterm, who had been in charge at Dachau, had a nervous breakdown. The officers left were unnerved when former Commandant Martin Weiss was called in to take his place. And even more of them ran away. Then, news arrived at Dachau that changed everything. The Allies had arrived, and they had liberated Buchenwald.

The Nazis who remained at the camp were panicked. They no longer permitted the inmates to climb the hill and bury the dead. Corpses were piling up everywhere around the camp.

One evening, as the men lined up for their soup, Max searched everywhere for Kaz. But he couldn't find him. Max and Adrien ate quickly, then returned to their block to see if Kaz was there. He was. Kaz was lying on his bed of straw, shivering.

"Oh, dear God, help us," Adrien said, shaking his head. "He's sick."

"What's wrong with him? Is it typhoid?" Max asked anxiously.

"I don't think so. Look at the puddle of blood and mucus by his mouth."

There was a thick glob of blood laced with mucus lying on the straw next to Kaz's lips.

"What is it? Why is he bleeding like that? Can you help him?" Max asked Adrien. Max's hands trembled, and he could hardly stand up; his knees were weak.

"I'm all right, *boychik*," Kaz said, but his voice was soft and cracking.

"I think it's tuberculosis," Adrien said. He put his hand on Kaz's head. "He's hot. My guess is he's got a fever."

"What can we do?"

Adrien shook his head. "Nothing. We have no medicine. There's nothing we can do to help him."

"Is he going to die?"

"Probably," Adrien said, looking away as tears filled his eyes.

Max put his arms around Kaz and held him. Then he began to cry. He wept hard, wrenching sobs like a child.

"You shouldn't be so close to him. If it's tuberculosis. He's contagious."

Max shook his head, and he continued to hold his friend close.

Kaz grew weaker through the night. He was already too thin for his stocky frame. Max stayed beside him; he didn't sleep. He gave Kaz water and held him, but by morning, Kaz was dead.

Adrien patted Max's shoulder. "I've had all I can take," he said softly. Max didn't know what to say. He saw the grief on Adrien's face. He, too, was grieving. Losing Kaz was a terrible blow to both of them. The three of them had become like brothers. They were all they had. "I'm going to get some air," Adrien said. Then he walked outside. Max felt something wasn't right. He knew Adrien would do something, but he wasn't sure what it was. A chill ran down his spine. He got up and left Kaz's body for a moment. Then he went outside to see what was going on. He arrived outside too late to stop Adrien, who was running as fast as he could toward the entrance to Dachau. It was as if he was trying to escape. The guard in the tower saw him and shot him instantly. He fell where he stood, silently. Then, one of the guards came down from the tower and threw his dead body on top of a pile of corpses. They treated Adrien's body as if it were trash and not the body of a man who had healed so many.

After the guards returned to the overhead tower, Max walked over to Adrien's body. He hoped that somehow Adrien wasn't dead. But he was. "You damn fool," Max said. "If only you could have tried to wait a little longer. The allies are coming. And now I am all alone. I don't have Kaz, and I don't have you."

Max put his head in his hands. He knew Adrien wasn't trying to escape. He was too smart to have tried to escape that way. He ran right in front of the overhead guard. *No, he wasn't trying to escape. He was committing suicide. And now, both of my friends are gone. I'm alone here.*

Everything was out of order in the camp. The guards were jittery. They even stopped taking roll calls. Max thought it was because they knew for sure that the Americans were coming, but they didn't know when they would show up or what to expect when the Allies arrived. They stopped paying attention to the work details. The guards that still remained at the camp were too busy destroying evidence. Nightly food service also ceased, and the prisoners raided the kitchen, taking whatever they could find. The prisoners were anxious but also hopeful. They knew the Allies were coming, but they were constantly afraid that at any time, the guards would receive an order that told them they must speed up the mass killings so as not to leave any of the inmates alive. Max overheard several of his fellow prisoners talking to each other one night as he lay alone on his pallet, covered in straw.

"We are so close. If we can only survive until the allies get here," he heard one of them say.

"I'm afraid they will begin the mass shootings again. They don't want any of us to be free."

"I don't think they will bother. They want to get out of here before the allies come. I've noticed that they have stopped killing us. They aren't even paying attention to us anymore. They're worried about their own survival. If they are still here when the allies come, they will suffer, and they know it."

Max listened to them, but he was detached. The only thing that kept him from doing what Adrien did and ending his own life was the memory of hearing Margot's voice. He often wondered if that night had really happened as he recalled or if hearing Margot was just a dream, something his tortured mind imagined. *Maybe she's dead, and what I heard was her spirit. But why would she have been talking to the guards as if she were in the camp with Richter? I don't understand any of it. I might be going mad. That could be it. The near starvation, all the loss, and all the tragedy I've endured could have driven me out of my mind.*

And then, late in April, on a chilly day, the Americans entered Dachau. When Max saw them in their uniforms, he stood paralyzed. It was the most glorious thing he had ever witnessed. Hot tears ran down his cheeks. He was laughing and crying at the same time. *Is this real? Are the Allies really here? Is this all really over? If only Kaz and Adrien had lasted another two weeks.*

When they entered Dachau, the American troops looked around

the camp in horror. Max tried to see the camp through their eyes and realized how unbelievable the sight was. There were so many piles of dead skeletal bodies everywhere. The smell of death and human excrement was overpowering, and the ground was covered in ashes from the bodies that had been burned in the crematorium. As Max watched the soldiers, he could see that they were horrified. Some of them covered their noses and mouths with handkerchiefs. Then his eyes fell upon an American soldier, a baby-faced young man with the clean, good looks of healthy living. The soldier ran away from the others in his troop to hide behind a building. Max saw that he was vomiting. Some of the Americans were crying.

The American soldiers began to round up the Nazi guards and SS officers that were still in the camp. They forced the guards out of the overhead tower. And they began to beat the Nazis. They kicked them and shot them. A few of the Americans found the kennel of attack dogs that the Nazis had trained to kill. They shot them.

The prisoners who were still strong enough to participate began to join in the beating of the Germans. They kicked the guards who had tortured them for years. Max saw one prisoner throw a guard to the ground and then stomp on his face until he was dead.

For several minutes, Max stood and watched in disbelief. The tables had finally turned. The Nazis were finished.

CHAPTER 79

When Kurtis Richter saw the Americans enter Dachau, he stood still for a moment. His thoughts turned to his wife and son, who were at home. He considered going back to get them. But he was far too frightened to worry about them. He saw the Americans beating the guards, and he was not willing to risk them finding him. He knew that if he tried to leave by the front entrance, he would be caught by the Allied soldiers. So, he gathered all of his things and valuables he'd stolen from the prisoners over the years and began to make his way out of the camp by a back entrance that almost no one knew existed. *I am going to have to leave Margot and Barrett behind. Going back to the house will only slow me down. I have to get myself out of here. I'll see about them later if I can.*

Kurtis' heart was thumping. He was running as fast as he could, but it had been a long time since he had done any physical activities. He had gotten lazy and put on weight, and his running was not fast enough to protect him.

As soon as Max regained composure, he went to Richter's office, waiting and watching. When Richter came out the back door, Max followed him. Then, right before Richter was about to escape through a back entrance, Max overtook him. He knocked Richter's gun out of his hand. Then he jumped on top of Richter. The bag of stolen valuables, which had meant so much to Richter, flew out of his hands and fell. It opened, and its contents scattered all over the ground. There, on the grounds of Dachau, lay family heirlooms. Men's fine watches, gold wedding bands, and diamond cufflinks. Max felt a burst of strength come over him. He stood over Richter with his foot on Richter's chest.

"Running away like the miserable weakling that you are," Max said, disgusted. He had Richter's gun, which he now pointed in Richter's face.

Richter thought the gun might be empty, but he wasn't sure and wasn't willing to take that chance. "Let me go, and you can take whatever you want from this stuff," Richter indicated the jewels in the dirt. "Take a look at it. It is all very valuable, and it will help you to build a new life."

"You are a maggot," Max growled. "But I will not kill you if you tell me how you know a girl by the name of Margot Kraus. And don't you dare tell me you don't know her."

The *Kommandoführer* was nervous. *How did this prisoner know Margot?* "She is my wife," he said.

Max trembled. "What? What did you say?"

"She is my wife."

"Your wife?"

"Yes. Why?"

"You're not asking the questions anymore. I am. I'm the one with the gun, not you. Not anymore. Where is Margot now?" Max asked.

"Are you going to hurt her?"

"No. I am not. But you are going to tell me where she is, or I am going to kill you. Are you ready to die, *Kommandoführer?*"

"All right. All right. I tell you where she is. Then you promise that you will let me go?" Richter asked.

"Yes, I will. Now tell me because I am losing patience."

Richter thought for a moment. This prisoner might kill Margot and his son. And although he would hate to see that happen, Richter cared about his safety more than theirs. *He might kill me anyway, but this is my only chance. I must tell him and hope he will keep his promise.* Richter thought. "There is a house that is located right outside of the camp. It's on a street where all of the officers live. Margot should be there waiting for me. Let me go, and you can go there right now and find her."

"Which house is it?" Max asked.

"The third from the corner on the right side. The one with the brown and yellow brick," Kurtis said.

Max nodded. "Third from the corner," he repeated.

Kurtis looked at Max, then he said, "I've told you what you wanted to know, so now you must keep your promise. You are a man of your word, aren't you?"

Max laughed heartily. He hadn't laughed so fully for so long that the laughter caused him to start coughing. "I lied." He could barely catch his breath. "Just like every Nazi I have ever known has lied to me."

"I'm not lying. You will find Margot at that house."

"You might not be lying, but you were a louse all these years. You caused the death and misery of so many. I'd like to stay here and torture you. It would give me pleasure. But I must go to Margot before the soldiers get there. You didn't care to protect her. But I do," Max said, and then he pulled the trigger. The gun happened to have a single bullet. Kurtis's face exploded into a mass of bone and blood. The blood splashed onto Max's stripped uniform, but he hardly noticed.

Max quickly picked up as many valuables as he could fit into his pockets. Then he ran towards the entrance. His heart was pounding. *Could it really be possible that I am about to see Margot? Could it really be possible that she was so close to me all this time, yet I was unable to get to her?*

Even though Max was severely underweight, and his feet and body ached, it was as if he had suddenly grown wings. Knowing Margot was only a few feet away, he ran through the camp. As he made his way to the entrance, he saw a group of GIs standing outside the barbed wire. They were throwing cigarettes and candy bars at the prisoners. Max wondered if they were afraid of disease, so they stood outside and didn't enter the camp. Other GIs were already inside Dachau. He saw prisoners embracing the soldiers, and others had fallen to their knees, kissing the feet of their American saviors. It was chaotic, but Max found it to be beautiful, even when he saw prisoners and soldiers beating up or murdering Nazi guards. If he hadn't been on his way to see Margot, he would have stopped and taken great pleasure in the torturing of these miserable Nazis. But right now, nothing was more important to him than getting to Margot, and each step was a step closer to the woman he loved. And it had been so long since he had touched her, looking into her eyes. So very long.

When Max arrived at the house where Kurtis told him Margot would be, he rushed to the front door. All around him, women were standing outside their homes, crying and holding their children in their arms. *These must be the wives of the SS officers. They are frightened now. Their husbands are not here to protect them. They are alone. I should pity them. After all, they are only women, and they weren't involved in the torture at the camp. But I have no pity for them. I don't care what the soldiers do to them as long as Margot is safe.*

Max pounded his fist on the door to the yellow and brown brick house where he thought he would find Margot's, but there was no answer. He pounded again. Max was losing faith. *He lied to me. That louse lied to me. She's not here.* Then, in desperation, Max cried out, "Margot, Margot, it's Max."

Margot was hiding inside. But when she heard him, she ran to the door and flung it open.

It was Margot. There she was. His breath caught in his throat. She was older. Her face was lined with worry lines, and her bleached blond hair had streaks of premature gray. But none of this mattered to him. It was Margot. His Margot. The love of his life. She was trembling as he took her into his arms. Then she began to weep. And he wept, too.

"The Americans are here. They've liberated the camp," he whispered as tears ran down his face.

"I know," she said as she pulled him inside and locked the door behind them. "I am afraid that because I was married to one of the Nazis, they are going to take their anger out on me."

"He looked at her, puzzled. Why? Why did you marry Richter?"

"I had to Max. I needed his protection."

"Please explain."

She nodded. Then she called out, "Barrett, come in here. I want you to meet your father."

Max stared at Barrett in disbelief. He was trembling. A smile slowly came over his face. Then he turned to Margot, and in a soft voice, he said, "My son?"

She nodded, "Yes."

"My son," he repeated. "You were pregnant when you ran away from Trudy's house. I was afraid you might have lost the baby."

"No, he is right here," she lied.

Max put his hand to his heart. "My son, my boy," he said.

She nodded, but she was still crying. "I married Richter to keep him safe. I lied to Richter and told him that he was Barrett's father. I had to do it. Forgive me, Max. Please."

"Come here. Let me see you better," Max said to Barrett.

Barrett was frightened. He hid behind his mother. "It's all right," she said. "Go and let him look at you. Go on."

Barrett slowly walked up to Max, who embraced him.

"I understand why you did what you did. I am proud of you for finding a way to protect our son. But you don't have to worry about Richter anymore. He's dead."

"Are you sure?"

"Very sure. I killed him." Max said.

She had never loved Kurtis, and sometimes she hated him, but she was shocked to hear that Max had killed him. For a moment, she didn't speak. Then she said, "Were you living with Trudy for a while?"

He nodded. "Yes, I had to. I did whatever she asked because she threatened to tell the police about you being Jewish and about my killing Rudy. Then, after all that I put up with from her, she had me arrested anyway. That's how I ended up here in Dachau. Someday, I would like to find her and make her pay for everything she did to us," Max said.

Margot shook her head. "You're too late. She's dead. She died in a fire. I am not sure, but I believe it was arson."

He cocked his head. "Whatever happened to her was well deserved."

"I agree with you. But I must tell you that I am afraid for my safety and Barrett's, too, because I was married to an SS officer. I will be punished by the Allies if they find me. Some of the wives of the guards and the officers have been saying that the Allies are raping German women to punish Germany for the deaths of their fellow soldiers."

"Don't be afraid," he assured her gently. "I promise I won't let anything happen to you or Barrett. We will run away from here. I will keep you safe from now on," Max promised. "Hurry, we have to get out of here. Gather anything you think you will need. We must go right now."

Margot took a few items of clothing for her and Barrett. Then she took all the money and jewelry she still had left from Ben and everything of value that Kurtis kept in a box in their room.

CHAPTER 80

On April 29, 1945, in an underground bunker known as the *Führer Bunker* in Berlin, Hitler married his longtime girlfriend, Eva Braun. As the Red Army advanced through the city, Heinrich Himmler, knowing that Germany had lost the war, attempted to surrender to the Allies. Hitler took this as a betrayal and put out an order for Himmler's arrest.

Realizing that his beloved empire was falling, Hitler commanded his physician to administer cyanide capsules to Blondi, his German Shepherd, to test their effectiveness. After the dog died, the rest of her pups were taken into the yard and shot along with Eva Braun's dogs. And then, afraid to be taken alive, fearing he would endure torture and shame, Hitler, along with Eva Braun, committed suicide.

The following day, despondent at losing his beloved *Führer*, Joseph Goebbels, who was staying in the bunker with the *Führer*, and his wife Maga gave their six young children juice drinks laced with morphine. Once the little ones fell asleep, cyanide was administered to each of the children. They died in the bunker. Then, their parents, Joseph and Maga, took their own lives. General Wilhelm Bergdorf and Franz Schädle, who was one of Hitler's bodyguards, also died by suicide in Hitler's underground bunker.

By the time Hitler died, Max and Margot had sold all the valuables they owned on the black market. Then they took the money they made, and although it cost them almost everything they had, they secured passage. They were on their way to a new life. In June, two months later, along with their young son Barrett, they boarded a ship headed for America.

EPILOGUE

Margot and Max held hands together in the large auditorium at the University of Chicago Medical School. Max beamed with pride. Their fifteen-year-old daughter, Erika, named after their son Erik, sat beside her father.

Max squeezed Margot's hand as Barrett walked down the aisle in his cap and gown. Barrett was not tall. But he was a handsome, slender, intelligent-looking, dark-haired, dark-eyed boy. "I'm so proud of him," Max said. "Our son is a doctor."

"Yes, so am I," Margot agreed, her eyes watery with tears of joy. However, Margot had been feeling guilty about lying to Max. At night, she had been having dreams of her parents. After the war ended, she wrote to her sister Mattie and asked about Mattie's family and about their parents. Mattie wrote back to Margot and told her that she was currently working as a secretary, but she was sad to have to tell her that her husband had been killed when the Russians entered Berlin. Mattie also said that both of their parents were gone. They died of illness during the war. It broke Margot's heart to know that she would never see them again or have a chance to explain why she disappeared or say goodbye.

The years had been kind to the Kraus family in America. Life wasn't perfect or easy, but her marriage to Max had been good. When they first arrived, Max had gotten a job bussing tables in a restaurant where Margot was waitressing. They hired a teenager who lived in the building to watch Barrett while they worked. And together, they saved every penny they could. Finally, after ten years, they were able to start their own business. It was a small German restaurant in the German section of Chicago. They worked hard, and although they weren't rich, they had a nice home and plenty to eat. Coming from war-torn Europe, this was more than they had ever dared to hope for. However, there was always something not quite right between them. Margot knew Max loved her, and she adored him, but the intimacy they had shared before the war was gone. And Margot longed for it. She thought that perhaps Max did, too. And lately, she had begun to wonder if all the lies between them had ruined their closeness.

When her parents came to her in dreams, they would tell her she was not being fair to Max. They insisted that she owed it to Max to tell him the truth about Barrett being Ben's son. They said this was what was standing between them. At first, she ignored the dreams, hoping they would stop. Instead, they became more frequent. And because of this, her guilt about lying to Max grew every day. It was driving her mad, and she began to think that she would go completely out of her mind if she didn't tell Max the truth. So, on the night following Barrett's graduation, she decided to tell him everything once they were alone. Margot knew she was taking a terrible risk. Everything was going fine right now. Once Max knew the truth, he might not be able to handle it; in fact, he might leave her. She realized that. But she had to do it. She couldn't go on this way. And no matter what happens, there will be no more lies.

After the graduation ceremony, the family went out for a celebratory dinner at an established Italian restaurant called the Como Inn. It was a family favorite where the Kraus family always went to celebrate special occasions.

Margot watched Max and Barrett discuss the Chicago baseball

teams, the Cubs, and the White Sox. Max liked the Sox; Barrett liked the Cubs. This was a constant, friendly argument between them. Erika chimed in, "We should go to a game this year. You should take off work, Dad. It's only one day."

"Of course, I'd love to. I'll have the cook come in early," he said. "But your mother won't be able to come with us. One of us always has to be at the restaurant."

"It's all right. I don't mind at all," Margot said. "You three haven't been to a game in years."

"Well, we wanted to go this year but couldn't do anything until Barrett finished his finals."

"Now that he's graduated, and our son is a doctor," Margot said, "I think he deserves a day out with his family."

Max and Barrett were so different, yet they were as close as a father and son could be. For a moment, Margot thought she might cry.

Because the family regularly ate at the restaurant, the owner bought drinks and desserts for everyone to celebrate Barrett's graduation. Margot ate and drank more than she normally would have. But this was a huge accomplishment, and it was late when they all got home. Barrett and Erika went to bed, leaving Margot and Max alone.

"Max," she said.

"Yes?"

"I have to talk to you about something."

Margot couldn't bear to look him directly in the eye. She knew that once she revealed the secret she kept from him, he would be broken by the words she would say. In fact, it might end everything for the two of them. For a moment, she silently contemplated whether to tell him or let him go on in blissful ignorance. She considered keeping her secret hidden, burying it forever in the deepest, darkest recesses of her heart. And yet, she knew she could not. It was not fair to her husband, who had always been a good man, to live a lie. He deserved to know the truth. *No, I will not spend what time we have left on earth lying to him. If we are to go on as a couple, then I must tell him everything, all of it. Everything that happened, regardless of how difficult it is. It is either this or I must leave, walk away from him forever.*

"I have something I must tell you. I cannot keep this a secret if we are to stay together."

"What are you talking about? Everything is fine," he said.

"But it isn't. Believe me, I would like to keep things the way they are. I wish I could just let you go on believing the lie, but I can't. Not after all we have been through. In my heart, I know that I owe you this much. I owe you honesty," she said, gazing at the small window across the room.

There was a long silence. She could hear her own heartbeat. A cold shiver ran through her like a lightning bolt, and she trembled, but neither moved. Then he walked over to her, gently took her hand, and, nodding his head, said, "No, you're right. It must be hard for you to live with a lie. It's all right. Go on and tell me everything. I know it's hard, but I love you, Margot, and whatever you tell me won't change anything."

She could feel his hand trembling in hers. She wished she could protect him from what she was about to say. After these words were said, they would either be closer than they ever were, or their marriage would end, and they would never speak to each other again.

"But…" she said, feeling a pain in her heart. "I know that what I am about to say will hurt you. I wish I knew the right thing to do."

"I know. I realize that is why you are so hesitant. Is it about the past? Is it about something that happened during the war?" he asked.

"Yes."

"I thought so. So much of what we both have gone through is unpleasant. If we want to try to rebuild our lives together, we must leave the past behind. But it seems that you can't do that until we share our secrets and clear away any lies we told. I agree with you. Only in the open air can wounds heal." He reached up and touched her cheek. His hand was warm and clammy. But she wished she could hold his hand close to her heart. If she did, she thought that somehow he would be able to feel all the love she still had for him.

Hot tears stung the back of her eyes. "And you?" she said in an angry voice. "Maybe this wouldn't be so hard if you weren't so damn good. You were always so damn good. You never broke the rules. You never did bad things. Oh no, not you. You were not like me," she said, shaking her head, and the tears spilled down her cheeks. She looked away from him. Then she whispered in a small voice, "I've always wished I could be more like you."

"Oh no. I am far from perfect. You see, that's where you're wrong. I'm not so damn good. In fact, I've done things too. Things I know will hurt you. But if you want to know, I will tell you. And I hope you will find it in your heart to forgive me." He looked away for a moment. Then, softly, he added, "That war did these things to us all. It tore us apart, and although we lived through it, we are not the same. Don't think that I am so good. Believe me, I have things to say, things I need to get off my chest. And, like you, I wondered if it would be better if I told you these things or if I should leave them unsaid. But if you think this is best, I will do as you say."

She nodded. "Yes." Tears ran down her cheeks. She had to touch him. She had to find the courage to talk and tell him all she'd done and why. Her hands were trembling, but she knew they both needed the physical touch of the other, so she took his hand and squeezed it. Then she put it to her lips and kissed it. She began to sob hard. Tears of guilt, but not of regret. If only she could regret what she had done, perhaps she would allow herself to believe that she deserved forgiveness. But she didn't regret it. She couldn't. "You tell me what you have done. And I will tell you what I have done."

He reached down and turned her face gently to gaze into her eyes. "And what will happen to us if what we are about to tell each other changes everything between us? Once we tell each other, we can't go back," she asked.

"It won't change things. It can't. You and I have a long history together. We can't be broken so easily," he said.

"I hope you're right," she shrugged.

"We must lay it all out on the table and let fate take its course."

He began. "There was a young woman who worked in the office at the camp. Her name was Rivka…" Margot listened in silence as he told her everything. When he had finished, she nodded.

"Did you still love me, even when you were in love with her?"

"Yes, I always loved you. I will always love you."

"Then you are going to understand when I tell you that I loved two men at the same time. You and Ben." She sighed and looked away. Then she grabbed his hand and held it tightly in both of hers. "Max, when I ran away after Rudy's murder, I did miscarry. Ben saved my life. I went into hiding with him until he died." She hesitated, and then she began to cry. "I have been lying to you. I've been telling you that Barrett is your son. He's not. He's Ben's son."

He touched her cheek. "I know. I've always known," he said. "It's all right. I understand, and I love you. Barrett may not be my biological son, but he is my son nonetheless, and I love him too."

The End.

AUTHORS NOTE

I always enjoy hearing from my readers, and your thoughts about my work are very important to me. If you enjoyed my novel, please consider telling your friends and posting a short review on Amazon. Word of mouth is an author's best friend.

Also, it would be my honor to have you join my mailing list. As my gift to you for joining, you will receive 3 **free** short stories and my USA Today award-winning novella complimentary in your email! To sign up, just go to my website at www.RobertaKagan.com

I send blessings to each and every one of you,

Roberta

Email: roberta@robertakagan.com

ABOUT THE AUTHOR

I wanted to take a moment to introduce myself. My name is Roberta, and I am an author of Historical Fiction, mainly based on World War 2 and the Holocaust. While I never discount the horrors of the Holocaust and the Nazis, my novels are constantly inspired by love, kindness, and the small special moments that make life worth living.

I always knew I wanted to reach people through art when I was younger. I just always thought I would be an actress. That dream died in my late 20's, after many attempts and failures. For the next several years, I tried so many different professions. I worked as a hairstylist and a wedding coordinator, amongst many other jobs. But I was never satisfied. Finally, in my 50's, I worked for a hospital on the PBX board. Every day I would drive to work, I would dread clocking in. I would count the hours until I clocked out. And, the next day, I would do it all over again. I couldn't see a way out, but I prayed, and I prayed, and then I prayed some more. Until one morning at 4 am, I woke up with a voice in my head, and you might know that voice as Detrick. He told me to write his story, and together we sat at the computer; we wrote the novel that is now known as All My Love, Detrick. I now have over 30 books published, and I have had the honor of being a USA Today Best-Selling Author. I have met such incredible people in this industry, and I am so blessed to be meeting you.

I tell this story a lot. And a lot of people think I am crazy, but it is true. I always found solace in books growing up but didn't start writing until I was in my late 50s. I try to tell this story to as many people as possible to inspire them. No matter where you are in your life, remember there is always a flicker of light no matter how dark it seems.

I send you many blessings, and I hope you enjoy my novels. They are all written with love.

Roberta

MORE BOOKS BY ROBERTA KAGAN

AVAILABLE ON AMAZON

Margot's Secret Series

The Secret They Hid

An Innocent Child

Margot's Secret

The Lies We Told

The Blood Sisters Series

The Pact

My Sister's Betrayal

When Forever Ends

The Auschwitz Twins Series

The Children's Dream

Mengele's Apprentice

The Auschwitz Twins

Jews, The Third Reich, and a Web of Secrets

My Son's Secret

The Stolen Child

A Web of Secrets

A Jewish Family Saga

Not In America

They Never Saw It Coming

When The Dust Settled

The Syndrome That Saved Us

A Holocaust Story Series

The Smallest Crack

The Darkest Canyon

Millions Of Pebbles

Sarah and Solomon

All My Love, Detrick Series

All My Love, Detrick

You Are My Sunshine

The Promised Land

To Be An Israeli

Forever My Homeland

Michal's Destiny Series

Michal's Destiny

A Family Shattered

Watch Over My Child

Another Breath, Another Sunrise

Eidel's Story Series

And . . . Who Is The Real Mother?

Secrets Revealed

New Life, New Land

Another Generation

The Wrath of Eden Series

The Wrath Of Eden

The Angels Song

Stand Alone Novels

One Last Hope

A Flicker Of Light

The Heart Of A Gypsy

Printed in Great Britain
by Amazon

50160650R00158